The Mario Mystery

Also by John MacDonald

The Widow Esposito

The Cassiatorre Quartet

The Mario Mystery
Deadly Secrets
The Oligarch Murders
Get Me Moretti!

The Mario Mystery

A Dino Moretti Novel

JOHN MACDONALD

Cassiatorre

First published 2025
by Cassiatorre

The right of John MacDonald to be identified as author of this work
has been asserted in accordance with Section 77 of the Copyright,
Designs and Patents Act 1988.
Paperback ISBN 978-1-917862-01-1
Ebook ISBN 978-1-917862-10-3

For Carol –
who gave me Italy.

ACKNOWLEDGMENTS

With thanks to everyone who has shaped my writing and given so generously of their time to read my work and share their experience.
Myra Duffy, Richard Louden, Malcolm MacDonald, Margaret McMillan, David Pettigrew, Helen Williamson.
My editor, Christine McPherson.
And my wife Carol for believing.

CHAPTER ONE

Commissario Dino Moretti turned his head and inhaled slowly as if he could scent the molecules of evidence in the darkened room.

Nothing. He exhaled. When the accustomed lump formed in his gullet, he swallowed and cleared his throat before he spoke in a reverential tone that matched the sombre surroundings.

'My fear is that we're in a murder scene without a body.'

'Or we could be looking at a kidnapping, or a runaway, capo,' said Agente Gennaro Santoro. 'Who knows.'

Moretti checked the windows and sills – no cobwebs.

'Closed tight. The shutters, too. Is upstairs the same?'

Santoro nodded. 'The whole place. Locked like they were going on vacation.'

Moretti unlatched and opened the windows and the squeaky shutters. Light and warmth streamed into the room. The shadows of the wrought iron window bars folded over the furniture.

'What do you notice, Gennaro?'

The older man shrugged. 'It's brighter.'

'Yes, but what do you see?'

Santoro sighed. 'Don't start this, capo, just tell me.'

The commissario drew a shape in the air, causing the floating particles to swirl. 'The sunbeam. The dust hasn't settled.'

Moretti drew his gloved finger across the top of the sideboard and assessed the thin trace in the dusty surface.

'The usual ten Euros?' Santoro mumbled.

Moretti nodded. 'Two… no, three days at most.'

Detective Santoro referred to his notebook and shook his head. 'That seems about right. I'll owe you the cash.'

Moretti stamped on the terracotta floor. 'What about the cellars? Any access from there?'

'Padlocked from the outside, and we checked the roof as well. No access into the loft except for a skylight, but that was bolted and padlocked, too. Do you want to look for yourself?'

Moretti glowered at Santoro and crossed to the fridge.

'Sorry, capo.'

'Outbuildings?'

'The uniform cops searched them, the fields, and a pond. Everywhere. They got a locksmith to let them into the house and took a video of their searches. The kid was nowhere.'

Moretti assessed the contents of the fridge against a mental inventory. Milk, orange juice, salad, a plastic box with leftovers. Nothing out of the ordinary present, nothing important absent.

'Tell me about the outbuildings.'

'One's a workshop, there's a barn, and a couple of animal sheds from when the place was run as a farm.'

The commissario opened and sniffed the carton of milk. 'Find anything in the outbuildings?'

'No. The usual collection of tools, old paint tins, wine demijohns, and oil bottles. You see the same junk everywhere.'

Moretti closed the fridge and studied the magnets and child's drawings stuck to the door. 'Nothing out of place? Odd?'

'Nothing.' Santoro flicked over some pages. 'Unless you call dried flowers odd.'

Moretti jerked round to face the agente. 'Tell me about the dried flowers.'

'There's a wooden wine box. You know, the size that holds three bottles.'

Moretti nodded.

'It has a few dried flowers in it.'

'And that's it?'

'And there's a plastic bin with a lid. That has a heap of dried flowers in it, too. A mixture.'

'The same mixture in both containers?'

'Yes.'

Moretti poked about in a waste basket and found nothing except a crumpled piece of a newspaper, a couple of tissues, and a Kinder Easter egg wrapper. He took off his glove and preened his walrus moustache with a finger and thumb, then ran his fingers through his untidy grizzled hair.

'The boy – Mario, isn't it?'

'Yes. Mario Rosati. Father, Domenico. Mother, Chiara.'

Moretti tutted. 'Mario's somewhere. The parents must have taken him with them.'

Santoro shrugged and leafed back through his notebook. 'According to this, they left him here on his own.'

Moretti walked over to the sink and turned on the tap, letting water splash over his hand. He sniffed then tasted the water. 'And this was a regular thing? They left their son alone, locked up every day?'

'According to the anonymous call we received, yes. They both work down the hill in Maghicchio. They sometimes arranged for somebody to babysit, but they either forgot or didn't want to bother anyone.'

The commissario wiped his hand almost dry on the hem of his linen jacket, blew into his glove to pop the fingers out and put it back on. 'What kind of people are they?'

'They get by financially; ordinary, nothing unusual. They aren't from here originally. They bought the place about twelve years ago, a couple of years before Mario was born.'

Moretti opened a cabinet above the marble worktop and counted the glasses and crockery inside. 'Do they socialise?'

'Early word from the uniform guys is that they pass the time of day with the neighbours or shopkeepers in Cassiatorre, but apart from that, they pretty much keep themselves to themselves.'

The commissario closed the cabinet door and picked up a photograph from the sideboard. A familiar sliver pierced his heart. 'Does Mario have friends?'

'We've still to interview his teacher and classmates, but that won't be straightforward because of the Easter holidays.'

Moretti studied the photograph, reading the boy's smiling face for clues, willing him to speak.

Nothing.

He replaced the photograph and folded his arms. 'I wonder if

3

he visited his friends?'

Moretti removed his gloves, tucked them into a pocket and scratched his stubble. 'It had to be the parents. Either they hid him somewhere on the podere or they took him with them in the car.'

Santoro shook his head. 'They brought in the canine team to help with the search. He's not on the farm.'

'Must be the car, then.'

'They stopped to buy fuel on the way to Maghicchio. The attendant checked the oil and the tyres, including the spare in the boot. The boy wasn't in the car.'

Moretti outstretched his palms, shrugged and stepped out. He squinted in the unseasonable hot spring sun, deepening the creases around his dark brown eyes, and sauntered around the outside of the house.

Against the wall, whose stucco wore a patchwork of repairs in sun-faded yellows from zabaglione to a wheatfield ready to harvest, a lavender plant in full flower filled the warm air with its heady perfume. Moretti bent to break off a sprig when he noticed a large hummingbird hawkmoth struggling to escape a web. He reached past the feeding bees and, tongue protruding beyond his moustache, used his fingertips to tease apart the moth's silken chains until it managed to escape and thrum past his face to freedom.

'They're a good omen,' said Santoro. 'Should bring us luck.'

'Let's hope so. Looks like we'll need it.'

CHAPTER TWO

'Be a good boy, Mario. Play quietly and we'll see you tonight.' Chiara Rosati smiled and pulled her son close. 'Give me one of your killer hugs.'

Her son looked dejected but encircled his mother's waist and squeezed it tight. Chiara stroked his dark hair, thanked God, and took pleasure in that simple embrace. She wished her ten-year-old would hug her like that for ever, that she didn't have to leave for work, that she didn't have to leave him alone. But most of all, she wished they didn't have to lock him in the house all day.

Chiara's husband Domenico broke the spell.

'That's enough, you two,' he said, tousling Mario's hair with a calloused hand. 'We'll be late for work. We need fuel.'

Chiara held Mario's face in her hands and kissed him on the lips. She knew that he would wipe them when she left. 'Love you.'

Mario looked downcast. 'Love you, Mamma.'

Domenico stood holding the door. His stocky frame and pasta belly left little space for her to pass. 'Come on. I can't be late today.'

She stood, paused in front of the hallstand, looked in the mirror at her face devoid of makeup and at the dark shadows under her eyes. She frowned, smoothed her short hair behind her ears, picked up a carton of eggs from the stand, and popped them in her bag.

'All right, all right,' she said, as she squeezed past him and made for the car.

She settled herself and buckled up while Domenico locked the front door. Three turns of the key slid the long steel bolts home. Mario was safe. She turned for one last look and saw him closing the shutter at the kitchen window. Now the house looked deserted, locked up, secure. Mario was safe.

As they set off down the track Domenico snatched a look at the bag on her lap. 'Who are the eggs for?'

'One of the women at work – Francesca – I bought them from Signor Giusti.'

'Make sure she pays you,' her husband mumbled.

Chiara sighed. 'Not again, Domenico. You Genoese, you're all so tight. It was only a couple of Euros.'

He nodded and lifted a hand from the wheel to make his point. 'Better in our pockets than hers.'

They joined the main road.

'Was there no-one?' There was a tightness – almost an accusation – in his voice.

Chiara turned away from him and looked out of the side window. 'No-one. I called everybody. Well, everybody dependable.'

Domenico tutted. 'Maybe if you tried harder to make friends with some of the other mums, you'd have a bigger pool to call on.'

Chiara gripped the handles of the bag. 'You're one to talk. You never socialise.'

'I do.'

'I don't only mean hunting or fishing.'

They drove in silence for a short time.

'I don't like leaving him any more than you do, Chiara, but there's no alternative.'

She turned to face her husband. 'We could pay someone… or I could stop work.'

He puffed his cheeks and exhaled with a groan. 'Don't start that again. We can't afford a babysitter, and we sure can't manage without your wage.'

'Only until after the Easter holidays. I could ask my supervisor.'

He lifted his hand off the wheel, fingers splayed. 'Don't. These days we're lucky to have jobs. If you reduce your hours, somebody will snap them up and you won't get them back.'

They avoided eye contact and conversation until the filling station where Domenico got out and chatted with the attendant. Chiara knew he was right but was still thinking of a solution when they set off again, following the series of curves down to the valley and into the early morning mist. They took a tight right-hander.

'Domenico!'

He saw it too late. 'Shit!'

They hit the wild boar hard enough to kill it outright.

Domenico twisted round, eyes bulging. 'Are you okay?'

Chiara's hand shook at her throat. 'I'm fine, you?'

He grabbed the steering wheel and shook it violently. 'Sod it. We're going to be late. Stay there, I'll check the outside.'

Chiara ignored him, laid her bag on the floor, and stepped out to inspect the damage.

Domenico looked up and down the road. 'The damn thing was standing in the middle of the road looking at us.'

Chiara put her hands on her hips. 'You were going too fast.'

Traces of spittle appeared in the corners of his mouth. 'I always drive at that speed, it's not fast.'

She folded her arms. 'I didn't say it was fast, I said it was too fast for this stretch of road. You know that with the trees so close to the road deer or boar can suddenly dash out.'

He shrugged, hands outstretched, palms up. 'But it didn't run out. It was standing there.'

Domenico kicked the dead animal. Its muzzle had penetrated the front grille, breaking and horribly displacing its still-attached lower jaw. 'Shit. Shit. Shit. There's supposed to be a fence along here.'

Chiara crouched down. 'The front of the car is mangled, and all covered in blood, and there's water underneath. What are we going to do? Didn't the law change? Don't we have to report it?'

He looked down at her.

'And spend the morning filling in forms, giving statements and being breathalysed? What if they find out that we've left Mario on his own? More questions, statements, maybe a fine, court. No. We'll shift it and get to work.'

She stood up again. 'How? These things weigh a ton.'

'Watch.'

He went to the boot of the car and brought out a tow rope.

Chiara shook her head. 'Someone will see us.'

'Not if we hurry. Help me free its head and tie it up.'

She gave Domenico a hand to truss up the boar. He passed the free end of the rope around the nearest tree.

'Come on, grab the rope.'

Chiara stood behind him and picked up the loose end. They pulled, not quite together. At first the animal refused to budge, and when it did, it jerked forward a fraction.

Domenico dropped the rope. 'You get in front.'

He changed places with his wife and wrapped the end of the rope around his waist.

'Right, hold it tight and try to pull while walking back in time with me.'

This time they managed to pull the carcass off the road and right up to the tree.

'Fetch some branches to cover it up while I untie the rope.'

Chiara quickly collected an armful of dead wood and laid it on top of the boar, tearing up grasses to help disguise it while Domenico looped up the rope.

'You can still see it, Domenico.'

'Well hide it better.'

'I can't.' Chiara sobbed. 'I've tried my best. It's too big.'

Domenico threw the rope into the boot and pulled a large knife from his tool bag and strode towards her.

'What are you doing?' she said, wide-eyed.

'Cutting the brute up. Give me a hand to chuck the bits into the trees.'

Domenico sliced huge chunks of boar, and Chiara threw or carried them over a wide area. Her husband finished the job by jumping on to the animal's ribs to break them, before covering the carcass with wood and leaves.

'How's that?'

'Much better, but my uniform is all bloody. I can't go to work like this.'

'Chiara, if I don't get there on time I'll have to stay late. The job's already behind schedule.'

She wiped her hair off her forehead with her wrist. 'That's not your fault. Your boss agreed too short a timescale.'

He wiped his hands on a rag, glaring. 'Chiara, the job finishes today. I'll be there until it's done or get the sack.'

Her mouth gaped wide. 'What? I didn't know it was that important. You didn't tell me.'

He stuffed the rag in the bib of his overalls.

'Well, you know now. But it means I can't come and collect you from work until then, and Mario's alone at home until it's done.'

Chiara wrapped her arms around herself, threw her head back and yelled.

Domenico reached out to her, but she recoiled from him.

'All right, I'll take us home,' Domenico said. 'We'll get cleaned up, I'll quickly hose down the car, and we'll get to work. It'll be okay.'

He turned the key, but a warning light lit up on the dashboard.

'The damn radiator!' He slammed his hand on the dashboard, undid his seatbelt, got out and checked. 'Empty.'

'What'll we do? Can we call somebody?'

Domenico took out his phone. 'We're stuffed. No signal.'

He put the phone in his back pocket and walked up and down, hands pressed into the sides of his head, scanning the road again.

'I can't think, but we can't leave the car here in this state – they'll find the boar.' He spun around. 'Wait. I know how to fix it. We need water.'

They found plastic shopping bags and bottles in the boot and headed towards a nearby stream. A couple of trips was enough to fill the radiator.

'Sit in the driver's side, Chiara. Start the car and pass me those eggs.'

'What?'

'The eggs. I need them.'

He took the carton from her and carefully cracked and separated two eggs, pouring the whites one at a time into the radiator.

'What are you doing?'

He pressed his lips together as he screwed on the radiator cap. 'When the water in the radiator heats up, it'll cook the egg whites. They'll find and block the leaks.'

'Will it get us home?'

He thought about it. 'Back up the hill? No, I don't think so, but I've an idea. There's a cave cut into the tufa near here. It's one that hunters use when they're caught out in bad weather. We can hide the car there and come back for it later.'

'What about work?'

'Let's hide the car first and I'll think of something.'

They swapped places and Domenico drove off slowly.

'How do you know about the cave?'

'Some of the guys were talking about it. It was used by the partisans during the war. They used to store supplies and hide vehicles from the Germans there.'

After a couple of false trails, Domenico found the cave and drove the car to the back. When they emerged, they could hear traffic on the road, so the bloodied couple headed home cross-country, taking care to avoid all farm buildings, and sticking to the woods and margins of the fields where the shrubs and trees gave them cover. Domenico carried his heavy tool holdall on his back, with his arms through the handles like a rucksack.

'Chiara, this bag's heavy. Why don't we take a handle each?'

'I don't know why you had to bring it.'

He wiped his arm across his brow. 'It's bad enough that I'm going to be late. I can't turn up to work without tools.'

'Did you have to bring them all?'

'Look, will you help me or not?'

'The track isn't always wide enough to walk two abreast.'

'So that's a no, then.'

'It's too awkward.'

'So are you sometimes.'

As he stopped to adjust the load, Chiara strode off. He watched her go as he caught his breath and decided to take a shortcut that would get him home first. He'd show her.

CHAPTER THREE

Santoro sank into the wobbly rush chair at the oilcloth-covered table, opposite the grizzled old farmer, flipped open his notebook, and licked the point of his pencil.

'Signor Di Vittorio, thanks for seeing me. This shouldn't take long. Your podere joins on to the Rosati property, yes?'

The old man nodded and moved his hands from the table onto his lap. The oilskin glistened where his fingertips had rested.

Santoro held his notebook awkwardly at chest height in the gloom. 'When was the last time you saw the parents, Signor Di Vittorio?'

Di Vittorio hesitated slightly. 'The day they left. About three days ago.'

Santoro wrote it down. 'Did you speak with them?'

'No, I thought that they were heading out to work, as usual.'

Santoro watched the farmer closely. 'What time was that?'

'A little after seven.'

'How about Mario?'

Di Vittorio fidgeted with his shirt cuff. 'I never saw him.'

'Was he still indoors?'

The farmer undid and refastened the cuff button. 'I suppose he must've been.'

Santoro lowered his notebook and pencil. 'You suppose? You seem a little anxious, Signor Di Vittorio.'

Di Vittorio placed his hands on the table in front of him again.

'I've never been interviewed by the police before.'

Santoro smiled. 'Relax. We're only trying to build up a picture of your neighbours' daily routine.'

Di Vittorio leaned towards the agente. 'But isn't it against the law to leave children at home unsupervised?'

'Yes, it is,' agreed Santoro. 'And that's why you made the anonymous phone call to report them, isn't it?'

*

Domenico turned off the track and began to climb up a gentle slope, through the trees and out to where the gradient became steeper, and the ground underfoot changed from scrubby grass to rocky outcrops and fissures. His chest heaved as he used the rocks as handholds to pull himself up, balancing carefully around and over the deep cracks in the rocks. He reached a point where he couldn't go forward and had to turn back a little to traverse a particularly deep fissure. As he inched forward over the loose scree, he lost his footing and fell awkwardly down into the crevice, hitting his head on the sides as he fell.

When he came to, Domenico was lying face up, his arms wedged tightly in the narrow space, the tool bag preventing him from moving them. He tried to wriggle his legs but almost passed out again with the pain. His left leg was broken. He knew that he didn't have much time. Fighting unconsciousness, he called out for Chiara. The sun had slowly risen until it was now shining straight down on him. He could feel his thirst building.

*

Carmela Perri put the armful of textbooks onto her desk at the front of the airy classroom. Her dark eyes twinkled under naturally arched eyebrows; her tanned skin and vivid red lipstick accentuated the whiteness of her wide smile.

'Moretti? Like the beer?' She giggled and wiped imaginary froth from a non-existent moustache.

He sighed. 'Yes, Maestra Perri, Moretti like the beer. May I have a word?'

She nodded and the smile left her face. 'It's about Mario, isn't it? I've heard the rumours.'

Moretti waited until she sat down then did the same.

'Maestra Perri, how long have you been Mario's teacher?'

'I took the class over at the start of the session, so a little over

12

six months.'

'What's he like?'

Mario's teacher smiled wistfully. 'He's such a sweet boy. Always bringing me little presents.'

Moretti raised his brows. 'Oh?'

She leaned forward shaking her head. 'Nothing expensive; more thoughtful. A flower, an empty snail shell – things that he finds in the countryside.'

'I see, and is he a good student?'

She nodded her head, and some long black corkscrews of hair fell across her face. She pushed the thick hair back with both hands, collected it into a low ponytail, took a band from her wrist, and fastened it. Her dark eyes now commanded his attention.

'He's a very inquisitive boy. A bit of a daydreamer.' Her gaze shifted to a spot behind Moretti. 'I had to move him into the centre of the room, away from the windows.'

That smile again. 'I'd say that he's above average. Maybe in the top third in the class.'

'Who are his friends? How does he get on with his classmates?'

'He gets on fine with everyone. I don't know who are his friends, though. I don't think he has friends over to play. I get the impression that once he's home, he's home. He's an only child, so I guess he's used to playing on his own. Maybe that's why he has such an imagination.'

'Have you met the parents?'

The smile faltered on her lips. 'I've seen them both at open evenings and concerts, but I've only ever spoken to his mother.'

'What's she like?'

A thick coil of hair had worked itself free, so she tucked it back in place. 'She seemed more concerned with how he ate at lunch and who he played with than how he did in his classwork.'

'A bit overprotective, would you say?'

She placed her hands together on her lap. 'I don't know if I'd go that far, but I did think it rather odd.'

Moretti tried to read her thoughts but failed. 'You said earlier you'd heard the rumours. What exactly?'

She looked down at her hands. 'Oh, I don't know, you know.'

Moretti tilted his head. 'What do I know?'

'About his parents.'

'What about them?'

'That they left him alone in the house and never came back.'

'Anything else?'

'That somehow Mario disappeared.'

'How do you think that happened?'

Without raising her head, she looked up at him. 'I can't imagine.'

'No?'

'I can't imagine how he must have felt when they didn't come home. I can't bear to think of that poor boy, on his own, locked in. What did he eat? How long was he alone? Why did no-one check sooner?'

A large tear rolled down her cheek and left a dark circle where it splashed onto her blue dress.

'Do you have a contact number for the mother, perhaps?'

'No, but if you call this number, they'll give it to you.'

Moretti saved the number to his phone.

'Thank you.' He handed her his card. 'If you can think of anything else, Signorina, call me right away.'

Her hands scrunched up the material of her dress. 'Is he dead? Do you think he's dead?'

'At the moment he's a missing person. Like I said, if you think of anything else, call immediately. We might not have much time.'

CHAPTER FOUR

Chiara marched on, head down, holding the front of her dirty and bloodied uniform off her body. The warming air had brought out the flies. A persistent little swarm followed her, landing on the congealed blood on her uniform, buzzing in front of her face and landing on her bare arms. She snatched up a stick and switched it around her as she walked, now heedless of the touch of the fabric on her skin.

She paused to listen, but Domenico wasn't behind her. *The idiot was trying to race her home. Typical.* She pushed on, determined to beat him, until she realised that she'd left her bag in the car. She cursed and hurried on to a point that she knew he'd have to pass, where she sat down, still swishing her stick around her head, and looked down the track at the way she had come. Her angry tears made little dark, wet, craters in the dry soil beneath her.

After half an hour, Chiara stood up. He should have arrived by now. Her anger became uneasiness, and she retraced her steps looking for him. She'd even help him with his stupid tool bag if he asked. A thought occurred to her and she started to climb, scrambling over the increasingly broken terrain while calling his name over and over. She ignored the flies feasting on the boar's blood and sweat on her uniform and passed very close to the place where her husband was trapped – but not close enough.

*

Agente Santoro knocked for the third time and waited. He knew that his old friend Enzo Giusti was home because his car was parked under the vine pergola at the side of the farmhouse.

'Coming.'

Giusti opened the door a crack and his puffy, dark-circled eyes squinted into the light. His breaths were shallow and quick, and he seemed to take a moment to recognise Santoro.

'Hello, Enzo, how's things?'

'Ah, Gennaro, it's you. Come in. I was settling Rosaria.'

Santoro followed him into the cool, dimly lit entrance that led to a large open plan kitchen and dining room.

'How is Rosaria?'

Giusti raised his eyebrows and tilted his head. 'You know. Much the same, although her good days are fewer now. Can I offer you something? Water, coffee, wine?'

'Some water, please.'

'Tap?'

'Tap's fine, thanks.'

Giusti poured and passed him a glass. 'Is this social or official?'

Santoro blushed. It had been a while.

'Official.' He sipped the cool water. 'It's about the Rosati boy, Mario. Their property runs on to yours.'

'He plays here sometimes. Nice kid. Polite.'

'When was the last time you saw him?'

'Playing here, or at all?'

'Both.'

Giusti rubbed the side of his cheek. 'Playing here, maybe a month, but I saw him on his own place about three or four days ago. His mother Chiara bought some eggs from me about the same time.'

Santoro put down the glass and took out his notebook. 'Which was it?'

'How do you mean?'

'You said you saw Mario three or four days ago. Which was it, three or four days?'

Giusti sagged. 'Gennaro, I don't know. Things haven't been good here. Rosaria needs so much that I don't ever get a full night's sleep these days. I'm losing all track of time.'

Santoro looked at his friend. He'd aged and lost weight. Better to ease up.

'It's not important. How's the family?'

'Okay. Lucia's in Germany, Roberto's in New York. I never see them.'

Santoro had a few more questions but now was not the time.

'Enzo, it was good to see you again. I won't leave it so long next time.'

They walked to the door, Santoro's hand on Giusti's shoulder. 'Tell Rosaria I was asking for her.'

Giusti nodded. 'For all the good it'll do, but okay.'

Santoro stopped in the threshold and turned.

'One last thing, how was Mario when you last saw him? How did he seem?'

His question put years on Enzo.

'Gennaro, I was driving past. Going to collect Rosaria's medication. I saw the boy out of the corner of my eye. I don't know. Sorry.'

As they shook hands, Santoro squeezed his friend's forearm. 'It's me that's sorry, Enzo.'

*

Domenico was unsure of what was real as he slipped into and out of consciousness. At one point he thought that he saw, or rather felt Chiara pass by the opening of the crevice. He tried to call out, but the sun had dried up his voice. A lizard that had been basking on the sheer side of the crevice, now approached, tongue flicking, and nestled in the shade somewhere between his shirt and the rocky wall. He felt it move briefly past him before he passed out.

CHAPTER FIVE

In Bar Italia, the banter and laughter of the six older men playing *briscola* at the table furthest from the door drowned out the talk at the other tables. At a couple more, men sat alone reading their newspapers. Immediately inside the door, at their usual table, three women – Fausta Racano, Rosalia Seccavigne, and Donatella Luchia – spoke quietly just in case.

'Well, it's a disgrace,' said Fausta, a very plump, dark-haired woman whose tiny dog poked its head from her bag towards the table. 'Someone should have reported them long ago.'

'I thought you had, Fausta,' said Rosalia, arching her brows. 'You've threatened to often enough.'

Fausta dabbed her brow with a small, white, lace-edged handkerchief. 'So, it shows that I was right.'

Donatella stroked Fausta's tiny dog's head with a finger. It closed its eyes and tilted its head.

'They're such a nice family, the little boy is so polite,' she said.

The other two looked at their smiling companion.

'Where did you meet them?' asked Rosalia.

'How do you know he's polite?' pressed Fausta.

'I've met them in church,' Donatella replied. 'I dropped my purse, and my loose change spilled out under the pews, everywhere. Mario collected it all, put it back in the purse, and handed it back to me.'

'Are you certain he put it all back?'

'Yes, Rosalia, every centesimo.'

Fausta moved her bag a touch so that her dog was out of Donatella's reach. The little animal strained briefly against its faux-leather prison but admitted defeat and snuggled down inside instead.

Rosalia bent closer to the others, caught a whiff of something, recoiled slightly, then leaned back again.

'But what are the parents like? They don't take part in anything.' She produced a little linen lavender bag and held it under her nose.

At the appearance of the lavender bag, Fausta winced, slipped her hand past the dog, and dipped into the bottom of her bag. She found a fan, held it between her and Rosalia, and began to waft it vigorously.

Rosalia tucked the lavender bag into her cuff.

'I think they work hard and keep themselves to themselves,' said Donatella brightly.

'Well, I think she's stuck up,' said Fausta. 'Thinks she's better than everybody.'

Donatella shook her head. 'How can you say that? You don't know her.'

'Maybe not but, I know her type.' Fausta insisted.

'What do you mean, her type?' said Rosalia.

Fausta closed the fan and placed it on the table. 'Goody two shoes.' She wrinkled her nose. 'All scrubbed and snobby – and she's no reason to.'

She found her handkerchief again and dabbed her temples. 'Who does she think she is, anyway? I mean, she only works in a supermarket.' Her excitement made her little dog pop its head up out of her bag again. 'Never wears a scrap of make-up, and she should, you know – at least something to cover up those dark rings under her eyes.' She picked up the fan again, using it to emphasise her points. 'She never gets her hair done; I'm sure she cuts it herself.'

Fausta splayed the fan again and began to waft it slowly. 'You know, I'm surprised she's even married, looking like that, let alone with a child.' She leaned across the table and whispered. 'I bet she keeps her husband on short rations. I wouldn't be surprised if he doesn't play away.'

Rosalia and Donatella gaped.

'What?' said Fausta, pausing her fanning. 'Don't tell me you're not thinking the same.'

'Actually, I was wondering how you describe me to other people,' said Rosalia.

Fausta now fanned furiously, her upper arm wobbling in time. 'You're different. You're a friend.'

Rosalia said nothing. Instead, she collected the things from the table and took them to the counter.

'I'll get this today,' she said. 'I must head home, and I've some shopping to do first.'

'I'm off, too,' said Donatella with a sigh.

Fausta looked perplexed and fanned her face, while the little dog looked from one to another, tongue out, panting.

'What?' said Fausta. 'What?'

The two women left. The card players were too absorbed in their game to notice.

*

Chiara searched frantically now – running, scrambling, slipping, crawling over the broken ground. She descended and made her way back the way they had come, trying in vain to find the car. She climbed again, hoping for a view of the track from the ridge. A couple of hours later she found the deep fissure where her husband lay pinioned. Chiara's relief exploded in a gasp, and she crossed herself and pressed the back of her thumb to her lips.

She called down, but there was no reply.

Then shouted. No response.

She dropped a pebble to rouse him. It ricocheted down past him. Nothing.

Panicking, she dropped a slightly larger stone. He made no response when it landed on his chest.

Chiara sank to her knees and doubled over, clutching her belly. She swayed back and forwards crying, mouth agape, unable to wail or make tears. Now she saw that he'd lost blood and the flies had found him too. He was dead.

Mario.

Chiara winced as she pushed up to her feet, unaware of the cuts and scratches covering her hands, arms, and legs. Her only instinct now was to get back to her son, but before that she had to get back to the car for her house keys and phone. Yet all the trails looked the same, and with the sun higher in the sky, she lost her orientation and with it any chance of finding the car again.

Still avoiding the main road, she walked in circles, not knowing what to do, fighting fatigue and thirst. She spread her fingers into her short hair and twisted them until it hurt. Who could help her? Domenico was right – who did she know? Who could she trust? Maybe the parish priest. She closed her eyes, ignoring the sting of the salt, thought about Mario, then knew what she had to do. She left the thinning trees and started off again.

CHAPTER SIX

Back at the Questura, Moretti pointed to the screen. Santoro leaned in.

'Stop there,' Santoro said. 'Can we zoom in on the main lock?'

The technician gave them a close-up view. The lock looked as though a spider had made its home inside the keyhole and covered the whole of the front in its web.

Moretti stared hard at the full-screen view of the keyhole and lost himself in his thoughts.

After a bit, Santoro brought him back into the room. 'Capo?'

Moretti started a little.

'Pan to the other lock, please,' said Moretti.

The image moved slowly and stopped on the Yale lock. It, too, was covered in web.

'Now the hinges, please.'

The technician obliged.

Moretti rubbed the nape of his neck. 'They're intact, too.' He sighed. 'So how did the locksmith get in?'

'He picked the Yale and drilled the other one,' replied the technician, and switched to a view of the door after entry.

Moretti patted the technician's back. 'Okay, thanks, I've seen enough. Let's go to my office, Gennaro.'

They sat on opposite sides of Moretti's desk.

'Go over the timings with me again.'

Santoro consulted his notebook. 'Three days ago Di Vittorio

saw the parents leave shortly after seven.'

'Without Mario.'

'Without Mario. They got to the petrol station at ten past seven. The security camera picked them up. Like I said before, the garage guy filled the tank and checked all five tyres. Mario wasn't in the car.'

'Could they have dumped his body along the way?'

'The local cops checked. They would only have had time to dump it at the roadside. Somebody would've seen it.'

Moretti opened the French door, stepped out on to the tiny balcony, and lit up a small cigar.

'Capo, you're killing me,' said Santoro.

'I'm blowing the smoke outside, Gennaro.'

'It's not that. I still get the craving, that's all.'

Moretti leaned further out, twisted his mouth downwind and exhaled. 'How reliable is Di Vittorio?'

'Not sure. His hands were sweating. His fingers left wet marks on the table when he moved them.'

'Nerves?'

'Maybe.'

Moretti rubbed his cigar out on the stucco, came back in, and stood looking down across Piazza Garibaldi with his back to Santoro.

'Was he telling the truth?'

Santoro's lips shrugged. 'I think so. Maybe. Aw, who knows these days. What would he have to gain from lying?'

'Nothing, if he's innocent. Plenty, if he's guilty.'

'I don't take him for a murderer. He was the one who made the anonymous call.' Santoro closed his notepad. 'How did you get on with the schoolteacher?'

Moretti turned to face the agente. 'Have you met her?'

Santoro shook his head.

'I never had a teacher like that when I was young,' Moretti continued.

Santoro laughed. 'Maybe it's as well, or you wouldn't have made commissario.'

'She's young, very beautiful, and clearly very upset by the whole situation, but knows nothing. She gave me a number to call tomorrow.'

Santoro stood and put his hand on Moretti's shoulder. 'You look tired.'

'We're missing something, Gennaro. The place was locked up tighter than a vault. It had to be the parents. Maybe they smuggled him out at night. Di Vittorio must have missed it.'

'Pity we can't ask them. It's early days. We'll have better luck tomorrow.'

'We'd better; it might already be too late.' He sighed. 'You go on home, Gennaro. I'm going to have another look at the video. I'm missing something.'

The agente reached into his pocket and took out a note from his wallet. 'Here's the money I owe you. Don't work too late.'

'Yes, dear,' said Moretti.

Gennaro smiled. 'I mean it, Dino.'

*

Moretti surveyed the kitchen worktops.

'Have you eaten, Maria?'

His slim wife, face cleansed and already changed into pyjamas, appeared from the sitting room. A plain headband pulled back her shoulder-length black hair. He stifled the urge to kiss her.

'Sorry, Dino, I was starved and couldn't wait. I left you some *pici all'Aglione*. Go and change and I'll heat it up.'

He nodded and touched her shoulder as he passed, noticing the almost imperceptible turn of her head away from him.

When he returned to the kitchen, Maria was serving the pasta and had already poured him a glass of wine.

She sat opposite him. 'How was your day?'

He twisted up a forkful of pasta coated in the thick tomatoey sauce suffused with the sweet subtle flavour of the Valdichiana's huge Aglione garlic.

'Not great,' he said, fork poised in front of his mouth. 'A child disappeared from a locked house three days ago, and I don't know how it's possible.'

They exchanged a guilty look and Maria hesitated before speaking. 'Three days ago? Why did nobody report it sooner? Why was the child alone?'

Moretti chewed the pici and avoided eye contact. The sliver twisted inside his heart.

'It's a young boy. Ten years old. Mario. The parents didn't or

24

couldn't find a babysitter. Seems it was a regular thing.'

Maria fidgeted with her wedding ring, turning it and sliding it up and down over the finger joint. 'What about the parents? What are they saying?'

'We don't know where they are. Neither turned up for work. The three of them have vanished.'

Their conversation came to a familiar threshold, but neither of them wanted to open the door and deal with what was on the other side. The room closed in on the pair, exaggerating the space between them.

Moretti put down his fork and took a sip of wine. 'So how was your day?'

Maria sat up. 'Oh fine. You know, the usual. Nothing much.'

She chatted about the people that she'd met who sent Dino their regards, filling the time it took for him to finish his meal.

'Thank you,' he said. 'I'll tidy away. I've some thinking to do before I come to bed.'

Maria smiled and nodded. They never went to bed at the same time these days. It was easier for them both if one of them could feign sleep rather than spurn intimacy.

She stopped and placed her hand on his shoulder. 'You will find him, Dino, won't you? You'll find Mario?'

Moretti looked up at her and covered her hand with his. 'I promise.'

CHAPTER SEVEN

Moretti stepped into Bar Italia at his usual hour and addressed everyone and no-one. 'Good morning.'

A few of the regulars mumbled a reply.

Carla smiled, placed his cappuccino on the counter, and held out his cornetto. 'Good morning, Commissario.'

'Thanks, Carla.'

He bit into the sweet pastry and took a slurp of the tepid coffee, letting the tastes mingle as he chewed.

The mirrored shelves behind the counter displayed the usual liqueurs and spirits. The racks above him held neat rows of glasses by their stems. Behind him, today's tubs of multicoloured, freshly-made gelato already filled the cold display.

The locals, gulping down espresso or cappuccino ignored him. No leads. No new ideas. Nothing.

At the till, Carla had already counted out the change of the ten Euro note he always presented. This time she also smiled, held out a paper napkin, and tapped her top lip.

He took it and wiped pastry flakes from his thick moustache.

'Thanks, Carla, what would I do without you?'

He stepped outside and called the number Carmela Perri had given him and asked for the emergency contact details of both Rosatis then he tried the numbers in turn – both unavailable.

Santoro's podgy figure approached down the little slope of the Piazza Garibaldi with his lopsided, one running step, one walking step, gait. He waved his arms up and down in front of him as if calming a crowd or ordering Moretti to slow down.

'What is it, Gennaro?'

Santoro bent over with his hands on his thighs, catching his breath. 'She's here.'

Moretti inclined his head to look at Santoro's face. 'Ispettore Furlan? How does she look?'

Santoro angled his head up to meet Moretti's gaze. 'Tall.'

'Tall. Is that it? Tall. You're supposed to be a detective.'

Santoro straightened up and slid his hand up across his forehead. 'Believe me, you won't have any trouble detecting her.'

'Age?'

'Late twenties.'

Moretti shook his head. 'That young? *Cavolo.* That's my replacement, Gennaro. Believe me, a couple of years getting to know the area, and I'll be out. Innocenti will find something.'

'Nonsense, capo. Anyway, she seems nice.'

Moretti sighed. 'Okay, let's get this over with.'

The detectives stopped at the front desk of the Questura. Moretti scribbled the two numbers on the desk officer's pad.

'Alfiero, keep calling these two numbers and let me know immediately if you get a reply. And while you're at it, call the hospital in Maghiccio in case any of the Rosatis have been admitted.'

Although he was several centimetres taller than the average Italian, a few minutes later Moretti saw that Ispettore Cristina Furlan was, by some margin, taller than everyone in the building. Blonde hair tied back in a loose bun, long legs, and an athletic figure, she held out her hand and shook his with an unexpectedly firm grip.

'Good morning, Commissario. Cristina Furlan. I am so very pleased to be able to join you here.'

Her singsong accent confirmed her origins in northeast Italy.

Moretti became aware of his strong Tuscan accent.

'We're all glad that you have joined us, too. May I present my colleague, Agente Gennaro Santoro.'

'I saw you earlier. Pleased to meet you.'

She smiled. 'Call me Cristina, and I'll call you Gennaro.'

'Good, now that we've all made friends, I'll catch you up with the case we're working on,' said Moretti.

'No need,' said Cristina. 'I came in early and read the reports. Where did it happen, and have you called the parents? Where do the people you've interviewed live? Has anyone been assigned to track down relatives or friends of the family? Were they planning a vacation? Did they maybe get an urgent call about a sick family member that made them dash off without telling anyone?'

She responded to their surprised looks with a blush.

'We from the north believe in pushing on with things, I'm afraid. I hope I haven't broken any protocols on my first morning.'

Moretti's eyes widened but he recovered quickly. 'No, no,' he said. 'That's good, Cristina. Initiative. That's what we like to see, eh Gennaro?'

'Initiative – yes, capo, that's what we like around here.'

Feeling at a height disadvantage, Moretti suggested that they all sit. It was of little use, though; he still found himself looking up at her.

'We have called the parents, but both calls went to voicemail. It's a puzzling case,' said Moretti. 'Parents go off, allegedly leaving their son in their locked house – unless you're right, Cristina, and they left suddenly, taking Mario with them without telling anyone. It's possible that the neighbours didn't see them return for Mario. Or, sticking with our initial thoughts, they don't return, and three days later when it's reported, the cops break into the house, but the boy is gone.'

'You've no way of knowing when during those three days Mario disappeared.'

'None.'

'You've done three interviews so far?' asked Cristina.

'Yes, with two neighbours and Mario's teacher.' Moretti stood and moved to a large-scale wall map and pointed to a spot outside of the town. 'The Rosatis live here, surrounded by five other properties.' He circled a wider area. 'The whole area around Cassiatorre and down the valley as far as Maghicchio is all farmland.' He tapped the map. 'This is the Di Vittorio farm, and beside it here is the Giusti farm. We've already spoken to them. Up here is the Mancini place, with the Erpicone podere down here. This huge estate on the other side of the Rosati place is the Ricci agriturismo.'

'Quite an area,' said Cristina. 'And tricky terrain, by the looks of it.'

'Now that you're here, we should be able to push on with things,' said Moretti. 'I want you to go with Gennaro this morning and speak to Erpicone. I'll call on Mancini, and we'll meet back here later.'

Gennaro gave him a resigned look and led the way outside to his car. He put the bag containing his lunch in the door storage and waited until Cristina pushed the passenger seat to its lowest and furthest back position before he drove off. He found it easier to look at her in the mirror than to turn his head back when speaking with her.

'Ispettore, eh? Must be something of a hotshot.'

'Not really, I work hard.'

Gennaro made a noise, something between a cough and a growl, in the back of his throat.

'Married?'

He sensed her hesitate and look out of the window at her side.

'No. Not married.'

He picked up on it. 'Ah, that'll be why,' he said. 'Marriage and kids take so much of your time.'

'Are you married, Gennaro?'

'Widower. Children have all moved away. Spread all over the place. Grandchildren, too. Never see them.'

'That must be hard.'

'Well, I'm retiring in a couple of years and going back to Puglia. I expect when I settle down there the family will be queuing up to visit.' He didn't sound convincing, even to himself.

They left the main road and followed a white dirt road to a stony yard surrounded by farm buildings and rusting harrows and ploughs. The car was met by a chorus of barking dogs, the smallest of which snapped at Cristina's door until she stepped out and stood up. It continued to bark, but from a safer distance.

Santoro was welcomed like a friend. The dogs crowded close, tails wagging, as he crouched down to them, reached into his pocket, and produced strips of dried pork crackling which he broke and divided among them. The dogs withdrew to the shade with their spoils.

'Local knowledge,' Santoro said.

Cristina smiled and looked around. Paint of similar hues, but different degrees of flaking and weathering, covered the walls in a patchwork of neglect. Several tiles had slid off the roof's shallow slope and had detached the rusty gutter above the door.

'So you're prepared, Ispettore, Ettore Erpicone is a farmer and one of the most unpleasant people you'll ever meet. His wife killed herself a while ago, but he refuses to acknowledge it. He says, and I'm sure that he believes, that she abandoned him.'

'Any family?'

'Four grown-up children – three boys and a girl. They've all gone, too. The girl hung around longest to look after him following the death of his wife, but eventually even she left. Probably driven away by his attitude, or more likely that he didn't want her to go out with boys.'

Santoro knocked on the substantial door.

No reply.

He thumped it with his fist.

'Ettore, its Gennaro. Open up. I know you're in there.'

A curse preceded the sound of scraping bolts and clunking locks. The heavy door opened.

'How in hell did you know I was here?'

Ettore Erpicone was short, squat, and dressed in blue dungarees and a checked shirt unbuttoned enough to reveal a thick mat of greying chest hair. He looked up at Cristina.

'And who the hell is this? The Queen of the Amazons? Ever get struck by lightning, *tesoro*?'

'Now, now, Ettore. This is Ispettore Furlan, so watch your tone.'

Cristina held up her ID.

'It's no use,' said Santoro. 'He can't see it, can you, Ettore?'

'I can see fine. But your girlfriend casts such a shadow everything's gone dark.'

Santoro tutted. 'He needs cataract operations in both eyes and refuses to leave the podere long enough to have them done. Isn't that right, Ettore? That's why I knew you were at home.'

'I'm a busy man. What do you want?'

Santoro turned to Cristina.

'What Ettore means is, "Go away, I don't want you poking around and finding the illegal immigrants who I have working as slave labour in my fields and sleeping in a run-down shack or a barn that's no longer good enough to keep my animals in.'"

He turned back to the irate farmer.

'I have no slaves,' Erpicone said with a snarl. 'No-one's in the barn. There were pigs there, but I moved them. You can move in if you like. I'm sure it's better than the hovel you can afford on a cop's salary.'

Santoro ignored the jibe and pulled out his notebook. 'We're interested in what you know about your neighbours the Rosatis.'

'Nothing.'

Santoro tapped his pencil on the notebook. 'You see, that's not helpful. That's the sort of reply that makes me want to drive down to the bottom vineyard where the vines are probably being pruned by your illegal workers.'

'Spring pruning's finished.'

Santoro made a note.

'Or they're hoeing in between the rows of vines. Look, do you really want me to go and find out for myself?'

Erpicone glowered at him.

'The Rosati family,' repeated Santoro. 'We had a report yesterday afternoon that the parents had left their boy alone in the house.'

'Not interested.'

'He's ten years old and that was three days ago.'

'I haven't seen him.'

Santoro turned to Cristina again. 'Looks like we'll have to find these illegal workers and interview the lot of them, after all.'

Erpicone snarled again. 'Come inside.'

They followed him into the dark, cool, surprisingly clean and tidy interior – mirrors and surfaces were free of dust, there were plumped cushions, and the merest background hint of plug-in air freshener.

'Wait there.'

The farmer left them and returned a moment later with a scrap of paper that he pretended to pass to Cristina before snatching it back.

She grabbed at the empty air and the old man grinned.

'Too slow, snow line,' he said, handing her the note. 'The pruning was done by a gang from Siena. Legitimate. They come

31

every year and do the vines and the olives. Cost me a fortune. That's their number. Call it and find out where they're working now. If anybody has seen anything, it'll have been them.'

Cristina photographed the phone number and dropped the paper as Erpicone reached out to take it.

'Oops, clumsy,' she said.

'That's right, beanstalk, make fun of the old blind guy,' said Erpicone. 'And I've a bad back. Pick it up and hand it to me properly, there's a good girl.'

'But you're so much closer to the ground than I am, Signor Erpicone,' said Cristina. 'I'm sure you'll find it.'

Erpicone cupped the groin of his dungarees in both hands. 'Find this, pine tree,' he said. 'I'll cut you down to size.'

Cristina couldn't help herself. 'I'm afraid that would take an axe, not a nail file,' she said.

'Enough,' said Santoro, snapping his notebook shut. 'Let's go.'

The farm dogs followed Santoro to the car, tails wagging, but he ignored them. They returned to the shade while Cristina folded herself into the passenger seat.

They drove off and parked a little way along on the dusty track before it joined the main road. Santoro opened the bag containing his lunch and pulled out a sealed plastic bag of raw carrot sticks.

He offered the bag to Cristina. 'Like some?'

'No thanks.'

He began crunching. 'My new diet,' he said. 'Raw carrots twice a day for a fortnight. Guaranteed.'

Cristina still glowered straight ahead in silence.

'Don't let him get to you,' said Santoro.

She unclenched her jaw and her fists. 'I know I should be used to it. I've heard it all my life. I'm sorry.'

'What did you make of him?'

'Every bit as unpleasant as you said.'

Santoro fished out another piece of carrot. 'What else?'

'You mean his hands?'

'Go on,' he said, before biting into the carrot.

'Either he has Parkinson's or something similar, or he's a drinker.'

Santoro paused mid crunch. 'A drinker. He starts the day with *caffè corretto*, then sips grappa or wine all day. I guess he's never completely sober now.'

'Since his wife died?'

'Even before that,' said Santoro. 'But he's certainly much worse now. That's another reason he stays on the farm; he knows he couldn't drive.'

'He keeps a tidy house.'

'Before she left, his daughter got social services involved. There's a woman from the town who visits every day. She tidies up and does his laundry. Brings a hot meal every day, too.'

'Why doesn't he get the cataract operation?'

'He deludes himself that his kids will come back some day. He doesn't want to be away when they do, so he stays on the farm.'

'Do you think he'll report me for the way I spoke to him, Gennaro?'

Santoro chuckled. 'Relax, he'll have loved the way you spoke to him.'

CHAPTER EIGHT

The roof of the two-storey farmhouse had been recently redone. The original lichen-covered pantiles, which were in the majority, were cleverly interspersed with new ones whose bright red terracotta was lost in a mosaic that seemed to have always been there. Traditional green shutters stood out against the zabaglione-coloured walls.

Moretti parked in the shade, leaving the windows down.

As he arrived at the heavy chestnut wood door, he could hear the steady rhythm of a woman's low staccato gasps issuing from the open window above him. Envy made Moretti ring the bell for much longer than necessary.

Unfeasibly quickly, fully dressed Signor Mancini opened the door a little.

'Good morning,' he said. 'Can I help you?'

Moretti looked Mancini up and down. Handsome, and about the same height but leaner than Moretti, clean shaven with dark hair greying at the temples.

'Sorry to disturb you,' he said, in a tone that he might have used in a bar when asking someone to pass the sugar. 'Commissario Dino Moretti. I wonder if I might have a word with you.'

He held up his ID. 'If I'm not interrupting anything.'

Mancini smiled.

'Of course, please come in.' He opened the door wide and stood back to let Moretti enter.

The room was simply and tastefully furnished in a modern, anonymous style.

'Please take a seat. May I offer you a cold drink? Coffee?'

'No, thank you.' Moretti perched on a sofa while Mancini sat in an armchair opposite.

'How may I help you?'

'I'm investigating the disappearance of a family from one of the neighbouring properties. You might have noticed something.'

'Sorry, no, I haven't.'

'This is rather serious, Signor Mancini,' said the commissario. 'A ten-year-old boy has gone missing from a locked house.'

Mancini crossed his legs, pinched the crease of his trouser leg to hitch it up a little and assumed an open posture with his hands relaxed over the end of the armrests.

'Perhaps the parents have taken him on vacation for Easter.'

'A witness said the parents left for work without him three days ago.'

'I understand, and I don't mean to trivialise the boy's disappearance, but I don't know anything about it. I have no way of knowing anything about it, so I don't know how I can contribute to your investigation.'

Moretti leaned forward. 'When did you move into the area, Signor Mancini?'

'A few years back,' he replied with the merest wave of a hand.

'And from your accent, I'd say you're originally from the south.'

'Yes.'

'What do you do? Do you work locally?'

'I'm retired.'

'So, you have plenty of spare time.'

He studied Moretti's face. 'Yes.'

'Do you travel much, or do you stay here?'

'I'm sure you know that I hunt with some of the local guys during the season.'

'And when it's not the season?'

'I'm mostly at home.'

Upstairs, a toilet flushed.

Moretti looked at the ceiling. 'I'm sure that you find plenty to occupy your time.'

Mancini flicked a non-existent piece of fluff from his trousers.

35

'Yes.'

'Do you know where the Rosati property is, Signor Mancini?'

'I'm sorry, I'm a very private person and I keep myself to myself, so no, I don't.'

'You share a common boundary.'

'Really? I didn't know.'

'How about the boy, Mario Rosati? Have you ever met him? Seen him around, perhaps?'

'No, sorry.'

'That you haven't met him, or that you haven't seen him around?'

'Neither.'

A woman in her twenties appeared at the door. Her silk robe was tied at the waist but gaped open, revealing most of her cleavage and a thick dark tuft. She ignored Moretti and ran a hand through her messy hair.

'Pino, have you nearly finished?'

Mancini smiled at Moretti and shrugged. 'Is there anything else?'

'That'll be all for the moment,' said Moretti, rising to his feet. 'I'll let you get back to… whatever you were doing. I'll see myself out.'

He took a card from his wallet and placed it on the arm of the sofa. 'Here's my number if you think of anything.'

*

Vice Questore Innocenti called them into his office. He nodded at Santoro, tightened his lips at Moretti, and beamed at Furlan.

'Sit down, all of you.'

Santoro pulled over a seat and they sat in order of height at Innocenti's desk: Cristina, very tall and athletic, thick blonde hair, blue eyes; Moretti, taller than average, lean with a slight paunch, unkempt grizzled hair, brown eyes, and a dark walrus moustache; and Santoro, shortest, darkest, and podgiest of the three.

Innocenti pulled out a handkerchief and dabbed his lip. 'How's the Rosati case going, Moretti?'

'Slowly, Vice Questore. We've interviewed the neighbours and Mario's teacher. Nobody's seen anything, nobody knows anything.'

Innocenti mopped his brow. 'Or they're not talking.'

'There's that too.'

'What's next? Any clues or leads?'

'The Rosatis are not answering their phones and they've not been admitted to hospital. We're trying to track down any relatives, but they were a very private couple, so nobody really knows much about them. There are some migrant workers on Erpicone's place and the pruning squad from Siena. We've still to talk to them, although the pruning guys come around every year so I'm thinking that they're less likely to be involved.'

'But you're not ruling anything out at this stage?'

'No, I'm not ruling anything out at this stage, but what we need is a thorough search. Would it be okay if I pulled together a big search party using our own uniformed guys and the cops in Maghicchio and surrounding towns? We could cover the entire area in a day.'

'What?'

'I'll organise everything if you sanction it, of course.'

Innocenti held out his palm towards Moretti and turned to Cristina.

'You see, Ispettore, everything's on the grand scale with Moretti. No thought about the overtime costs, no concern about taking law officers away from their duties elsewhere to search for a family who are probably on an Easter vacation.' He turned back to Moretti. 'I'll sanction no such thing. How about,' he looked to the ceiling. 'I don't know, searching that massive property next door to the Rosati podere – the Ricci agriturismo? Have you spoken to him yet?'

Moretti was suddenly aware of the quickening pulse in his neck. 'Not yet. We'll visit today, probably. I heard he's out of town.'

'Get over and check, and make sure you get the guest list and contact details for the last three weeks.'

Moretti looked wide-eyed at his superior. 'Oh, the guest details for the last three weeks. Thanks, Vice Questore, we'd never have come up with that, eh Santoro?'

Santoro smirked. 'Just writing that down.'

Innocenti twisted the cotton material as if wringing a neck.

'Maybe you want to write this down as well, detectives. I want this case solved, and soon, otherwise I'll call in the carabinieri or regional guys. Is that understood? You wouldn't want your careers to end in failure.'

Moretti and Santoro nodded.

'Ok, you two, get on with it. I want to talk to Ispettore Furlan.'

When the detectives had shuffled out, Innocenti relaxed into his chair.

'How's the case going?'

Cristina cleared her throat.

'It's like Commissario Moretti said, slowly. We're still working on it, and so you know, he'd already said about interviewing Ricci and getting the guest details.'

Innocenti smiled.

'Very loyal. I know. But he's such a hot shot with all his awards that I like to put him in his place from time to time, in case he gets too big-headed.'

'Ah.'

'Has he told you yet that he's solved every case?'

'No, Vice Questore.'

'He will. But tell me, Cristina, his methods are... well, old school. What new perspective can you bring to the case? What sort of things do they do in the north?'

'I don't think that I'd be doing anything different, to be honest. Commissario Moretti is thorough and has great local knowledge, something that I lack.'

Innocenti mopped his forehead.

'Hmm. People talk about his stubbornness. Have you noticed that?'

'Maybe it's his determination to see a case through.'

He narrowed his eyes. 'How about his judgement? Is he always a hundred percent focused on the job?'

'I've spent more time with Agente Santoro, Vice Questore. I couldn't really comment.'

'No, I see. Moretti sometimes seems to be preoccupied with matters of his own. I'd hate to see a case compromised because he was dealing with personal matters. Understand?'

'Yes, Vice Questore.'

'And you'd report to me if you felt that was the case?'

'Of course, Vice Questore.'

'Cristina, you're the new face of policing. I see you as Moretti's replacement. It's only a matter of time before he slips up and spoils that perfect record. Learn what you can from him, get to know the local area, and when the time comes, I want you to take over – a seamless transition.'

Cristina opened her mouth to protest.

'But keep this between us, and make sure that you go with him when he interviews Ricci.'

CHAPTER NINE

The white gravel of the agriturismo's car park was lined on one side by a low hedge of lavender and on two sides by oleander, their floral and musky perfumes a heady mix in the still, hot air. The open side gave access and views to the main building and the pool area with its surrounding chalets.

Giorgio Ricci came to reception. He was taller than the locals – as tall as Cristina – with a tanned complexion and sunglasses perched on top of neat black hair that was greying in a distinguished way at the temples. From his designer basket-weave loafers to his tailored slacks and shirt, everything about Ricci spoke of money. He wore his white, impeccably laundered shirt with open collar and sleeves turned back, showing off his gold Rolex.

'Commissario Moretti and Ispettore Furlan to see you Signor Ricci,' said Alicia the receptionist.

'I've been expecting you,' he said, holding out his hand to Moretti, who gripped it, pumped it once up and down, and released it. 'Giorgio Ricci. I'm the owner of this agriturismo.'

He offered his hand palm up to Cristina, as if to kiss hers, but stopped abruptly with the force of her grip and settled instead for a normal handshake.

'Let's go through to my office.'

One wall in the tidy room was covered in framed certificates of the awards his various wines had won in international competitions, another held a large-scale map of the estate detailing where different grape and olive varieties were planted out.

'May I offer you something?' said Ricci, motioning them to sit.

Moretti answered for both. 'No thank you.'

Ricci smiled.

'How can I help you, officers?'

'We're investigating the whereabouts of your neighbours, the Rosatis. What can you tell us about them?'

'Not much, really. We share a common boundary, so I imagine that the youngster played on my land sometimes. I can't recall seeing him, though.'

'But you have seen him?'

'I suppose so; I can't be more specific. So many people arrive during the season that it's hard to keep up. Some bring children, too, so I really couldn't say.'

'What about the parents? His father does building work.'

Ricci looked past them as if the prize certificates held the answer.

'Maybe he's done some for me in the past. I'll have to check with the estate manager. He'd have a record.'

Moretti mimed writing for Ricci's benefit. Cristina was already noting everything on her phone. He focused closely on Ricci's face but spoke nonchalantly.

'His mother, Chiara?'

Ricci's eyes gave the merest flicker, then steadied.

'I'm certain I haven't. When I'm not away on business, I'm tied up here and don't get off the estate much.'

Moretti hid his annoyance at Ricci's evasion.

'There's something else,' he said, pausing, scrutinising Ricci's expression, but in vain. Ricci's eyes were fixed on some detail on the wall.

'Yes?'

'We'll need to interview everyone staying here at the moment, and we'll need the names and contact details for your guests for the last three weeks.'

Ricci now broke his gaze and looked at Moretti.

'Of course. Ask Alicia at reception on your way out.'

'With full addresses, phone numbers, and passport details?'

'I'll get those sent on to you.'

'It's alright, we'll wait.'

Ricci rose to his feet.

'Very well, if you wouldn't mind waiting in here, I'll see to it and get on with the rest of my day. Oh, sorry. If you've finished with me, that is.'

'For now, yes. Thank you, Signor Ricci.'

Ricci closed the door behind him, leaving the two detectives in his office.

'A cool customer, wouldn't you say? Fancies himself as a bit of a ladies' man.'

'A creep is how I'd describe him, Commissario.'

'What did you make of him?'

'He's hiding something – something about Mario's mother.'

'You saw it, too? We can come back to that at some point. Meanwhile, we'll go over the list of visitors and make up an interview schedule. Maybe decide who we can call and who we'd like to speak to face-to-face.'

'Commissario—'

The receptionist knocking on the door interrupted Cristina.

'Excuse me. Signor Ricci asked me to help you.'

Moretti smiled.

'Alicia? Yes, we need to speak to all the guests. Can you tell me which are currently here, and which are out for the day?'

'Of course.' Alicia counted on her fingers. 'The American couple, the Belgian couple, and the English tourist are all here, either at the pool or somewhere on the estate. The Dutch couple left after breakfast. I think they are visiting Pienza and Siena today.'

'Any idea when they're expected back?'

'They usually get back after lunch, but I can call and let you know.'

'Thank you. Is that everyone?'

'Everyone here. An Australian couple left three days ago.'

'Do you know where they were heading?'

'Yes, they were going down to Puglia. I think I have the address of their hotel at the desk.'

'Good, I'd like to see that, please. And would you tell the estate manager that I'd like a list of all the work carried out on the property over the last three years?'

'What sort of work, Commissario?'

'Everything done by outside contractors – pruning, grape and olive harvest, building and repairs, electrical work; anything that involved outside firms or individuals.'

'He's somewhere on the estate now. I'll call and ask him. When do you need it?'

Moretti's phone buzzed. He looked at the screen, put the call on hold, and stood.

'Excuse me, I need to take this. I'll send someone this afternoon, Alicia. That should give him enough time. Thank you.'

'You're welcome.'

Moretti turned as he reached the door.

'And Alicia, don't let the guests know that we'll be speaking to them. Understood?'

'Of course, Commissario.'

Outside in the car park Moretti unpaused the call.

'Hello, Dino, it's Achille Donati. How are you?'

Moretti grinned wryly. 'Hello, Achille. I'm fine. Are you asking as a friend or as the sindaco?'

Donati chuckled. 'Both, as always. You're working on the Rosati case?'

'You know I am, Achille. That's why you called. If I were to guess, I'd say that you've spoken with Giorgio Ricci.'

'Ever the detective. No comment.'

Moretti heard the smile in Donati's voice and smiled himself. 'Ever the politician. What do you need?'

'Dino, is this a case of a family going on holiday or is it something more sinister?'

'I wish I knew, Achille. We're hoping they're safe but so far no-one can verify their whereabouts, so until we get a lead, we're treating their disappearance seriously.'

'The timing of this case couldn't be worse. We're at the start of the tourist season, and I'd like it cleared up quickly and quietly.'

'You and me both. But when you say quietly, what exactly do you mean?'

Donati sighed. 'You know I don't want to tell you how to do your job.'

'But?'

'But go easy on the tourists, please, okay?'

Moretti exhaled loudly. 'Achille, it was three days before we were alerted. If it is bad news, time's not on our side.'

43

'Dino, I know why this is so tough on you. All I'm saying is do your job but go easy.' The sindaco ended the call.

Moretti rubbed the nape of his neck and walked to the car.

*

Cristina paused after Moretti left the office.

'Alicia, how is Signor Ricci to work for?'

The young woman's eyes checked that Moretti was gone.

'I don't want to cause trouble. There's not a lot of work around here.'

'It's okay, I'd like to know – woman to woman.'

Alicia looked at the floor. Her hand stroked the hair just behind her right ear, and she replied without looking up.

'Woman to woman, don't ever get yourself into a situation where you need something from him.'

Cristina pulled out a card and placed it in Alicia's hand.

'Thank you. If you ever need to talk to me, call. Any time. Okay?'

Alicia nodded.

Cristina rested her hand on the young woman's shoulder. 'Any time.'

*

The air was still warm when the three detectives returned later that afternoon. The agriturismo guests were called to the dining room and seated at separate tables where Santoro waited to ensure no collusion.

Moretti and Cristina were in Ricci's office and asked Alicia to bring through the visitors one at a time. An English stock market trader was first followed by a same sex Belgian couple and finally an American couple. No-one had seen Mario or his parents. No-one had been near their place.

Someone was lying.

CHAPTER TEN

'Thank you. Now leave us,' said the older, grey-haired man. 'And we don't want to be disturbed.'

He waited until he was certain that the waiter was out of earshot.

'No names, just in case, alright?'

The younger man, equally elegantly dressed, smiled. 'Understood.'

'Good, now enjoy the truffle ravioli. They go well with the Brunello.'

The two men sat in their booth at the narrowest and furthest part of the trattoria, whose painted walls still showed the marks where the space had been excavated from the rock. They could observe the whole place from here and enjoyed a few mouthfuls in silence. The younger man spoke first.

'Do you think there is enough to interest my partners?'

The older man nodded and finished chewing his pasta. 'I've been doing this kind of work for rather a long time.'

'Since before I was born, is what I usually hear at this point,' the younger one said with a smile.

'I can imagine. But I can reassure your partners that this is a sound prospect. The candidate I have in mind fits the criteria, and there is soon to be a considerable infrastructure investment in the area.'

'These ravioli are fantastic. Are they stuffed with pheasant?'

'Guinea fowl, I think. Less seasonal.'

'The candidate?'

'Owns a large agriturismo, so there's plenty of opportunity for moving money through his business. He already has contacts with local builders, suppliers, and couriers.'

'Leverage?'

'He's a former banker. Retired early – very early. There were rumours of impropriety, but no charges brought.'

'So he's done it before?'

'I'm sure of it.'

'You have proof?'

'I know people who know him. They have proof.'

'Anything current?'

'He sleeps with some of his guests. Nobody important, and they're all very willing, apparently, but it's something we could use later. He also takes advantage of his female workers – they're not so willing. Nothing major, but enough to cause him some difficulty if it were to be made public.'

'What about the current sindaco?'

'Local man, well liked, trusted, honest – not the sort we can work with at all.'

'Have you approached the candidate yet?'

'Not yet, but if you're interested, we need to act soon. You need to organise the transfer of funds, and there's the usual bureaucracy to go through to register him as a candidate.'

'And you're sure he'll accept our offer?'

'How could he refuse?'

The younger man burst out laughing. 'You watch too many movies.'

CHAPTER ELEVEN

Later that day, Moretti and Cristina returned to Ricci's office to interview the two Dutch tourists. Knowing that they would already have spoken to other guests, they took them together.

'I'm Ispettore Furlan and this is—'

'We know,' the robustly built Dutch woman interrupted with a smile. 'Commissario Beer.'

'…Commissario Moretti. Thank you for taking time from your evening to speak with us. We won't keep you long.'

The couple sat across from the detectives. The husband was lean and considerably taller than Cristina.

'I'm Sabine, and this is my husband Jaap. We heard a young boy has gone missing from a locked farmhouse. Is there any news update, or is he still missing?'

'Still missing, I'm afraid, as are his parents. I understand that you run in various parts of the estate. We're interested in this part.'

She pointed to the boundary between the agriturismo and the Rosati house.

'You've run near there?'

'Yes, with the American, Daniel Cooper, but we went out early, around six-thirty in the morning – we didn't expect it to be so hot at this time of the year – so we saw no-one except the estate manager one morning. He was already out tending the vines over at that bit.'

'Can you remember which day that was?'

'Two days ago. The day of the pool party.'

'Pool party? Tell me about it.'

Sabine laughed.

'It was all very sedate at the start, with people standing around the pool area eating nibbles and having a tasting of some of the estate wine. But the longer it went on, the more boisterous it became. The wine changed from white to red, to very strong red, to Vin Santo, then to grappa. I'm sure there were a few sore heads the next morning.'

'Including you two?'

'I had a great time. Daniel and I were out running the next morning – a little later, but still before breakfast.'

Cristina turned to Jaap. 'And you?'

'I tasted the wines, but I prefer beer, so I stopped and left the party early.'

'Before it became boisterous?'

'Exactly.'

'One final question, have either of you seen an unaccompanied ten-year-old boy when you've been out?'

'No,' they answered in unison.

Everyone stood. Cristina looked up at Jaap.

'Thank you for your help. Enjoy the remainder of your stay. How long do you have left?'

They all shook hands.

'We're here for another couple of days – maybe we'll bump into each other,' he grinned broadly. Sabine hooked her arm into Jaap's and led him out.

Moretti spoke for the first time.

'Well, Cristina, it's been a long day. Alfiero texted to say that the Rosati phones are still going to voicemail. Do you want to join Commissario Beer for a drink?'

'Maybe another time. I want to put together a report about today's interviews.'

*

Moretti wiped his moustache of any remaining traces of beer froth, paid up, and stepped out to his car. He didn't notice the fish until he started the engine and was about to drive off. He switched off, stepped out and looked, first back into Bar Italia, then up and down the street. Carla's son Gigi was watering the tubs of geraniums outside the bar, locals were drinking aperitivi, having a passeggiata, or hurrying home after work as usual.

He bent closer and sniffed – an anchovy, raw, fresh, whole, stuck under his windscreen wiper. Scanning the street again, he searched for a sign, a facial expression, a smirk, something that would reveal the culprit. Again nothing. He pulled an evidence bag from his pocket, eased back the wiper, picked the oily fish up by its tail, and popped it head first into the bag to keep the inside of his car fresh.

A few kilometres out of town he pulled off the road, stopped, and got out. The angry knot in his gut twisted tight. The agriturismo interviews hadn't been helpful.

The meeting with Innocenti had bothered him all day – telling him how to do his job, like a rookie, and in front of Cristina, too. And what was she – a colleague? Maybe she was a spy; she had been kept back, after all. She was definitely his replacement.

Innocenti resented his success. It was always Innocenti that collected the commendations – *his* commendations – 'on behalf of the department'. Bullshit! The Vice Questore was waiting for a mistake, just one, to pension him off, and if anything bad happened to the Rosatis, this could be the case to do it.

How the hell did the kid get out of that house? Where are the damn parents?

Moretti surveyed the landscape that dropped before him to the wide valley.

Somewhere out there is the answer.

The cicadas started up their ratchet chorus, and Moretti headed back to the car.

Why a bloody fish? Who the hell did it?

The divergent mind that made him such a successful detective instantly offered answers, from the banal to the bizarre and, of course, linked it to the other thing – the thought that was always there no matter how he strived to contain it, to lock it away behind an unbreachable wall, never to be confronted or spoken of, never to be free of.

At least I can get rid of the damn anchovy.

He tossed the fish, still in the evidence bag, under a shrub, cleaned his hands on a tissue, and stuffed that, too, where it couldn't be seen from the road.

*

A wonderful combination of cooking smells welcomed Moretti home.

'Maria?'

'In here, Dino,' she called from the kitchen.

'You're home early.'

'The prosecution case fell apart, so I decided to finish for the day and come straight home.'

She held out a glass of wine. 'How was your day?'

He sipped his wine.

'Confusing. The sindaco told me not to upset the tourists. Innocenti treated me like a novice in front of Cristina. She insisted on coming with me instead of Gennaro to talk to Ricci.'

He looked for a reaction from his wife but there was none.

'How did that go?' she asked, as she turned to the dresser.

'I'm not sure. Cristina thinks he's hiding something.'

Maria brought out two plates. 'Oh? Why's that?'

'He was being his usual self.' He watched her set the plates on the table. 'You know.'

'No, I don't know.'

'He was all fake charm. Sleazy.'

'Some women appreciate that.'

'Well, luckily Cristina is one of those women who can see right through his facade.' He took a long sip of wine and studied his wife closely. 'She called him a creep.'

Still no reaction from Maria.

'We did get to speak to some of Ricci's guests, though. That was more interesting.'

Now she stopped and gave him all her attention.

'Oh? Are you closer to finding out what happened to Mario and his parents?'

'I don't think so, but I'm not sure. Maybe. We've started looking for relatives or friends of the Rosati's outside Cassiatorre, because they don't really socialise with the locals.'

'Where do they work?'

'Both in Maghicchio. So we're making enquiries there, and we've also involved the regional and national guys to widen the search through the whole of Italy.'

Maria raised her eyebrows.

'Good luck with that, Dino. In my experience the national service isn't fit for purpose. There isn't a national database; they don't even use the same software systems and equipment. You'd be as quick going door-to-door yourself.'

'Well, that's what we have, and we don't have the manpower to do anything more. I asked Innocenti if I could organise a combined search party, and he refused.'

'No surprise there. What about your informal informants?'

'What do you mean?'

'Those women who spend most of their time in Bar Italia.'

Moretti squeezed his eyes shut.

'Ah, the busybodies. No, I haven't spoken to them yet. Usually I don't have to – one or other of them makes an anonymous call to the Questura – but their information is typically little more than spiteful prejudice.'

'If you don't have anything else, you need to chase every lead.'

'Now you're starting to sound like Innocenti.'

'Just saying.'

'Anyway, I've asked the others to meet me at six-thirty tomorrow morning to try to push on.'

'Do you think they'll come in?'

'Furlan definitely – she's from the north. Santoro, who knows. But he has children; he wants to find the boy.'

He put down his glass and fetched two napkins and placed them on the table.

'Cristina did all the talking today. Her English is very good.'

Maria took a casserole out of the oven.

'So maybe it was as well that she insisted on coming with you today. Put a trivet on the table, we can serve it from there.'

'Smells great. What is it?'

'I was able to find some lovely fresh fish in the market today, so I've made anchovy parmigiana.'

Moretti was speechless.

CHAPTER TWELVE

The darkness under the trees took the shape of a tall, thin figure, which made its silent way across the open space to the shack.

'Psh. Psh.'

'Come in.'

Yusuf pulled aside the tarpaulin that almost covered the door space and entered. The eight men inside made space for the newcomer, who shrugged off the dark blanket he wore over his shoulders and sat cross-legged on the earth floor among them.

'What's happening, brother?'

Yusuf held out a plastic container.

'I've brought you some ewes' milk, and some news.'

The men decanted the milk into an assortment of containers fashioned from fizzy drinks cans and cut-down water bottles and gulped it down.

'What's the news?' asked the milk-moustachioed leader.

'A young boy has gone missing. Police are searching and asking questions.'

The leader wiped his mouth and furrowed his brows.

'What has that to do with us? We keep ourselves to ourselves. We speak to no-one and hide from the local people. We know nothing about a boy.'

Yusuf nodded.

'We are black,' he said with a sigh. 'We are different; foreign, Muslim, and we are illegal. In their eyes we broke the law to come here, so they do not trust us and will not believe us. If a bad thing has happened to the boy, someone will find a way to blame us.'

The workers nodded and muttered agreement.

'But you speak their language, you can speak for us. You know us – know our story.'

'Nobody knows I speak their language,' he said in a whisper, as if someone might overhear. 'That way I'm invisible to them.'

Yusuf looked around, holding each man's gaze.

'Brothers, if any one of you has done anything to this boy,' he said in a level, measured tone, 'he must leave, lest we are all punished. If any of you has even as much as seen the boy, he must tell me so that I can think about what to do. These are not easy times for us, and we must think of the thousands like us who are hiding in this country. None of us wants to be the reason that we are all rounded up and sent back. Our families have sacrificed much to send us here.'

He paused and searched their faces.

'Very well.' He addressed the leader. 'I will leave it to you to talk to your men. I must go, but I shall return soon.'

Yusuf stood, raised his hand in farewell, wrapped his blanket over his shoulders and left as silently as he had come, his eyes closed to slits so that he once again became part of the darkness.

CHAPTER THIRTEEN

Moretti sat against his desk, facing the two seated detectives. Now he was taller than Cristina.

'Sorry for asking you to come in so early, but I'm afraid that we're getting nowhere fast with this case. So, where are we? You start off, Gennaro.'

Santoro popped the carrot stick he was about to eat back into its plastic bag and opened his notebook.

'The neighbour Signor Di Vittorio saw the parents leave at the usual time, about seven in the morning. He knows that they often left Mario at home on his own.'

'Was that who reported it?' Cristina asked. 'What exactly did he say?'

Santoro read from his notebook. 'These are Alfiero's notes. Di Vittorio says, "The Rosatis went to work and locked their boy inside their farmhouse." Alfiero asks, "When was this, sir?" "Three days ago. They usually get home about six o'clock." "You haven't seen the boy or his parents for three days?" "No, and their car hasn't been back." "So the boy has been alone for three days? Why didn't you call earlier, sir?" Caller hangs up.'

'That was when the cops investigated and brought us in,' said Moretti.

'Do you believe Di Vittorio?' Cristina asked.

'No reason not to at this stage.'

Santoro flipped a page in his notebook.

'Enzo Giusti, another neighbour. Mario plays on his property sometimes, but that's all. We can rule him out – he spends every minute looking after his sick wife.'

'Sure?'

'Certain. I've known Enzo for years. Absolutely not him.'

'How about the garage guy?'

'He fuelled the car, checked the oil and tyre pressure; only the parents were in the car. Nothing different from usual.'

'There's something different and we're not seeing it. I spoke with Mario's teacher. She's another one who knew that the parents used to leave him alone. What's wrong with these people? Erpicone?'

Cristina and Gennaro looked at each other.

'You go,' she said.

Gennaro smiled.

'Erpicone was his usual charming self. He denied even knowing Mario, and we've still to follow up on the pruning squad that he uses and his gang of illegal workers.'

'Do you believe him?'

'Capo?'

'About Mario. Do you believe that he doesn't know the boy?'

'No. He's lying, but that might be because he is such an uncooperative—'

Cristina flushed. 'And obnoxious.'

'…and obnoxious person.'

'Could he be involved?'

'Not directly, he's in self-imposed house arrest – never leaves. As I said, we've still to check on his workers.'

Moretti looked at the ispettore.

'Cristina.'

'Our visit to the agriturismo has thrown up a few possibilities. I've pulled together what we discovered yesterday from our interviews.'

She passed the others a spreadsheet.

'These are the guests who were there during the time that we think Mario went missing. None of them admit to seeing him, although certain parts of their stories are contradictory. We still need to follow up on that.'

The men scanned the sheet. Moretti nodded.

'Yes. Sabine's account contradicts Daniel's version. Good work, Cristina.'

'I've also been through the information from Ricci.'

She handed out another spreadsheet.

'Here is a list of the guests over the last few weeks, and on the other side a note of all the people who've done work on his place over the last year or so. You'll see that Mario's dad Domenico Rosati is there, and also the pruning squad that Erpicone uses.'

'The workers and tradesmen we can contact. What about the visitors?'

'Some of those who have left are Italian, so we can reach them. Others are foreigners and will be back home by now, a few are still on vacation elsewhere in Italy. I've some officers working through the list, and I'll update you later.'

Moretti pursed his lips.

'I think that Ricci and the agriturismo will give us our prime suspect, but we have no motive. And the sindaco doesn't want us to press the tourists hard.'

'He knows it's a possible murder inquiry, doesn't he?'

'Politicians look at things differently.'

'So why is Ricci a strong suspect?'

'Just a gut feeling, Gennaro. I think that's maybe where we concentrate our searches.'

'What about Mancini?'

Moretti smoothed his moustache with finger and thumb. 'Mancini's an interesting character.'

'How do you mean, capo?'

'It's the way he speaks. He's from the south, somewhere. He doesn't say much – like a cop giving evidence in a court. You know what I mean; nothing that could lead to a supplementary.'

'Do you think he's lying?'

'Or maybe hiding something?'

'Why do you say that, Cristina?'

'I hope you don't mind, but I used my initiative again.'

Moretti and Santoro exchanged a glance.

'I ran his details through the computer and reached a dead end.'

'How do you mean?'

'The records are detailed going back about ten years or so, but then nothing.'

'Nothing?'

'It's like that's when he arrived on the planet. I think he's been given a new identity, and whoever organised it didn't go back far enough.'

She looked from Moretti to Gennaro.

'Gennaro?'

Santoro snapped shut his notebook and picked up his bag of carrot sticks again.

'Interesting,' he said with a smile. 'Computers don't know everything. You say he's from the south? I'll make a few calls to some friends down there and see what I can unearth.'

'Good. Update me as soon as you know anything. Any progress on finding the parents?'

'Not yet,' said Santoro. 'I've been in touch with some of my contacts in the national organisation, but this is so low level for them that I don't think it's even registered on their radar. All I ever get from them is how under-resourced they are – which is true – how antiquated and incompatible the various systems are – which is also true – and how they respond to whichever political dog barks loudest.'

'And I suppose our dog is a chihuahua,' said Moretti.

'Capo, I hate to say it, but as far as the national crime guys are concerned, we don't even have a dog.'

'Nevertheless, Innocenti and the sindaco want this case closed quickly before it destroys the tourist season, so I'll speak to Innocenti again about recalling some of the uniformed boys from leave. And, Santoro, you call the local hunters' groups to help. If we can get enough of them, we'll start a thorough search of the area between the filling station and Maghicchio this morning. Cristina, during the search, I want you to check on all CCTV coverage radiating in every direction out of Cassiatorre, in case for any reason they took a different route. Are we clear?'

'Yes,' they chorused.

CHAPTER FOURTEEN

What looked like a chaotic abandonment of vehicles had instead a clearly defined order. The more modern and larger SUVs and pickup trucks with their chunky tyres were arranged to one side of Piazza Garibaldi, while the smaller, older, 4x4 Pandas clustered together in front of Bar Italia. What each of the vehicles had in common, though, was a transport box – purpose-made from aluminium, or a homemade wire mesh contraption with a camouflage canvas cover for the dogs.

All the dogs were hunters. The lean, tireless Segugi, descendants of ancient Egyptian hounds bred to track and kill their quarry of rabbit and hare, could run all day in any terrain; the stockier Spinone, capable of penetrating the thorniest bushes thanks to their thick, wiry coats; and the large Bracco, or Pointer, hunter retrievers, with their coats spattered with characteristic patches of orange, amber, and chestnut.

The personalities of the dogs reflected those of their owners. Some noisy, fidgety, and eager to hunt, others throwing their heads back to howl or bark challenges at the other dogs, while a few lay, paws crossed but alert, waiting to be unleashed. The men, dressed in a mishmash of camouflage gear, drank coffee, smoked, whispered, and joked in pairs, trios, or larger groups, comparing dogs, swapping stories, and managing the adrenaline that coursed through them all.

As Moretti, Santoro, and Furlan approached down the slope of

Piazza Garibaldi, the hunters, and most of the dogs, fell silent.

'Men, thank you for being here,' Moretti said grimly. 'The Rosati family – Domenico, Chiara, Mario – have disappeared, and we need your help to try to find them. We need to cover the terrain between here and Maghicchio, the Rosati's usual journey to work, but I also want to search all the surrounding area to a radius of ten kilometres. Ispettore Furlan and Agente Santoro are passing out the phone number that you should call if you find anything.'

He paused as Cristina's height and looks prompted chatter and ribald remarks. 'So you are all clear,' he said with a smile. 'It's my phone number, not Ispettore Furlan's.'

Groans and some laughter from the crowd.

'You know the area better than I do, so I'll leave it to you to organise yourselves into teams. Please remember these important points. First, if you find something, call me immediately, and under no circumstances touch anything at the scene. We're already a couple of days late in starting out so our forensics might already be compromised. Don't make it worse by contaminating the scene.

'Second, the church bell will be the signal that the search is called off. If you hear that, either head back here, or go home.

'Third, no-one should be carrying a gun, but if you are, do not under any circumstances use it. With so many people out there, I don't want there to be any accidents.'

A few hands raised.

'No, there are no exceptions. I don't care what type of exotic game wanders in front of you, no shooting. Any questions?'

'What about our fuel costs?'

Moretti shook his head. 'Seriously? Look, nobody is forcing you to search, but if anyone feels that they need reimbursed for their fuel, report to the Questura with your number plate details and we'll give you a voucher for half a tank. Fair enough?'

There was general agreement, and several men hit the one who'd asked the question over the head.

One of the hunters, Corrado, handed Moretti a walkie-talkie.

'Here, Commissario, take this. We'll be searching in places without a phone signal.'

Within five minutes, the hunters had organised themselves and left, leaving a counter full of empty espresso cups in Bar Italia, scattered cigarette butts on the ground or stubbed into the soil of the geranium tubs, and an acrid mist of diesel exhaust in the air. A couple of men reading their newspapers, two mums with buggies, and three women at a table immediately inside the door were the only remaining customers.

'All we can do now is wait,' said Santoro.

'Tell the Forensics guys and the uniforms to stand by.'

'Yes, Commissario.'

*

The warming air carried the baying of hounds set to work by the search parties closest to the village.

Inside the Questura, the detectives managed the situation in different ways. Cristina studied CCTV recordings, Santoro stepped out of the office to call south, and Moretti sat staring at his phone, willing it to ring. He jumped when the walkie-talkie squawked.

'Moretti. Where are you? What have you found?'

'Commissario, it's Sandro, we're halfway between Cassiatorre and Maghicchio. The dogs are going crazy. They've found the remains of a boar carcass. Someone's cut it up and spread it about. I don't know if it's important, but it's queer.'

'Okay, don't touch anything. Keep the dogs under control and stay there. I'm sending down a Forensics team. Make sure someone flags them down from the roadside. Over.'

Moretti called through on the desk phone.

'Send Team One down the road to Maghicchio. Look out for one of the hunters at the roadside.'

The walkie-talkie crackled as he finished.

'Moretti. Where are you? What have you found?'

'Tommaso here. We're at the old partisan cave. We've found a car.'

'Anyone inside?'

'No, it's empty.'

'Good work. Don't touch anything and keep the dogs leashed. Where exactly is the cave? Near the road?'

'No, it's hidden in the woods. Send Corrado. He knows where it is. Tell him to come in from the top road.'

'Will do. Thanks.'

He picked up the desk phone again. 'Find Corrado and send him with Team Two to the partisan cave. They've to use the top road.'

60

Santoro drove his car, with Cristina in the passenger seat and Moretti squeezed in the back.

'Stop at the roadside first.'

On the way they passed a police car blocking the road and diverting traffic, and when they arrived, white-suited officers were already busy taking samples from the tarmac and the verge.

'What have you found?'

'On the road surface, dried blood, hair, and fragments of glass and plastic. Someone hit a boar then dragged it off the road over there – it's a mess.'

'Any idea of how long ago?'

'Not precisely, but it fits the timeframe if it was Rosati. Stay outside of the taped area if you're going over there.'

The three made their way towards the trees.

Moretti immediately pictured the accident.

'Looks like they had a rope around that tree. They dragged the boar off the road but figured the carcass could still be seen, so they butchered it.'

'The car must have been in a mess,' said Santoro.

'If it's theirs, that's why they hid it in the partisan cave.'

Cristina pointed to a stinking pile of entrails in the grass.

'Why?' she asked. 'Why not simply report the accident?'

Santoro smiled.

'That's what you'd do in the north. You like bureaucracy up there. The further south you go, the less we like it.'

'Remember,' said Moretti. 'This is a couple who were too busy, or late, or badly organised to arrange a babysitter for their son. I think from the moment they hit the boar, they panicked. They didn't think things through. Okay, I've seen enough. Santoro, give me your car keys and stay here. Cristina, you come with me.'

Corrado met them at the end of a dirt track, and they followed his car to the taped-off partisan cave where another Forensics team was busy working.

'Is it Rosati's car?'

'Yes, Commissario. Registered to Domenico Rosati. The front is badly mangled and covered in blood and hair. We think they dumped it here and set off cross country. Tommaso and the rest of the hunters set off following trails rather than hanging around here.'

The sound of hunting dogs seemed to come from every direction around them.

Cristina tried to peer into the far end of the cave. 'Can you tell if Mario was in the car that morning?'

'No, Ispettore. We'll have a better idea once we have analysed all our samples.'

'Find anything unusual?' asked Moretti.

'Apart from the damage, no, except there's a woman's bag in the footwell passenger side.'

'May we see?'

The officer handed them rubber gloves. 'Sure, come this way.'

The bag held the usual bits and pieces, including purse, identity card, and keys.

Moretti looked grim.

'This isn't good,' he said, pointing to the house keys. 'It means that Signora Rosati couldn't have let Mario out of the house.'

The walkie-talkie squawked.

'Moretti. Where are you? What have you found?'

'It's Tommaso, we've found Rosati. It's not good news.'

'Where are you?'

'Tell Corrado to bring you to the Stag Leap, but you'll need a mountain rescue team to examine and retrieve the body.'

'*Porca miseria*, that'll take hours.'

'No, it won't, Commissario,' said Cristina. 'Does anyone have a rope?'

CHAPTER FIFTEEN

The crevice was known to the local hunters as the Stag Leap because many a day's hunting had ended at the point where a red deer could easily jump from one side to the other, leaving dogs and hunters behind. There were no trees close enough to the opening, so Cristina passed one end of a rope around a large boulder and knotted the two ends together.

'Clear away the stones and debris,' she said to Moretti and the others. 'I don't want anything to fall on my head while I'm descending. And lend me your jackets.'

She put on two long-sleeved jackets, then threw the knotted end of the rope down towards Rosati's body and checked that the top end passed freely around the boulder.

Moretti placed his hand on her arm. 'Are you sure about this?'

'Yes, Commissario.'

Cristina stepped between the two strands of rope, passed them under her armpits, and crossed them behind her back. Then she stepped over each strand so that the rope passed between her legs.

'That looks uncomfortable,' said Moretti.

'It's only a short descent. The friction burns on my back and arms would be more of a problem without the extra layers.'

She wrapped the free rope around her forearm and gripped tightly to support her weight as she leaned back into the void. Using her free hand to hold the top part of the rope, she began her slow descent. Halfway down, the rope above her slipped and dislodged a loose piece of stone that fell directly at her. She saw it coming and used her free hand to bat it away.

'Are you okay?'

'No problem, Commissario.'

When she reached Rosati, she planted one foot flat on the rock behind her and crouched, bracing her knee against the other wall as she assessed the situation.

'He fell with what looks like a tool bag on his back.'

She tried to move him.

'The bag weighs a ton, that's why he couldn't move. Oh, and I think his leg's broken.'

'Can we bring him up?'

'Not with the tool bag.'

'Can you cut it free?'

The bag clanked into the darkness of the fissure. Cristina reached underneath Rosati.

'Okay, I think we can lift him now. Toss me another line.'

A rope snaked down, and Cristina expertly changed position around Rosati to pass it under his body and knot it securely.

'Right, try that.'

The officers at the top took the strain but nothing happened.

'Hang on.'

Cristina moved to Rosati's feet, grabbed a handful of trouser leg and hauled it up so that the broken leg rested on top of the other.

'Now try.'

This time the body moved a little. She moved to the head end, lowered herself as far as she could and placed her own shoulder under the dead man's and pushed.

The body moved and rose freely.

'Slow down! I don't want sideswiped by his legs. Let me get back into position.'

Cristina clamped her ropes at her ankles and pulled herself up, keeping pace with the body. Once at the top, she helped the others to pull up and untie the corpse. When they'd finished, everyone clapped and patted her on the back.

'Let's get someone up here to examine the body and organise a stretcher to move the body down. Are you all right, Cristina?'

'Yes,' she replied, removing the borrowed jackets. 'But if that offer of a drink is still on, I'd like to take it up.'

Moretti grinned.

'Absolutely. Wherever did you learn to climb like that? You were amazing.'

She carefully coiled the ropes.

'I've been climbing in the Dolomites since I was a child, but that's my first time with a corpse.'

'Let's go and get Santoro. He'll never believe this.'

*

Bar Italia was busy.

Some of the hunters who were searching that morning had returned and taken up their usual seats outside against the wall facing out to Piazza Garibaldi, others were inside chatting to the three gossips or playing cards.

Moretti ordered drinks then joined Gennaro and Cristina at a table outside. He took in the scene. Nothing suggested that the day was other than ordinary – nothing reflected the grim find they had made that morning or Moretti's rising feeling of urgency about the missing boy and his mother.

The Dutch couple, Sabine and Jaap, raised their glasses from a nearby table as Carla appeared with three small beers and a selection of snacks and small sandwiches.

Moretti nodded and turned to his colleagues.

'Cheers,' he said out of habit, as they clinked glasses and sipped.

'Coming here was a bad idea. Now that we've found Domenico's body, the public will expect us to press on with the search.'

Santoro's bag of carrot sticks lay unopened on the table as he picked up his second salami sandwich.

'The public will be fine with the idea that we're human, and we're having a quick drink before we get back to work.'

'We're allowed a lunch break, Commissario.'

'Exactly,' said Santoro. 'And if by the public you meant the three busybodies inside, I wouldn't be worried. Today's work has given them plenty to talk about. Look at them in there, interrogating the guys who were on the search party.'

'All the same, I'd feel happier if we finished up and got back to the Questura.'

As he rose to go inside to pay, Cristina nodded and finished her beer in a mouthful. Santoro did likewise, stuffed another sandwich into his mouth, and grabbed a last handful of snacks.

Several of the hunters rose to shake hands with Cristina. One called into the bar and the others came out to do the same. As she left, Jaap raised his glass again, smiled and winked.

The gossips tutted as Moretti headed back outside.

'Good day, ladies,' he said, smoothing each side of his thick moustache with an index finger. 'If you're not careful I'm going to co-opt you into my detective team to help us with our interviews.'

*

Back in the Questura, the three detectives looked at the large-scale map on the wall. Pins showed where the boar was killed, the position of the partisan's cave, and where the body was found.

'What happened to the mother? Where is she?'

'The Forensics teams are still working across that whole area,' said Cristina. 'I'm sure they'll come up with something.'

Moretti closed his eyes, imagining the scene.

'But that might be too late. Where would she go? Her boy was locked indoors. Her keys were in her bag.'

Santoro indicated on the map.

'The trackers found her trail heading home. They also found traces of her at the site where her husband fell.'

Moretti opened his eyes. 'They split up.'

'Commissario?'

'For some reason they separated. She went off one way and he another. She waited for him and doubled back when he didn't show up. She probably realised she had no keys and went back to look for them.'

'Why would they split up?'

'An argument, they fought, who knows, but that would explain the traces that the dogs found.'

'Okay, capo, the dogs have found traces of her all over the place, but why haven't they found how she left the area? She couldn't just disappear.'

'Right, Gennaro, you go to the deceased's work. Ask his workmates what sort of person Domenico was. You know what we're looking for. Cristina, you come with me, and we'll do the same at the supermarket where Signora Rosati worked. We'll meet back here later.'

CHAPTER SIXTEEN

After the short drive down to Maghicchio, Moretti and Cristina arrived at the supermarket and were allowed to use the manager's office and a small staff room for their interviews.

Cristina decided on a group interview and sat on the same side of the manager's desk as the women she spoke to.

'What can you tell me about Chiara?'

The women all spoke in turn.

'She keeps herself to herself – doesn't mix much.'

'She's from the south – they're different down there.'

'I don't really know her that well.'

'Yes, she's – I don't know – fussy, isn't she?'

The other women nodded.

'Yes, always tidying things – even in the canteen. She'll clean up the table, even though it's not her job.'

'Always neat and tidy, her hair is always short and well kept. She never wears make up – at least, not that I've ever seen – and her nails are always clipped short, she never wears nail polish.'

'I think she worries or at least has trouble sleeping. She always has dark rings under her eyes – I mean they're sunken anyway – but I don't know if she has an easy time at home.'

'Have any of you visited her at home?'

A chorus of 'No'.

'I took her home once. She was feeling ill, and her husband had their car, so the manager asked if anyone would give her a lift.'

'Did you go inside?'

'Yes. The place was spotless, you know, the way your nonna keeps house.'

The other women smiled.

'She's very houseproud. Even though she wasn't well, she noticed a piece of fluff on the floor, and she stooped to pick it up.'

Another woman chimed in. 'She hates germs. I think that's why she cleans so much, and why they don't have pets.'

'What about her son?'

'She adores him.'

They all nodded.

'Very protective. She won't let him have friends to the house in case they bring in dirt and mess.'

'She wants him to be vegetarian like her when he turns thirteen,' said another.

A woman who had yet to speak unfolded her arms. 'I don't think she likes sex.'

They all laughed.

'You mean as much as you, Roberta.'

More laughter.

'As much as normal,' replied Roberta. 'She loves her boy and would like another child, but she can't bring herself to it.'

Cristina leaned towards her.

'How do you mean Roberta?'

Roberta folded her arms again and the other women listened.

'I found her crying in the toilets once. She'd been in the canteen with the rest of us, and some of the men were, you know, mucking about and boasting about what they did at home and teasing us about our husbands. The usual stupid men stuff. Well, she took it personally and ended up in tears.'

'I never knew,' said one.

'Go on,' said Cristina.

'Even when we speak among ourselves about our husbands and boyfriends – you know, when they come home with a bunch of flowers expecting you to jump into bed, or when they send the kids out to play in the afternoon and they come up behind you at the sink and lift your skirt – she always leaves the room. So, I don't think she likes sex.'

The women were more serious now.

'That's right, she's very old-fashioned – like your granny almost.'

'Or a nun.'

'Who knows her best?'

'None of us. I think she used to talk to one of her neighbours, but I couldn't be sure.'

Along the corridor in the staff room, the men told Moretti a similar, if less detailed, story of how Chiara was prudish.

She can't take a joke was the consensus.

*

Santoro's interview with Domenico's workmates was less structured, as some of them were out on jobs and they returned in twos and threes.

'What kind of a worker was Signor Rosati?'

Each of the men offered some information.

'He was a good worker. He could turn his hand to most building jobs and was very good at painting.'

'He prided himself on having a set of expensive tools that he'd built up over the years.'

'Yes, he'd bring his tool bag to every job. It weighed a ton. I don't know how he could lift it. He was very strong.'

'How did he get along with you lot? Was he sociable?'

'Da Vinci? Sure. He made friends easily, liked a joke. He'd come for a drink after work sometimes.'

'Why was he called Da Vinci?'

The builder smiled. 'Everybody has a nickname here. I'm Pluto, he's Toothpick, our boss is Beatrice – don't ask – another is Maradona. Domenico shaved his head, so when he was working outdoors in the summer, he used to wear a white painter's hat. So we called him Da Vinci.'

'You said he came for a drink only sometimes?'

A few men grinned.

'What he means is he didn't join the fishing club,' said Pluto.

The grins turned to chuckles.

'The fishing club? You have a fishing club?'

'That's what we call it – but it's not the kind of fish you're thinking about.'

'Go on.'

'Every so often we go on a fishing trip. We pack up rods and clothes for a couple of days and we head off somewhere for a boozy weekend. We rarely bring back any fish – we tell our wives that we put them back or we buy some to keep up the pretence.'

'So it's an excuse for a drunken weekend.'

'And the rest,' said Toothpick.

They all laughed.

'What he means is we go for a drink, we have a laugh, we find some girls, we go dancing, and we have sex.'

'And we joke about our fishing poles and tackle. You can imagine.'

'And Domenico never went with you?'

'He'd have liked to. I think he was jealous of our exploits.'

'Not yours, maybe.'

They all laughed.

'I think he was short-changed at home,' said Pluto. 'His wife was a cleanliness fanatic. He once told me that whenever he did get a chance of hanky panky – and that wasn't very often; his wife either had a headache or a period – she got up right after, showered, then came back, stripped the bed, and remade it.'

Santoro waited until the comments stopped.

'How did he get on with his boy?'

'Mario? He loved him,' said Toothpick. 'He was very protective. Something had happened to him in his childhood, and he wanted to make sure that it didn't happen to Mario.'

'Do you know what that was?'

'No, but I can guess.'

'Did Domenico have any enemies?'

'I wouldn't say enemies,' said Pluto. 'But there were maybe a couple of people who had a grudge against him.'

'Why was that?'

'He sometimes did home jobs, and I remember that he did a job a few years ago where the price was so tight that he'd be working for nothing. Well, he used some recycled materials from a job here instead of buying new. The farmer was raging.'

'Can you remember who the farmer was?'

'I think it was old Erpicone, up near Cassiatorre.'

'The old skinflint threatened to shoot him, as I remember,' added Toothpick.

'Fat chance of that happening. The old coot's blind.'

CHAPTER SEVENTEEN

Late that afternoon, the detectives met in Moretti's office.

'It's been quite a day,' said Moretti. 'Let's see where we are now. Mario is still missing. His mother is missing. His father Domenico is dead. Have we any reason to believe his death was anything but an accident?'

Santoro consulted his notebook.

'The initial Forensics report says that he died from the fall, probably an internal haemorrhage when he struck his head.'

'So are we ruling out the wife as a possible suspect? She has gone missing, after all.'

'The impression I got,' said Cristina, 'is that they are a hard-working couple who loved their son, although there were difficulties in the bedroom. She felt that sex was messy and unfulfilling, so she avoided it, but I don't see that as sufficient reason to kill her husband.'

'The story I heard from Domenico's workmates confirms the sex thing, and I agree with Cristina that Chiara didn't have anything to do with her husband's death.'

'What else did Forensics say?'

Santoro rubbed the stubble on his chin.

'Well, they've come up with a probable cause of the accident.'

'Gennaro, we know that. Their car hit a boar.'

'Yes, but not a side blow – that's usually how they're killed, running across the road. This one was hit head-on.'

'Why didn't it move?'

'That's what Forensics found. The boar was off its face on cocaine.'

Moretti and Furlan chorused their surprise.

'What?'

'There were traces of cocaine on its tusks and in samples taken from some of the body parts they discovered. It must have been rooting around and found somebody's drug cache.'

'*Porca Maremma*,' groaned Moretti. 'Now we've a narcotics investigation as well.'

'They also found a stash of prescription drugs hidden behind the car in the partisan's cave, but they don't think they're connected either with the cocaine or the Rosati's car.'

'Find out what they are and check with the local pharmacy if anyone in the area uses them.'

'Yes, capo. Sorry.'

'But none of that changes why a mother wouldn't go back for her son, let alone disappear.'

'Commissario, one of Chiara's workmates said that she used to talk to a neighbour.'

'Which neighbour?'

'Well, I'm assuming that it's a woman, and the only two possibilities are Signora Erpicone – but I think she died too long ago – and Signora Giusti, before she became ill.'

'Good work, Cristina. Go and see her tomorrow morning. You go, too, Gennaro. What about Signora Rosati's handbag? Remind me what was in it.'

Santoro read from his notes.

'The usual stuff – purse, house keys, credit cards, phone, bits and pieces. Nothing unusual.'

'Gennaro, get someone – Moscardini maybe – to check if the keys match the locks at the house, and find out what transactions are on the credit cards.'

'Yes, capo.'

'Cristina, get the phone opened and checked for calls and messages. Go through her contacts and check for relatives and friends, and get someone to call them all to find out if anyone has seen her. We're looking for any clue about why Signora Rosati has disappeared and where she might have gone. There's still a chance that she got back to the house and took Mario with her. Did we recover Domenico's phone?'

'Yes, but it's a model that can't be opened,' said Cristina. 'We can request his call records from the phone company, though.'

'Good, do that.'

'Yes, Commissario.'

'I've been called to Innocenti's office first thing. Someone reported me for taking you two to Bar Italia at lunchtime. I'll see if he can push the national teams to find relatives of the couple.'

'We'll come, too, capo. Strength in numbers.'

Moretti placed his hand on Santoro's shoulder.

'Thanks, Gennaro, but the day I can't handle Innocenti is the day I'll retire. Go home, both of you, and we'll start fresh tomorrow. You did well today.'

When the officers left, Moretti put two more pins in the map to represent the drugs. He stood in front of it for ten minutes, his dark eyes following and crossing the contours, picturing Chiara Rosati's desperate wandering as she tried to get back to the cave.

Somewhere here there's an answer.

'I give up,' he said at last and left for his car.

'Shit.' He looked up and down the street. 'Shit.'

He lifted the windscreen wiper and removed the small squid that had been left there, taking care not to burst its ink sac.

Now he shouted to the culprit. 'Shit!'

CHAPTER EIGHTEEN

Moretti paused, his coffee cup halfway to his lips.

'So, when did you decide?'

'Almost immediately, Dino,' replied his wife. 'It's a career defining case.'

He put down the cup.

'But your career's already defined. You're a successful defence lawyer with more work than she can manage here. Why go so far south for this case?'

'You know why. For years, big business in the north has exploited the workforce in the south. They've paid them less, there are more accidents and deaths in the workplace, they work in intolerable heat in the summer, there's no Health and Safety, no proper medical insurance, they dump their waste there. Dino, the list is endless, where do you want me to stop?'

He took her hand in his.

'I remember when we'd discuss things like this – even an overnight away from each other. When did all that stop?'

'You know when, and you know why.'

He squeezed her hand.

'We can't... No, I'll speak for myself... I can't go on like this. What happened happened. We can't go back and undo it.'

'You're right, we can't. But neither of us can forget either, can we?'

He let her pull her hand free.

'How long will you be away?'

'Initially a week, then I'll come back here for some cases that are in the diary. After that, who knows, it could be a month, maybe more. I've asked my clerk not to take any further work and to look at the possibility of passing some of my cases over to colleagues.'

Moretti looked at his wife. Still almost as slim as when they met, and to him – no, to more than him – still beautiful. He admired, and feared, her resolve.

'Of course, you must go, Maria. There's no-one better than you. This case was made for you. Forgive me, I was being selfish.'

She took his hand and pressed her lips to the knuckle of his middle finger then gently bit it.

He smiled and brushed the fingers of his other hand over her cheek.

'You haven't done that in years.'

'Maybe we have to turn back the clock, Dino.'

*

Next morning, Moretti stood in front of Innocenti's desk.

'So, which one of the three was it? If I'm allowed to ask.'

Innocenti didn't look up.

'You're not allowed to ask, but even if you were, you'd be wrong. Plenty of other people saw you buying alcohol for your officers yesterday.'

'One small beer each.'

Now Innocenti looked at Moretti.

'Celebrating, were you? Really? Celebrating finding a dead body?'

'No, I was recognising Ispettore Furlan's prowess at climbing. She saved us hours in recovering the body, not to mention the expense of calling out the Mountain Rescue guys.'

'A simple well done would have sufficed. Now, where are you with this investigation?'

'The boy and his mother are still missing.'

'The drugs investigation? Someone buried a load of cocaine and who knows what else.'

'That's in hand. We'll run the two inquiries in tandem for a while.'

'Not the Narcotics Team, then?'

'Not yet. It could be a murder investigation, depending on fuller details from Forensics and the post-mortem.'

Innocenti made a shooing gesture. 'Better get on with it then.'

'Vice Questore.'

*

Moretti sat on the edge of his desk.

'Innocenti passes on his congratulations, Cristina. You did well yesterday, but we need to push on quickly because Di Vittorio didn't report it for three days. We're waiting for the Forensics guys to rule out foul play in Domenico's death. His wife and son have disappeared, so we could be looking at a murder inquiry. Our early evidence is that they did not have the happiest of marriages. Gennaro, did you find out about the prescription drugs?'

'Yes, capo, they match Signora Giusti's prescription.'

'A slight change of plan then. Cristina, visit the Giusti property and ask Enzo why his wife's drugs were in the cave, and find out all you can about Chiara Rosati.'

'Yes, Commissario.'

'Gennaro, chase up your friends in the south about the mysterious Signor Mancini, then check with the locksmith if anyone had a third set of keys cut for the Rosati house. I'm going to speak to Erpicone. Eventually someone is going to point the finger at his illegal workers about the drugs cache. Questions?'

'No, Commissario.'

'No, capo.'

'Good, we'll meet back here at midday.'

CHAPTER NINETEEN

Cristina knocked on the flaking paint of Giusti's door then turned to look around. A window was broken in one of the outbuildings, there was a gap to be fixed in one of the fences, and the yard needed tidying up. She was about to knock again when she heard movement inside. She faced the door and stepped back so that it would be easier for Signor Giusti to see her face. As it was, when he opened the door a little, he did the double take that she was accustomed to.

She smiled.

'Signor Giusti, I'm Ispettore Cristina Furlan. I wonder if I may come in for a moment.'

Her words did not seem to register.

'I'm a detective working with Commissario Moretti and Agente Santoro.'

Gennaro's name opened the door.

'I'm sorry, you caught me by surprise. Of course, come in, please.'

He stood aside and Cristina stepped into the cool, dimly lit room.

'Please sit, Ispettore. May I offer you something to drink?'

Cristina sat on the edge of the lowest seat she could see.

'No thank you, Signor Giusti. This won't take long.'

'If it's about the boy, I've already spoken to Gennaro.'

Cristina smiled again.

'I know,' she said softly. 'He told me how helpful you were. Thank you. I have a couple of questions for you, and then I'd like to speak with your wife, if I may.'

'Rosaria? But she's in bed. She's been housebound for years.'

'I understand, but I believe she knew Signora Rosati. I promise I won't tire her out.'

'Very well, what is it you want to ask me?'

Cristina leaned forward, her hands between her knees.

'Signor Giusti, where do you get your wife's medication?'

'From the pharmacy, why?'

'Well, we found some – rather a large amount, actually – of the drugs that your wife uses.'

He shook his head and wrung his hands. 'Am I in trouble?'

'I don't know. It depends on what you tell me.'

Giusti covered his eyes with his fists.

'I knew it. I should never have listened.' He uncovered his eyes and looked at Cristina. 'Will I have to go to prison? What about Rosaria?'

Cristina reached out and touched his arm.

'Tell me.'

He looked at the floor.

'Ispettore, we are poor. The podere makes no money. When Rosaria became ill, I began to take care of her, and I had to let all my workers go. I couldn't afford their wages. But to the authorities, I'm a rich man, with property, with a farm. I asked if Rosaria would qualify for free prescriptions, but they refused. So, we still pay a contribution. It's not much, I know, but we don't have anything – no savings, no income.'

'Go on.'

'I sometimes use workers that…'

'Yes?'

His voice dropped to almost a whisper. 'I sometimes use illegal immigrants. Not all the time, but for the grapes and the olives. It's too much for one person.'

'You're not the only farmer in Italy doing that, Signor Giusti.'

'I have one, though, who works full time. He looks after the sheep. He told me where I could buy prescription drugs cheaply, in bulk, so I did it. I admit it.'

Giusti looked up at Cristina, like a prisoner looking at a judge about to pass sentence.

'And where did you store this medicine?'

'I got someone to put it in the Partisan's cave. I couldn't risk having it in the house.'

'And you're sure that it is the same standard as from the pharmacy?'

'Yes, and I'm sure it was probably stolen, too.'

'But not by you, Signor Giusti.' She patted his arm. 'We've taken it into evidence at the moment, but I'll see to it that it is returned to you, and you can store it here.'

'Thank you.'

'Signor Giusti. The man who told you where to buy the drugs, is he the same one who put them in the Partisan's cave?'

'Yes.'

'What's his name and where can I find him?'

The farmer searched her face for motive.

'He's a good man, an intelligent man. I don't want to get him into trouble.'

'I understand, but we are investigating complex matters here, and time is short. We need to interview anyone who can help us.'

'He's called Yusuf. He has a place on the hillside where my sheep graze. He protects them against wolves.'

'So, we're looking for a hut?'

Giusti slumped into himself.

'Not even a hut – it's a very basic shelter that's open on two sides. Look, I'll draw a map.'

The old man picked up an envelope from a table, opened it out, and drew a rough sketch.

'If you find the sheep, you'll find his shelter.'

'Thank you, Signor Giusti. Now, if I may, I'd like to speak with your wife.'

Giusti led the way to a bedroom that smelled faintly of lavender, its closed shutters kept the room cool and dark. The high, metal-framed bed with its painted headboard faced the door. On either side of the bed, wooden cabinets were covered with bottles and bubble packs of medicine. Rosaria Giusti was half propped up on a small hillock of pillows. She touched the shade of a bedside lamp as they entered; its feeble light struggled to reach the dark corners.

'Rosaria, this is Ispettore Furlan. She's working with Gennaro to find the missing boy.'

Rosaria noticed something in Cristina's expression.

'Enzo, bring a chair for the ispettore, then leave us two women to talk.'

Enzo obeyed then left, closing the door behind him.

Rosaria peered up at Cristina then touched the lampshade again, bringing a little more light into the room.

'Sit here where I can see you, Ispettore.'

'Thank you for agreeing to chat, Signora Giusti. As you know we're searching for Mario Rosati, and we're trying to build up a picture of the family. I spoke to some of Signora Rosati's workmates yesterday, and they said that she confided in one of her neighbours. I'm guessing that was you.'

'We speak often. Her family live far away, and she misses having her mother or sisters to talk to. She's a good woman and a good mother.'

'I'm sure she is, everyone says so. Can I talk to you about how she is as a wife?'

The old woman's mouth pursed a little, and there was the slightest raising of her eyebrows.

'Her house is always spotless and there's always food on the table.'

'That's not what I mean. Signora Giusti, I appreciate that this is difficult for you, but I've already heard from the women at her work that she's a bit old-fashioned, modest, prudish even.'

The old woman sighed.

'It's true. Chiara finds her duties to her husband difficult. Not that Domenico is anything but loving, but she's fastidiously clean and thinks the whole thing is unnecessary. I remember one time when I reminded her of her wedding vows, she began to cry. She doesn't enjoy the physical side of marriage. She wants to, but she never has.'

'She has a son.'

'Yes, and she would dearly like more children, but it was at best a duty that she performed like a statue, or at worst a painful experience for her. It was never pleasurable. Her husband was always in a hurry.' The old woman looked away. 'I think he's also rather big.'

'So, neither of them had other partners?'

Rosaria crossed herself.

'God forgive me, I swore I'd never tell. She once went with another man to find out if it could be better. To see if she could learn something, perhaps, but that was no better. I don't know about Domenico.'

'Do you know who the other man was, the one she went with?'

'Yes. It was Giorgio Ricci from the agriturismo.'

Cristina messaged Moretti.

*

The bell suspended on its coil of brass above the door of the locksmith shop bounced and tinkled as Gennaro opened the door. Moscardini, a grey-haired sixty-something with a face lined with a lifetime's laughter, looked up from his paper, and his petite blonde daughter Sara glanced up from her phone.

'Good morning, Sara, good morning, Gianni. Can I have a word?'

'Oh, hi, Gennaro, sorry I'm heading out.'

'Okay, Sara, but I need to talk with you about the boy Mario.'

'Okay, later. Bye.'

The two men watched her dash out of the shop.

'Is she always like this, Gianni?'

'Always. She's young. Come through to the back shop and I'll make us coffee – or pour us something, if you prefer.'

'Coffee will be fine, thanks.'

Moscardini put the Moka on the gas.

'That was a tragic discovery yesterday.'

'Yes, he was a young man.'

'Any sign of Chiara?'

'No, nor Mario, and time's pressing. We need to get a breakthrough, and soon.'

Gianni poured hot water into two small cups.

'How can I help?'

'You told me that the Rosatis had changed all their locks.'

Coffee began bubbling into the Moka.

'Yes, and very expensive ones, too.'

'Could they be picked?'

'Not easily. I mean, any lock can be picked, but these ones only by an expert. Not even career burglars would bother to try – they'd find an easier target.'

'We found two sets of keys, one with Domenico and another in Chiara's bag. Did you make any others?'

Gianni emptied the hot water out of the cups and poured in the espresso.

'They only asked for two sets.'

'Could they have had a set cut elsewhere?'

Gianni passed a sugar bowl to Gennaro.

'There's a place down at the supermarket, they cut keys, but you would need to know the code number.'

Santoro stirred two teaspoons of sugar into the coffee.

'So stealing the keys would be no good. They'd have to have the code as well.'

'Exactly. The locks were top of the range, like I said.'

The two men drained their cups.

'Okay, thanks for that, and thanks for the coffee, Gianni.'

'You're welcome.'

'And tell Sara that I need to speak to her – urgently.'

'Will do. Take care.'

Less than half an hour later, Santoro was at the KeySoles key and shoe repair shop next to the supermarket. He held up the evidence bag and his ID.

'Good morning, I'm Agente Santoro. Could you tell me if you could cut a set of these keys?'

'Let me see them. I won't open the bag.'

Gennaro handed over the keys.

'Wow. Yes, but I'd have to order the blanks. We don't keep them in stock. We deal in higher volume keys. You'd also need the code.'

'Have you cut a set like this in, say, the last five years?'

'No. I'd remember for sure. Maybe one of the other guys did, though.'

'Could you check your records?'

'Sure, give me a moment.'

He handed the bag back, logged onto a computer, and searched.

'Nope, not this branch. You could try Montepulciano or Siena, they're nearest.'

'Okay, thanks. That's been helpful.'

Shortly after, Santoro tracked down the pruning squad a few kilometres outside of Cassiatorre. They told him that when they were working near the Rosati property that they hadn't seen a boy, only a stocky, well-built man at around four o'clock one morning. They also knew of Erpicone's illegal workers who were digging ditches and clearing scrubland.

The detective spent a few minutes writing in his notebook before setting off for the Questura.

CHAPTER TWENTY

Moretti parked as close as possible to Erpicone's house. The farm dogs surrounding his car barked until their master opened the door then they dispersed into the shade.

'Signor Erpicone, it's Moretti.'

The farmer squinted his cloudy eyes at the blurred silhouette.

'I know who you are. What do you want? I've already spoken to two of your flunkies. I know nothing about the boy.'

'This is about a different matter. I need to speak to your workers. Can you tell me where I can find them today?'

'I don't have any workers. The pruning gang were through, and I gave their details to that giantess you now employ. You should reprimand her for the way she spoke to me.'

Moretti sighed.

'Signor Erpicone, either you tell me where they are, or I take you to the Questura and question you instead. You'll probably be there a couple of days. Not very convenient if your family come back looking for you. So what's it to be?'

Erpicone snarled his reply.

'There might be some people squatting on my property down at the north boundary, I can't be certain. They're not my responsibility, mind, and if they've done anything illegal, it's nothing to do with me.'

Moretti nodded.

'And if there were people, as you say, squatting on your

property, how many of them might there be?'

'How the hell should I know! Maybe eight of them, but you won't get a word of sense out of them, they don't speak Italian.'

Grinning now, Moretti asked, 'And if they were still squatting on your property, how would I communicate with them?'

'Giusti has an illegal working for him. He's one of them but can speak a bit of Italian.'

'Thank you for your help, Signor Erpicone.'

'Finished? Then clear off.'

Moretti heard the door slam behind him as he headed for the car.

He drove slowly along the deeply rutted dirt road to the north boundary. Almost hidden under the trees, behind several large mounds of earth, was a ruined shack. Moretti spotted a movement out of the corner of his eye, and when he stopped, he leaned over to the glove box for his gun and stuffed into his waistband behind him.

He approached the rickety structure and called out, 'Come out, all of you.'

Silence.

He reached behind for his gun, cocked it, levelled it at the tarpaulin, and held up three fingers.

'One.'

He lowered a finger.

'Two.'

He lowered a second finger.

The tarpaulin moved and three men emerged, heads bowed, hands in the air, talking furiously.

Moretti put a finger to his lips and gestured them to sit. The three sat immediately, cross-legged, silent, still with their hands in the air.

'Does anyone speak Italian?'

They frowned.

Moretti put the gun away, pointed at them, and raised three fingers. He then raised eight fingers and questioned them with raised eyebrows.

No response.

He repeated his mime.

This time they nodded and pointed through the trees to the

fields beyond. Moretti smiled and signalled them to lower their hands.

'Yusuf?'

The three men smiled and nodded furiously, pointing to the hills behind Moretti. He raised a hand to stop them then called the Questura.

CHAPTER TWENTY-ONE

In the way of all small Italian towns, the locals had already heard of the rounding up of the illegal workers and had formed not so much a small crowd as a loose gaggle of onlookers near the Questura. Others watched from Bar Italia. Two police cars and two vans drew up outside the Questura, and the officers from the cars parked between the vans and the crowd. Although they shuffled for a better view, no-one pressed forward as the first of the black men was helped out of the vans. The two groups of thin, ragged workers merged into a single file and walked, heads down and mute, escorted but unhandcuffed, into the building.

The locals watched the last of the men disappear inside then either dispersed or swirled slowly and briefly into trios and quartets to comment on the proceedings before getting back to their day's business.

Inside the Questura, the men were split into two groups of four and given water and panini while they waited.

Cristina and Santoro arrived shortly afterwards with a tall, very lean black man and brought him to Moretti's office. Santoro sat beside him, and Cristina sat at the wall.

'Yusuf, I'm Commissario Moretti. I want to ask you some questions, and then I want you to translate for me while I question the others, okay?'

Yusuf nodded.

'You understand me?'

87

Yusuf nodded again.

'Yusuf, we know you can speak Italian, and we are investigating some serious matters, so we need your help. You can only help yourself and the other men if you speak to us.'

Yusuf answered in heavily accented Italian. 'I will do what I can.'

'Good,' said Moretti, passing him a bottle of cold water. 'First of all, tell us where you come from and how you are able to speak Italian.'

Yusuf opened the bottle and took a large gulp.

'I'm Somali. I was born in Mogadishu, as was my father, but my grandfather and great-grandfather came from Jowhaar, or as you know it Villabruzzi – the Italian colony established a hundred years ago. My great grandfather was a farmer, but he wanted something better for his son, so my grandfather learned Italian, studied hard, and eventually moved to Mogadishu to work in the Banca d'Italia there. He saw to it that my father was well educated. My father was in the export business and occupied himself with local politics, and he sent me to one of the best schools and then to university where I began to study medicine.'

Yusuf paused for another sip.

'The civil war ended all of that. Most of my family were killed by al-Shabaab, and I fled and made my way through Ethiopia and Sudan to Libya. My father had a business account in Sicily, and I knew that when I arrived there, things would be all right. But I didn't have much money for the journey, so I went on *tahriib*.'

'You went on what?'

'Tahriib. You agree with people smugglers to pay a certain amount after you arrive in Europe. For many men and boys, it leads to a kind of slavery – and it's worse for women. When I landed in Sicily, I was met by one of the smugglers' Italian contacts. He gave me clean clothes, took me to register as an asylum seeker, then went with me to the bank. He told me it would be better if I took out all the money from the account, because that way I would be free to travel wherever I wanted.'

Yusuf paused again.

Moretti looked at the other two detectives. 'I guess that the Italian took all of your money.'

'Yes,' said Yusuf. 'At least he left me with the new clothes.'

'How did you live?' asked Cristina.

Yusuf turned to face her.

'I worked on farms – picking tomatoes, aubergines, everything. I worked all the way up the peninsula.'

'Until you reached Cassiatorre,' said Moretti.

Yusuf faced front again.

'Until I reached Cassiatorre.'

'And you now work as a shepherd.'

'I keep the wolves away from Signor Giusti's flock.' Yusuf grinned. 'Before he found out I could speak Italian, he told one of his friends that I'm cheaper to keep than two sheep dogs.'

'And you can speak to the other men we've picked up? The ones working for Signor Erpicone?'

'Yes. Six are Somali like me, the other two are Ethiopian, but they can understand me or I speak in Arabic.'

A knock at the door interrupted them. A portly, red-faced man in his fifties came in.

'Sorry to disturb you, Commissario, but there's a bit of a problem.'

Moretti beckoned him in.

'What is it, Alfiero?'

'Two things – one minor, the other serious. The men haven't eaten their panini, so I don't know if they're on hunger strike.'

Yusuf raised his hand, and Moretti nodded.

'What was on the bread?'

'Prosciutto.'

Yusuf smiled. 'Then they are not on hunger strike. Prosciutto is *haram*, forbidden. It is pork meat, and we are all Muslim.'

Moretti looked at the officer. 'The other matter?'

'None of the men have fingerprints, Commissario.'

Moretti turned to Yusuf for an answer.

The man held up his hands. The pad of every fingertip was scarred.

'When we first arrive in Italy, our fingerprints are taken and sent to every country in Europe. That means we cannot leave until we have been processed through the Italian immigration system. That takes years, so we burn off our prints to destroy the record of where we landed.'

*

89

From their table in Bar Italia, Rosalia, Fausta and Donatella watched the men being taken into the Questura.

Rosalia held her little linen bag of lavender to her nose.

'That's the ringleader,' she said, as Yusuf was escorted from the police car that had brought him separately from the others.

'How do you know?' asked Donatella.

'Well, he's obviously their leader. He was brought in with his own special guard, wasn't he?'

'So, you've never actually seen him. You're guessing.'

'I agree with Rosalia,' said Fausta. 'He carries himself well – with authority. He's the leader all right. Pity, he's a good-looking man.'

Rosalia lowered her voice.

'I bet he has links to organised crime – the Mafia, or South American drugs cartels.'

Donatella frowned at her two companions.

'How can you say that? You can't even see him from here, and neither of you have met any of these poor men. Honestly, you two. The truth is more likely that they left war zones or countries in desperate poverty or famine and came here trying to make a better life for themselves and their families.'

Fausta's tiny dog poked its head out of the bag on her lap.

'But they're here illegally. They're illegal immigrants, they're breaking the law.'

Rosalia nodded.

'That's right. They're working and not paying any taxes. That's illegal.'

Now Donatella lowered her voice.

'You pair of hypocrites. Neither of you has a TV licence, and you both pay handymen cash-in-hand to avoid paying IVA. You, Rosalia, haggle with that poor old man who brings his vegetables to the market – his prices are already lower than everyone else, but you always ask for a discount and grab a handful of salad or peppers or something, after you've paid. And you, Fausta, do I have to remind you of the thing in the supermarket?'

Fausta flushed and produced her fan from her bag.

'I'm sure I don't know what you mean,' she said, fanning her face furiously.

'Oh, I'm very sure you know exactly what I mean,' said

Donatella. 'But if you're in any doubt, I can remind you – right here.'

Fausta now pulled a linen handkerchief from her cuff and mopped her forehead and temples.

'That won't be necessary,' she said, dabbing her throat and neck. 'I do have a vague recollection of something.'

Rosalia spoke from behind her lavender bag.

'Maybe you should say it anyway, Donatella, to make sure you're talking about the same thing.'

Donatella smiled.

As news of the detention of the illegal immigrants spread through Cassiatorre and beyond, a reporter from one of the local papers arrived and began to chat to the locals. The three gossips were uncharacteristically silent on the matter following Donatella's intervention.

CHAPTER TWENTY-TWO

A slim dark-haired woman, dressed in a pleated grey skirt, white blouse, and grey jacket, entered the Questura.

'Maria De Luca.' Moretti's wife introduced herself to the desk officer.

'Of course, Signora De Luca,' Alfiero said with a smile. 'I'll see if the commissario is free.'

'I'm here on behalf of the men who were picked up this morning. Please take me to them.'

The officer's smile faded.

'Ah, in that case, please wait a moment.'

He dialled through to Moretti.

'Sorry to disturb you, Commissario, but your wife's here.'

'Tell her I'm in the middle of something and that I can't see her now. I'll call her later.'

Alfiero felt suddenly that the bulletproof glass between him and Moretti's wife was insufficient protection.

'Commissario, she's here to see the detainees, not you.'

'Shit. I'll come out.'

The officer hung up.

'The commissario says please take a seat.'

Maria stayed put and punched something into her phone.

'I'm fine here.'

Moretti appeared at a door to the side of the desk officer.

'Come through.'

'I haven't been formally signed in yet.'

Moretti looked at Alfiero, who sheepishly passed the book and a pen to Maria while Moretti joined her on the other side of the desk and led her through to his office. He closed the door behind them.

'What are you doing?'

'I'm representing the men that you have in custody.'

'We're only making some enquiries.'

'And I'll be sitting there safeguarding their rights while you do that.'

'Look, we're trying to arrange for a translator and a duty lawyer.'

Maria smiled.

'I understand that one of the men speaks Italian. I'd like to speak with him now, to ascertain if they want my services.'

Moretti knew better than to argue. 'Come with me.'

He accompanied her to the room where Yusuf and four of the men were.

'Yusuf, this woman is a lawyer. She is offering to represent you and the other men. Would you like that? Please ask the others.'

Yusuf quickly translated, and an excited chorus confirmed that the men would like that very much.

'That's settled.' Maria nodded. 'Now I'd like some time alone with my clients, please.'

Moretti shook his head and left her with them as he returned to his office.

*

'Let's compare notes,' Moretti said. 'You start, Cristina.'

'When I spoke with Signor Giusti, he admitted that the prescription drugs in the Partisan's cave were his. They're short of cash, and he bought them from a dodgy source. I messaged you about Yusuf, Signor Giusti's shepherd. He organised the purchase of the prescription drugs, and your wife is talking to him now. Signor Giusti wanted to keep Yusuf out of it, and he admits that the medicines might be stolen, but he knows nothing of that. I believe him, and I think we should let this one go.'

Moretti looked to Santoro.

'Gennaro?'

'I agree. They're hard up and, if I may say so, hard done to by the regulations.'

'Okay, agreed. What else, Cristina?'

'I had a long chat with Signora Giusti. I think she was maybe Chiara Rosati's only confidante. I'll skip the details except to say that Chiara had a fling with Ricci at some point.'

That name, and the fact that his wife was right along the corridor, hit a nerve with Moretti.

'You see, I said he was a suspect.'

'Sorry, am I missing something? What's his involvement and motive in a missing person case?'

Moretti looked rattled. 'I think he's involved, somehow.'

Santoro shook his head.

'Do you think that Yusuf is mixed up with the cocaine business?' asked Moretti. 'Because if there's no connection with our case, I'll have to involve the Narcotics guys.'

'I honestly can't say. Signor Giusti told me that Yusuf spends most of his time on the hillside where we found him this morning, but that doesn't mean to say that he's not involved, given that he obviously has contacts who can supply prescription drugs.'

'Okay, get a Forensics team to check out his hut. Gennaro?'

Santoro flipped open his notebook.

'I visited Gianni Moscardini. The locks on the Rosati property were top of the range – as we discovered – and there were only two sets of keys. I checked at the key-cutting place at the supermarket. They said that the blanks were a special order, and that you'd need the code to cut the keys and they haven't in the past five years.'

Moretti leaned his face into his hands and massaged his forehead and temples.

'So how did Mario get out of a house locked up like a bank vault?'

Santoro shrugged. 'I heard back from my contacts in the south. I think you'll be interested in this.'

Moretti spoke through his hands. 'Go on.'

'It's about Mancini. My sources had some difficulty, but they found out that he was a cop. He was charged with child abuse, and although the charges were dropped for lack of evidence and the case never went to trial, it was thought that he should be retired and given a new identity for his own protection.'

Moretti frowned. 'A new identity is a bit of overkill, don't you think?'

'Not really. The child that he was accused of abusing came from a family of a Mafia clan. It seems that there's a contract out on him.'

'*Porca cane.* The Mafia is the last thing needed around here, and we're making no progress whatsoever with finding Mario and his mother.'

'What about Signor Ricci?'

'Given Gennaro's revelation, I think we should maybe switch our attention to Mancini, Cristina. There was a woman with him when I visited. Young, short black hair. Without letting on to Mancini, see if you can find out who she was and speak to her. See what she knows about Mancini, but don't give anything away about his background.'

'Yes, Commissario. How do you suggest I do that?'

'He goes hunting. Start with the Hunters' Association.'

Moretti stood.

'Okay, good work. Gennaro, you come with me. I'll need a friendly face in the interview room.'

'Capo.'

*

Moretti and Santoro sat across from Maria and Yusuf. A carafe of water and four glasses were on the table between them.

'Are you recording this interview?'

'No, it's an informal chat. No-one has been charged.'

'Is Yusuf or any other of my clients under suspicion?'

'No, they're helping with our enquiries.'

'So they're here on a voluntary basis and are free to go.'

Moretti sighed.

'Maria…'

'Signora De Luca.'

'Signora De Luca, we are running several investigations in parallel, and we're questioning many different people. Your clients are merely part of those enquiries.'

She crossed her legs.

'How many of the other people that you've questioned have been brought in vans to the Questura?'

'Signora De Luca…'

'How many?'

'None.'

Maria arranged the pleats on her skirt. 'So, you admit that you are treating my clients differently from everyone else. Is it because they're black, I wonder?'

Moretti's expression hardened.

'No, Signora De Luca, it's because your clients are here illegally. They do not have documents, they are working illegally, they do not pay taxes, they do not live in premises conducive to be used for interviewing, and in the case of Yusuf, we believe he has been involved with the illegal supply of prescription drugs, which we believe to be stolen, to the person he works for.'

Maria was unfazed.

'So, apart from the allegation of involvement, but for the absence of doubt, not the actual theft of prescription medication, neither Yusuf nor any of my other clients has broken the law. It very much sounds to me that this is nothing more than a fishing exercise, and that you have nothing concrete to justify your holding of my clients.'

Moretti poured a glass of water and took a long gulp.

'Unless they can show otherwise, they are all here illegally. They have not been processed; they have even destroyed their fingerprints. So, yes, they have broken the law.'

'And are you aware that the immigration system is broken, that it cannot cope with the numbers of refugees entering Italy or, indeed, being returned here from other countries because of the Dublin regulation? And are you further aware that there is an amnesty scheme, *Sanatoria Immigrati,* passing through parliament which, when it is adopted, will remove the illegal status of my clients?'

In that moment, Moretti both hated and adored her. A warrior fighting for the underdogs. Of course she had to take the case in the south – there was no-one better.

CHAPTER TWENTY-THREE

Cassiatorre's Castello dated from the tenth century and had withstood attack since the war between Siena and Florence. With two thick-walled stone towers, it commanded an elevated position dominating the landscape, surrounded first by two concentric walls, then by the town's houses.

The outermost houses of Cassiatorre's historic centre were themselves part of the fortifications. Their windows were several metres from ground level because the base of their walls was also thick and, if breached, gave access only to cantinas and cellars whose narrow stairs could be easily defended or blocked. These houses formed a continuous perimeter so the town was accessible only through large gates, each with a portcullis that would have been closed every night. The houses behind the walls were laid out in a way that they, too, formed part of the town's defences. The streets and *vicoli* between them were narrow, twisting mazes where an invading force could be slowed down or ambushed in dead ends before arriving at the first of the castle walls.

It was in a large cantina in an alley off one of the wider streets that Cristina found what she was looking for. A brass plate fixed to a double door of cypress wood identified the Hunters' Association of Cassiatorre. The doors were reinforced by horizontal black metal bands, and where they met, two large rings were mounted as handles. She used one of the rings to bang on the door.

A large bolt scraped along its barrel then the huge wrought iron hinges creaked, and one door opened.

A head appeared, shaved on top, sporting a scruffy, thick, salt and pepper beard.

'Ispettore?'

'Good morning. May I come in? I'm interested in joining the Association.'

A voice from inside called, 'Who's there, Carlo?'

Carlo opened the door wider so the others could see.

'It's the ispettore. She says she wants to join us.'

'Well, let her in,' shouted another voice from the back. 'Where are your manners?'

Carlo stepped back, opening the door fully behind him, letting some sunlight into the dimly lit cantina.

'Forgive me, Ispettore, please come in.'

Cristina entered, and her eyes adjusted quickly to the ambient light. Six men, dressed in unmatched camouflage gear, sat on benches at the long refectory table that ran down the middle of the space. Between them a bottle and chunky glasses of red wine sat beside dismantled parts of rifles, cleaning fluid, and rags. The taxidermied heads of wild boar, red and roe deer, and a sturgeon were fixed high up on the walls, while under them framed photographs, some of them very old, of hunters with their quarry.

She recognised one of the men as Corrado from the search party. He was a bear of a man, shorter than her, with a heavy jaw blackened by stubble, and muscular arms covered in thick black hair that ended in tufts along his fingers.

He smiled and held out the wine bottle and a glass.

'Here, take a seat and help yourself.'

Cristina raised her hand in refusal.

'So, you want to join us, eh?'

Cristina sat at the end of the bench. 'If that's possible.'

'Do you hunt? Can you shoot?'

'I have hunted and yes, I can shoot.'

'This is a man's club,' said one of the hunters as he poured another drop of wine into his glass. 'Always was, always should be.'

A couple of others nodded in agreement.

Corrado ruffled the untidy hair of the one beside him.

'You guys are still in the last century,' he said. 'You know women can vote now, don't you, Mauro?'

'One of the problems,' said Carlo, 'is that we don't let just anyone into the Association. We need to know that you can handle a rifle well enough to be able to kill an animal with your first shot. We don't want an injured boar suffering or attacking people while it takes days to die.'

'Yes, let's see how well the ispettore can shoot,' said another.

'What do you say?' asked Corrado. 'Are you up for it?'

Cristina stood and smiled. 'Let's do it.'

A short ride in trucks and motorbikes took them all to Carlo's farm, where they parked in the shade under the trees. There was a dead straight dirt track that was horizontal for a little over a hundred metres before it sloped up and round a bend.

Carlo fetched a target from a barn, sat with it on his lap, and rode his motorbike to a point in the track where there was a white painted stake at the side of the path. He set up the target and rode back to the others.

Corrado unlocked a gun box in his truck and took out two rifles. He offered them both to Cristina.

She took one, checked that it was unloaded, and then examined the scope and trigger action.

Corrado held out a handful of ammunition. 'Three shots each okay with you?'

'Let's make it two each,' Cristina said. 'It's more interesting.'

'Oooooh,' chorused the others.

Corrado grinned at them all. 'Right then. Ladies first.'

'It's your range, you have the honours.'

Corrado lay prone on the ground and settled into a comfortable shooting position. The air was still and hot. He took aim and fired his first shot.

Carlo looked at the target through binoculars. 'Slightly low and left.'

Corrado took the binoculars, checked for himself, and adjusted the scope. He relaxed into his shooting position and fired again.

'Centre but slightly right this time,' said Carlo.

The hunters applauded his efforts as Corrado stood up and dusted himself down.

'Okay, Ispettore, your turn.'

Cristina lay prone and assumed her position. As she was

squeezing the trigger, Mauro cleared his throat.

'High and right,' announced Carlo.

'That one doesn't count,' said Corrado, punching Mauro's arm. 'You still have two shots.'

Cristina squinted up at them all.

'One should be enough, thanks.'

She adjusted the scope, settled, and squeezed off her second shot.

'Dead centre,' Carlo shouted, passing Corrado the binoculars.

'Great shooting,' said Corrado, applauding and turning to the others. 'I guess that settles it then, the ispettore can join the Association. Any objections?'

He looked at Mauro.

'Anyone?'

'None here. The ispettore can join.'

They all shook hands with Cristina, who gave Mauro's an extra firm squeeze.

'Since you're all here,' said Carlo, 'why don't I organise some food? Corrado, go into the kitchen and bring out some cheese and salami.'

Carlo rode down to the end of the track to collect the target, while the others set up a trestle table and benches in the yard. Corrado reappeared with a young and a mature pecorino, a jar of set honey, and some home-made venison salami preserved under oil.

Carlo packed away the target and collected plates, glasses, cutlery, and wine, and they all sat down to eat. Everyone wanted to know where Cristina had learned to shoot, and she was happy to tell them. They cut chunks of bread, dipped them in the oil, and ate the cheese with honey or slices of pear.

Cristina was keen to find out if Mancini was in the Association, but she knew that she had to pick her moment. That moment came at the end of the meal, when Carlo appeared with a bottle of home-made grappa and some small glasses. Most took only a tiny drop, but Corrado mischievously poured a full glass for Cristina. All eyes were on her. She picked up the glass and drained it in one gulp.

'Now you, Corrado,' she said.

The hunters laughed and cheered him on. He filled his own glass up to the top and drained it.

'Again, Ispettore?'

'Again.'

To the cheers of the hunters, Cristina and Corrado went glass for glass with the strong liquor until, at last, Corrado held up his hands in mock surrender.

'You win,' he said. 'I can't go on.'

His defeat was met by applause and a huge cheer for Cristina. Mauro clapped loudest of all.

'You're certainly one of us now,' he said.

'Welcome to the twenty-first century,' said Corrado, slapping Mauro's back.

'I'll bring coffee,' Carlo said.

'Where did you learn to drink like that?' Corrado asked. 'I've never seen anything like it.'

'I grew up in the Dolomites,' said Cristina. 'That's where grappa was invented. It's like mother's milk to me.'

After coffee, the hunters split up into the different SUVs to sleep in the shade. Cristina went with Corrado.

'Who else is in the Association?' she asked. 'And do they all have to pass the shooting and drinking test?'

Corrado closed his eyes and grinned.

'Most of the hunters from Cassiatorre are in our Association or one of the other hunting groups. The shooting test was to convince guys like Mauro, and the drinking contest – well, you brought that on yourself.'

Cristina smiled. 'And I'm the only female?'

'Yes. A lot of the older members learned to shoot when they did their national service. For others, it's part of the culture.'

'So, I'm the only outsider then?'

'No, there are others, too, and some of them are good shots.'

'As good as you?'

'Yes, and better. Pino Mancini is a great shot. Much better than me. Maybe better than you.'

'Oh, did he learn during national service?'

'Perhaps. He's the right age, but he's so good that there are all sorts of rumours. You might have heard them.'

'No, I haven't. I'm new here, remember. What are the rumours?'

Corrado yawned and rubbed his eyes.

'Oh, that he was regular military, not just a conscript, or that he was in special forces or involved in black ops. You know how people exaggerate about anyone who doesn't talk about their past.'

'Ah, so he doesn't have any close friends then?'

Corrado laughed. 'Not among the hunters. He keeps himself to himself.'

Corrado reclined his seat.

'Look, if you want to find out more, you should ask one of the women he's been seeing – Paola or Luisa. But now I need to sleep and sober up before I drive us back to town.'

Corrado folded his arms over his chest and fell quickly to sleep.

Cristina tried to stay awake, but she also fell asleep a few minutes later.

CHAPTER TWENTY-FOUR

Moretti closed the door behind Yusuf and faced his wife. She was making notes, and he knew better than to interrupt her, so he stacked the empty water glasses and sat across from her.

'They're all innocent, Dino,' she said, head down, still writing.

'Maria…'

'And you know it.'

Moretti leaned back in his chair and stretched. 'I believe you. I believe them. I even feel sorry for them.'

'But?'

'But I'm going to have to report them and refer them to the Immigration Service.'

Now she stopped writing and looked at him, her dark eyes searching his soul for compassion.

'Maria, don't.'

'Don't *Maria don't* me. You brought these men in to question them about a missing boy. They haven't seen him, they haven't touched him, they don't know anything about his whereabouts. They've been as helpful as it was possible to be, and you're going to hand them over to the Immigration Service who'll put them in a truck and lock them up in some compound somewhere, no better than a concentration camp, until they're transported back home where they'll most likely be beaten or killed because they haven't sent back the money they owe to the people smugglers. So, don't *Maria don't* me, Dino.'

She stood up, packed her things, and left, leaving the door wide open.

Moretti closed his eyes, breathed deeply, and sighed. She was right and he knew it. He knew that the path he decided to follow would have serious consequences for the illegal immigrants, and no less serious consequences for his marriage. He reached into the top pocket of his linen jacket for the cigar he'd put there earlier, left the interview room, and headed for the exit.

As he was passing the front desk, Alfiero stopped him. He was holding up a plastic pocket containing an envelope.

'This came addressed to you, Commissario, while you were with your...' he paused and corrected himself, 'Signora De Luca.'

Moretti put the cigar back in its place and took the plastic pocket. He held it at eye level and examined both sides of the plain white envelope.

The words *Commissario Moretti* in black ink were all that was written on it.

'There's no stamp. Who handed it in?'

'It came with the regular post.'

'Who's touched it?'

'No-one here, Commissario. I took the bundle of post and began to sort through it as usual. This envelope was sandwiched between two larger manila envelopes. I saw it when I removed the top one and thought that it looked odd, so I put on a pair of gloves and popped it into the plastic pocket.'

Moretti nodded. 'Good work. Which postman brought it?

'Renzo.'

'Get in touch with Renzo and find out who at the Post Office could have touched it and ask them all to come in so we can fingerprint them. Do you know where the lightbox is?'

'I think it was in Agente Santoro's office the last time I saw it.'

'Thanks.'

Moretti found the lightbox, switched it on, and placed the envelope on it. Some of the words were backwards and upside down. He turned the envelope over, deciphered and wrote down what was printed inside.

BOY IS UNHARMED
TO KEEP HIM THAT WAY
EURO 250,000 CASH

USED SMALL NOTES
IF YOU AGREE
CLOSE OFFICE SHUTTERS

Moretti went to his office and looked out of the window. Below, Piazza Garibaldi looked as it always did. He closed the shutters and hurried back to the desk officer.

'Call Forensics and have them do their usual checks then bring the envelope back to me. Next, call Ispettore Furlan and Agente Santoro and get them back here immediately. Tell them to drop whatever they're doing. Give me five minutes then put a call through to Innocenti.'

*

The three detectives looked at copies of the note. Moretti had his unlit cigar between his lips, Gennaro held his bag of carrot sticks, and Cristina had opened a large bottle of water.

'Thoughts? Ideas?' asked Moretti.

Gennaro took a carrot stick from the bag and pointed it at the note.

'Can we believe it, capo? Is it really a ransom note or someone trying to throw us off course? I mean, there's no timescale, no drop off instructions, no *or else*. I mean, what is a ransom demand without threats and ultimatums?' He bit noisily into the carrot. 'But if it is genuine, it means that Chiara is not with Mario.'

'Cristina?'

She swallowed her large gulp of water and screwed the cap on the bottle.

'I agree with Gennaro, it looks odd, amateur even – but what if it is real? Isn't the important thing that Mario could still be safe and unharmed? I think that's what we can take from this, and I think you do, too, Commissario, otherwise why did you close the shutters?'

'Instinct, I guess,' said Moretti. 'The note looks amateur. My guess is that the person who wrote it hasn't done this before, because you're right, Gennaro, usually there's a time limit for raising the cash and something to say that there'll be further instructions or a phone number to call. The amount of cash is also odd – a quarter of a million – not a fortune. It's the kind of sum that we could raise very easily and quickly, and it's not enough to be able to buy a new identity or start a new life somewhere. You

105

know, the note strikes me as more reassuring than threatening. Who'd want to do that?'

'Someone who'd want a quarter of a million,' said Gennaro. 'It must be someone local, or at least someone who has been in Cassiatorre in person, because the note wasn't posted but handed into the Post Office somehow. Maybe we should ask at the bank if anyone is in financial trouble such that a quarter of a million would fix their problems.'

'I think a quarter of a million would fix most people's problems, Gennaro, but I agree, it's worth checking with the bank.'

'It has to be fake,' said Cristina. 'There's no hint of how we pass over the cash. And I'm not sure that it's a coincidence that it arrived precisely when we were interviewing the illegal immigrants, the hunters, and the pruning gang. I think there may be something that we've been told that's important, and this is a deflection, meant to take our attention away from a real clue.'

'Look, this is getting us nowhere,' said Moretti. 'If it's bogus, then ignoring it will lose us nothing. If it's genuine, then my closing the shutters ought to get a response. Let's wait until the Forensics team report back before we spend any more time on it. Gennaro, what did you get from the pruning team?'

Gennaro pocketed the bag of carrots and consulted his notebook.

'The gang were working on Erpicone's place on the day that Mario's parents had the crash. Remember that the farmer Di Vittorio saw the parents leaving about seven. Well, the pruning guys saw someone built like Domenico Rosati leaving about four in the morning and driving off somewhere. They'd moved to another part of the olive plantation, so they didn't see him return.'

Moretti tossed the soggy-tipped cigar into a waste bin.

'So where did Domenico go for those three hours and what was he doing?'

Gennaro shrugged. 'I don't know but they didn't see Mario.'

'Cristina, how did you get on with the hunters? You clearly had a drinking session with them.'

Cristina took another long gulp of her water.

'I'm now a fully-fledged member of the Hunters' Association,' she said with a grin. 'I managed to find out the names of two women that know Mancini – a Paola and a Luisa. I can ask around in Bar Firenze and Bar Italia tomorrow and see if I can come up with surnames and addresses.'

'Okay, Cristina but I need you to go over the witness statements from the agriturismo and pay them another visit. There's more to find out there, and your handling of the hunters has proved to me that you are capable.'

'And I speak English.'

'That too.'

'How did things go with your interviews, capo?'

Moretti tidied papers on his desk.

'I managed to establish that Yusuf and the other illegal workers had nothing at all to do with Mario's disappearance.'

The desk phone rang.

'Moretti… Uhuh… Wait till I grab pen, okay, go… Right, got it. Thank you.'

He returned the phone to its cradle.

'The team going through Chiara Rosati's phone contacts have found a relative of Domenico. I'll give him a call. You guys go home, and I'll see you tomorrow.'

The two officers left, and Moretti sat down and made two calls. One from the desk phone to Domenico's cousin, arranging for him to come and identify Domenico's body; the other from his cell phone.

He was tired and hungry but reluctant to go straight home. He picked the cigar he'd jettisoned back out of the waste bin and headed along the corridor, keeping his head down as he passed the front desk. Out in Piazza Garibaldi, he lit up the cigar and took a couple of puffs. The damp end felt unpleasant in his lips, and the smoke tasted funny. He stubbed it out, left it in the sand in a smokers' bin, and walked across Piazza Garibaldi to Bar Italia. He sat at one of the tables outside, next to a tub of geraniums.

When Carla arrived to take his order, her smile lifted his spirits.

'What can I get you, Commissario?'

'A small beer, please.'

'Right away.'

She tidied the glasses that were on his table and gave it a wipe.

A few minutes later, her son Gigi arrived carrying a tray with the beer, small bowls with crisps and peanuts, and a small plate with a few sandwiches. He carefully arranged everything in front of Moretti.

Moretti studied Gigi as he worked. He was a classmate of Mario's, and it occurred to Moretti to ask him about the boy's disappearance, but he decided against it.

'Thank you, Gigi.'

'You're welcome, Commissario,' Gigi replied, smiling an odd, lopsided grin.

Ragazzini, thought Moretti.

He sipped his beer, wiping froth from his moustache, and nibbled some of the snacks. The late afternoon sun was still strong, so he slid his chair under the shade of the parasol. Traffic flowed and bunched up on the road beside him as workers returned home. Some of the drivers and passengers tooted or waved at him as they passed. *Which of them knew something?* he wondered. *Which of them could help him solve the mystery? Where was Mario Rosati, and where was his mother?*

His gaze lost focus and memories of his own pressed in on him like a suffocating black pillow.

CHAPTER TWENTY-FIVE

'Hi, Commissario Beer, remember us?'

When Moretti heard the English-speaking voices, he turned to see the Dutch tourists Jaap and Sabine. Both were dressed in t-shirts and very short shorts.

Sabine rested her hand on his shoulder. 'Mind if we join you?'

'I'm sorry, my English is very poor.'

Sabine smiled and pointed to two seats at his table. 'We can sit here?'

Before waiting for his answer, she leaned close to his ear.

'Unless you're on a stakeout,' she said in a mock whisper. 'In which case, we can be a good cover story. I promise we'll act natural.'

She spoke slowly enough that Moretti could follow almost all of what she said. He felt awkward, but he was also glad of a reason to delay his return home.

Sabine sat down beside him before he had a chance to refuse. 'Jaap, go and get us a couple of drinks. What can we get you, Commissario? A Moretti?'

The couple laughed.

'Of course,' said Jaap. 'It has to be.'

Moretti managed a weak smile. 'A small one, thanks.'

Sabine called after her husband. 'Ask if they have some of those fennel Taralli, Jaap.'

'Okay.'

Sabine started to eat the bar snacks already on the table and put her hand on Moretti's arm.

'We were at a wine tasting today, so I'm starving. Don't you find that alcohol gives you an appetite?' She squeezed his arm.

Moretti panicked and glanced around him. In the cool interior of the bar, the three gossips were silent, listening to everything but pretending not to notice. Near them, further inside, two pensioners played dominoes. Alone, at an outside table against the wall, a man in a linen jacket sat reading his paper, while closer, and very much in earshot, two young mothers with toddlers in strollers were blatantly looking over. He hated being the centre of attention. He carefully, but decisively, lifted her hand from his arm.

Sabine pouted. 'Aw. Spoilsport.'

'I'm sorry, Signora.'

'Sabine.'

'I'm sorry, Sabine,' Moretti struggled with his English. 'But I think maybe the wine has made you a little free.'

Sabine laughed. 'Yes, you could say that.'

Moretti sipped his beer, using it like a shield between them.

She popped a handful of peanuts into her mouth and pointed to his moustache. 'Froth.'

He looked puzzled.

She pointed again. 'Bubbles.'

He wiped his moustache with a tissue.

Sabine reached drunkenly towards his face. 'I could have done that,' she said. 'I'm fascinated by your moustache. Can I touch it?'

As she stretched forward, Moretti leaned back and Jaap reappeared. He spoke to his wife like a parent scolding a child reaching for chocolate in a supermarket.

'Sabine, leave the commissario alone.'

She sat back, furrowed her brows, and munched the peanuts.

'We're a little bit drunk,' Jaap said.

'Your wife told me you tasted wine.'

He nodded. 'We overdid it, I'm afraid. Our guide took us to two different producers, and we tasted their full range.'

'Our local wine can be very strong.'

'Ah, here are our drinks,' said Jaap.

Gigi placed the tray on an adjacent table and carefully served first Sabine, then Jaap, then Moretti. He removed the original bar snacks and replaced them with fresh ones, including the Taralli.

Jaap beamed his approval. 'What a nice kid. Did you see how he served you first, Sabine? Manners, too.'

Sabine picked up her glass of Prosecco. 'Cheers.'

The men clinked glasses with her.

'We want kids,' said Jaap.

'You do,' Sabine said, as she gulped down her wine.

Jaap ignored her. 'That Gigi – such a great boy.'

Moretti nodded. 'He helps his mother.'

Jaap covered Sabine's hand with his. 'We could have a boy like that.'

Sabine pulled her hand away, leaned back in her chair and stretched, making it obvious that she wasn't wearing a bra.

'Jaap, we spoke about this. We don't need to tell the whole town that you want children.'

Jaap lowered his voice and leaned forward. 'Honestly, I can't believe that someone who likes sex so much doesn't want children.'

Moretti took refuge behind a sip of beer again.

'It's because I like sex that I don't want children,' she replied.

Gigi was clearing a nearby table. She called him by name and held up her glass. He nodded and took it inside.

Jaap drank and nibbled sulkily.

Sabine turned her attention back to Moretti and pushed her hair back off her forehead.

'How about you, Commissario Beer? Is there a Signora Beer and some baby Beers somewhere?'

She smiled at her own joke.

'I am married,' he replied.

'Any children?'

'Not now.'

For an instant Sabine hesitated, then Gigi appeared with a fresh glass of Prosecco.

'Ah, thank you.'

Moretti knew it was time to leave, but there was something that compelled him to stay and watch the slow-motion disintegration before him.

'So, Commissario.' She was slurring now. 'Do you swing?'

Moretti looked puzzled.

Sabine touched the thumb and index finger of her left hand and pushed the index finger of her right hand in and out of the circle. 'You know, with other couples?'

Moretti looked at Jaap. Instead of horror or reproach, Sabine's husband's face bore an expression of curiosity.

'I am sorry,' Moretti said as he rose. 'I must go home now. Goodbye.'

He left a ten on the table and hurried away to where his car was parked.

'You piece of shit,' he shouted.

A sardine was wedged under his windscreen wiper.

CHAPTER TWENTY-SIX

Back home, Moretti found Maria sitting typing up notes in the cool of her office. She had replaced her grey suit and blouse with a vest top and yoga pants, and her hair was twisted up and held with a pencil. Even though he had been shocked by Sabine's frank approach, he had found it exciting, and all the way home it had caused him to think about his sex life. He still found Maria attractive but had imposed an abstinence on their lovemaking. Their marriage had already been wounded by tragedy, but the thought that she might have been unfaithful was a debilitating poison that threatened to kill it completely.

She neither stopped nor looked up as he approached.

Moretti felt awkward and unsure, like a teenager making his first pass. He stood behind her, his hands hovering so close above her bare shoulders that she felt their heat.

'What are you up to?' she asked, still focused on the screen.

He looked at the little round mound of the bone that protruded at the base of her long neck. He leaned forward to kiss the wispy dark hairs at its nape.

Maria closed the lid of the laptop and turned abruptly, glaring at him.

'Dino, what the hell do you think you're doing? These are my notes of the interviews with the immigrants today. You can't read them. Get up.'

He recoiled immediately, horrified at her accusation. 'Maria, I wasn't,' he said. 'I was only…'

She folded her arms. 'You were only what?'

Dino noticed how the action emphasised her cleavage, and the feelings that he'd brought home returned.

'Maria,' he said. 'I was only going to kiss you.'

She looked puzzled. 'Kiss me?'

'Yes, on the nape of your neck. The way I used to.'

She noticed him looking at her cleavage and unfolded her arms. 'Why?'

'Why?' He started to turn away. 'Oh look, forget it. Go back to your work.'

Maria reached out and took his arm, stopping him.

Her lawyer's training drove her to follow through with her cross-examination, but her voice softened. 'Why?'

Dino noticed the subtle change but couldn't answer. He would have to admit to too much, open doors that kept feelings, and hurt, locked away.

Maria rubbed her thumb across the back of his hand.

'You feel guilty,' she said, rising. 'Mario's disappearance must be so difficult for you, given what happened to us. Your hours are unpredictable and impossibly long, and when you do get home, your mind is still sifting, sorting, and trying to impose order on the clues, false clues, hidden truths, and lies that fill your day.'

He opened his mouth, but she placed a finger on his lips.

'You come home exhausted and still thinking about whatever case you're on, instead of thinking about me.'

He nodded. 'Yes,' he said. 'It's all of that.'

She pressed against him and rested her head on his shoulder. Her warmth was like electricity through his body.

'Dino, I don't know where we are. I don't know where I am. I need time to work that out. I'm going to finish these notes and pass them on to a colleague to take over. She'll fight your plans to hand over those poor wretches to the Immigration Service. I've decided that I'm going to take the case down south to give us both a bit of space. I've already packed a bag. I'm leaving tomorrow morning.'

*

Moretti lay awake most of the night watching Maria asleep beside him, the way he had on the first night they'd spent together. While lying on her back, she still made the almost imperceptible 'p' sound as her lips parted a fraction when she exhaled. Shortly before dawn he fell into a deep sleep and woke a couple of hours later to find her already gone. He placed his palm on Maria's side of the bed. It had cooled, so he slid out of bed, got ready, and tucked away the ache of her leaving beside the bigger pain that he knew they both carried. He redialled the number that he had called the night before and set off for work.

He parked his car several streets away from the Questura and made for Bar Italia for breakfast. As he crossed Piazza Garibaldi, he saw Dante, the bank manager, and approached him with a smile and his hand outstretched.

'Dante, my friend, how are you?'

Dante smiled back and pumped his hand.

'What the hell do you think you're doing, calling me at home like that?' Dante said, grinning broadly.

Moretti continued the handshake and put his hand on the bank manager's shoulder for good measure.

'I need some help,' he said, nodding and still smiling. 'Quite a lot, actually, and strictly off the record.'

Dante threw back his head as if laughing. 'This is highly irregular, Dino.'

Moretti wiped away a non-existent tear of laughter.

'I know, Dante, but I need access to several accounts.'

Dante produced a handkerchief and blew his nose. 'You're crazy. We'll both end up in prison.'

Moretti shook his hand again, passing him a neatly folded piece of paper.

'More than likely, my friend. The names are on the paper. I'll call in to see you later this morning.'

They parted, Dante shaking his head, Moretti, still smiling, walking to Bar Italia.

Carla handed him his usual pastry and cappuccino.

'That must have been a good story,' she said, her smile as cheering as ever.

Moretti tapped the side of his nose. 'Not for mixed company,' he said.

CHAPTER TWENTY-SEVEN

Gennaro and Cristina were planning their day's work together when her phone rang.

'Furlan here, hello.'

'Ispettore, it's Alicia, from the agriturismo.'

Cristina's fingers mimed walking as she left the office and stepped out into the corridor.

'Alicia, hello. Is everything all right?'

'I can't speak now. Could you meet me here at the agriturismo? There are things that I think you should know.'

'Leave it to me, Alicia. Carry on with your work as normal, and I'll be there very soon.'

'Thank you.'

Alicia ended the call abruptly, and Cristina returned to Gennaro.

'That was the receptionist from the agriturismo. She wants to see me.'

'How did she sound?'

'Anxious, worried, maybe afraid. I need to go there right away. Would you do me a favour and follow up the leads on Paola and Luisa?'

Gennaro smiled. 'You're asking me to go to Bar Italia and Bar Firenze and track down two women? I'd be crazy not to. Off you go and find out what Alicia knows.'

Pausing only to upload the files on the agriturismo guests to her phone, Cristina hurried to Agriturismo Ricci. She stopped her car at the entry barrier, leaned out, and pressed the intercom.

'Yes?'

'Ispettore Furlan. I need to interview the staff and do a few follow-up interviews with some guests.'

There was a delay then the buzzer sounded, and the barrier lifted.

She parked under some trees at the side of the gravel courtyard, and a very tanned man crossed from reception to meet her.

'Ugo Boscolo,' he said, smiling and holding out his hand. 'I'm the estate manager here.'

Cristina stepped out of her car and shook his hand. Boscolo was nearly as tall as her, and his handshake was firm, but these were not the calloused hands of a manual worker. She reckoned that Signor Boscolo spent more time behind a desk than working on the land. She also recognised his accent.

'Cristina Furlan,' she said. 'Good to hear a different accent so far south.'

'I'm from outside of Asolo in Veneto. Where are you from, Ispettore?'

'Next province up, Trento. I guess you have experience with spumante wine?'

He swept his arm towards the reception, and they walked off together.

'Yes, I worked on some of the most famous estates producing Prosecco. Signor Ricci would like to produce a sparkling wine here to add to his range, but the climate is so different that we are still searching for suitable grape varieties.'

As they stepped into the cool interior, Cristina ignored Alicia at the reception desk.

'But you didn't come here to talk about wine,' Boscolo said.

'No, I'd like to talk to you about the missing boy.'

'Come with me, we can use Signor Ricci's office.'

Cristina found out when Mario's father had done work for the agriturismo, as well as checking the list of all external contractors. She also interviewed two kitchen staff, a gardener, and a handyman before it was Alicia's turn.

A slim, short-haired woman in her thirties, Alicia wore a black skirt and crisp white blouse. Her legs were bare, and she wore no make-up. When they shook hands, Cristina could tell she was used to working. Cristina moved Ricci's chair so that she sat on the same side of the desk as Alicia.

'Thank you for calling me, Alicia. What was it that you wanted to tell me?'

Alicia's hands were one on top of the other, fingers interlaced, on her knee.

'I might be wasting your time,' she said. 'It could be gossip or drunken talk, but I thought that you should know, and you can decide. It's about Mario Rosati.'

'Go on.'

'People doing my job are invisible. I mean, we're there, but guests ignore us. They don't acknowledge us; they don't speak to us.' She fidgeted with a ring. 'They say things.'

Cristina spoke softly to her.

'What did you hear, Alicia?'

'One of the guests, Signora Cooper, the American woman, is desperate for a child. She and her husband were arguing.'

'What about?'

Alicia touched the hair behind her ear. 'They were arguing because Signora Cooper had slept with Signor Ricci.'

'When was this, do you know?'

'It was after the pool party – after Mario went missing.'

'Did you hear what was said, Alicia?'

'I didn't follow all of it, but there was also something about a legal problem in America. She said with her colouring they could think about Africa or maybe Asia.'

'Do you think she was talking about adoption?'

Alicia shrugged. 'Maybe. I don't know. She said that they had been over it all before, and if he couldn't give her a child, it was time to go down another path.'

'Do you know what she meant by that?'

Alicia looked directly into Cristina's eyes. 'Ispettore, I can't shift the thought that she's maybe involved with Mario's disappearance.'

Cristina leaned forward and placed her hand on the receptionist's arm.

'Alicia, you've been a great help. This information might really move our investigation forward. I give you my word that I'm going to do everything I can to find him.'

Alicia nodded and left. Cristina put Ricci's chair back and followed her out, giving her only a nod as she passed reception.

Outside, several of the guests were relaxing around the pool. Daniel and Asia were face down on adjacent loungers, while Sabine was swimming lengths of the pool with an effortless, efficient, front crawl.

Jaap noticed Cristina and waved her over. 'Fancy a dip?'

She walked over.

'I'd love to,' she said. 'But I'm on duty, and anyway, the pool is for residents only.'

'How about a drink then?' Jaap asked. 'Non-alcoholic, if you prefer. We have a large cooler here.'

'Thanks. Only water, please.'

Jaap took a small bottle out of the cooler. It immediately frosted with condensation. He twisted open the cap, wrapped it in a paper napkin, and handed it to her.

'Thanks.' She sipped the water slowly to avoid a headache.

Jaap opened his mouth to speak when Sabine pulled herself athletically out of the pool. She walked over, skin shining with water and tanning oil, wringing the water out of her hair. She picked up a towel in passing and draped it over her shoulders when she reached them.

'Hi, Ispettore, back again?'

'I'm speaking to a few people that we missed last time. How was your swim?'

Sabine started towelling her hair. 'The water's great. It's thermal, you should try it.'

Cristina smiled.

'As I said to your husband, I'm not a guest, and anyway, I don't have a costume.'

'You're our guest, and I'm sure no-one would mind if you swam without a costume, eh Jaap?'

Cristina blushed.

A watch alarm beeped, and Asia and Daniel both got up and left the poolside.

Cristina lowered her voice. 'I wonder if we could have a few words in private.'

'Sure,' said Sabine. 'Why don't we all go back to our room? We can chat, have a drink, and I can dry my hair.'

Cristina followed them to a timber chalet set back a little from the pool. Jaap slid open the large patio doors, then closed the curtains when they were all inside. Sabine walked off to the bedroom.

'I'm going to change,' she said over her shoulder. 'You two make yourselves comfortable.'

'Please take a seat,' said Jaap. 'Can I get you a proper drink now?'

Cristina sat on the edge of a sofa and held up her bottle.

'I'm still on duty, so I'll stick to my water.'

Sabine returned with her hair up in a turban, wrapping herself in a large white bath sheet. She paused, long enough for Cristina to see that she had removed her swimsuit, then folded over the large open bath sheet and fixed it over her bust. Cristina averted her eyes and blushed again.

Sabine sat next to her.

'Pour me some white wine, please, Jaap. Now, what was it you wanted to talk about?'

Jaap filled her glass, poured himself a beer and sat opposite the women.

As Sabine shifted round to face Cristina, the bath sheet slid off her knee. 'You said you wanted a few words?'

Cristina sipped some water.

'I've been interviewing the staff about the missing boy, and I know it's not connected and probably nothing, but some of them told me that they had heard a couple arguing. I wondered if that's all it was, or if it was more serious.'

'And you thought it was us?'

'No, I know it was the American couple. That's why I wanted to speak in private.'

The couple exchanged a look.

'It's a long story,' Sabine said.

'I have the time,' said Cristina.

Jaap glugged his beer, his Adam's apple marking each swallow.

'Sabine and I have an open marriage. We can each see other people, or together we can see other couples, and it's okay for us. We're comfortable with it all.'

'Asia Cooper got drunk the night of the pool party,' said Sabine. 'Her character changed completely.'

'How so?'

Sabine sipped her wine. 'She's usually so proper and ladylike, but that's not really her. After a few drinks she became loud and very flirty.'

Jaap laughed. 'But not always with good judgement,' he said.

'How do you mean?' asked Cristina.

Sabine closed the towel over her knees.

'She was all over the English guy, David – you know, the one with the fabulous body – feeling his muscles, sitting on his lap, playing with his hair. And this in front of everybody.'

Cristina looked puzzled. 'But I thought that David was gay.'

The Dutch couple laughed.

'He is,' said Jaap. 'But Asia didn't know, and she couldn't understand why he wasn't responding.'

'She told me that it must be because he's English,' Sabine said.

'I don't understand what all this has to do with the argument,' said Cristina.

Sabine wiped away a tear.

'Asia is desperate to have a child,' she said. 'That alarm you heard at the pool? Asia has some kind of fertility app on her watch. When it beeps, they go and try. So far, she hasn't been able to have one with Daniel, so she wanted to get pregnant by David.'

'But he rejected her.'

'Exactly,' said Sabine. 'So she slept with Ricci instead.'

Cristina nodded. 'So that's what the argument was about.'

Sabine took another sip of wine.

'No, Ispettore,' she said. 'The argument was because her husband found out and had revenge sex with me.'

CHAPTER TWENTY-EIGHT

Moretti was shown immediately into the bank manager's office. They shook hands and Moretti glanced up at the camera in the corner.

'Relax, Dino, it's off.'

They sat at a circular coffee table on which was a small pile of folders.

'Thanks for seeing me, Dante. Do you have the information?'

The bank manager tapped the folders. 'I'll answer any questions, Dino, but the files stay with me, understood?'

'Understood. Let's start with Erpicone. What can you tell me?'

'His podere is losing money – has been for a while, but I don't think that will come as a surprise. Ever since his wife died and the family left, he's been in no condition to run a business.'

'When was the last time you spoke to him?'

'He's a recluse now, so I had to visit him. It must have been about six months ago.'

'Is he overdrawn?'

'He was, but that's not uncommon for farmers. They often have cash flow problems. They lay out money for stock and wages, but they recoup it after the harvest or when they sell off livestock.'

'Can I ask how much?'

'He borrowed a little over forty thousand.'

Moretti smoothed his moustache. 'Wow. Really?'

'As I said, Dino, it's not a lot. A well-run podere can more than make that up in a season, and he has access to some very cheap labour, I believe.'

Moretti's insides griped at the memory of Maria's leaving. '*Had* access is more accurate, and well-run is the key phrase.'

'But recently there have been a few deposits that have reduced the debt significantly.'

'Where from?'

Dante raised his brows. 'You know I can't answer that.'

'How about Giusti?'

'Giusti's problem is the time he spends looking after Rosaria. He borrowed a couple of thousand two months ago, but he said it was going to save him money in the long term. He's been making regular small payments. I don't expect him to default.'

'What about Ricci?'

Dante folded his arms. 'Signor Ricci is interesting. He's in the process of organising a sizeable loan.'

'How sizeable?'

'A quarter of a million Euros.'

'What does he want that for?'

'I can't go into detail, for reasons of commercial confidentiality, but it's a major expansion plan.'

'Are you going to grant the loan?' Moretti asked.

'We're in the process of deciding. He hasn't yet shown us an architect's or surveyor's plans or been to the town hall to ask for planning permission. There's a long, involved process, and securing the loan is only a small part of it.'

'I see. How are his finances otherwise?'

'You're the second person to ask that this week.'

Moretti frowned. 'Oh? Who else is asking?'

Dante held out his hands and shrugged.

'Again, I can't give details because of client confidentiality, but a third party is conducting due diligence, and I'm in the process of agreeing access to the agriturismo accounts with Signor Ricci.'

'Are they buying him out?'

The bank manager folded his arms again. 'Dino, I refuse to answer.'

'Very well, but you didn't answer my question about his current finances.'

'They're not great, but as I said before, a major part of his income comes from the land. So a good or bad grape or oil harvest can have a huge effect one way or the other.'

The desk phone rang.

'Dino, if you've more questions, I'll be glad to answer them – as far as I'm able. Otherwise, I need to chase you away and get on with things.'

Moretti rose to leave. 'One final question, Dante. Has my wife made any transactions or loan requests in the past few days?'

Dante smiled and placed his hand on Moretti's back as he opened the door.

'You can check your joint account, Dino. As far as Maria's personal account, you need to ask her, not me.'

CHAPTER TWENTY-NINE

Gennaro paused for a moment outside Bar Italia while his head and heart, or more accurately his head and stomach, had a discussion. Undecided, he entered and decided to let the pastries on offer resolve his dilemma.

'Good morning,' he said to the few customers.

The three busybodies smiled and replied. A man reading his paper looked up and nodded, a couple of tourists ignored him, and Carla stood smiling, hands on hips.

'Well, Agente, is it carrot juice or pastry today?'

Gennaro looked at the array behind the Perspex counter. There, among the usual assortment of croissants – plain and filled, the raisin twists, the fruit glazed pastries, and assorted biscuits – lay his nemesis.

'Carla, how could you?'

She followed his gaze to the cannoli shells.

'They're freshly made and ready to be filled.'

'Okay, I give in.'

'One or two?'

'Two. And may my heart forgive me.'

'Candied peel, pistachio, chocolate, or chopped nuts?'

'One with candied peel and chopped nuts, the other with pistachio and chocolate, please.'

Carla filled the first crisp cannolo shell with sweetened ricotta. She dipped one end in chopped pistachio and the other end in chocolate sauce, wrapped it in paper, and handed it to Gennaro.

He held the cannolo up at eye level to admire it, then bit into it. The crisp, pastry tube splintered and crunched as the soft filling oozed everywhere. He leaned forward so that the ricotta didn't fall on his clothes or shoes, and held his other hand underneath, in time to catch a drip of the chocolate sauce.

'That's where all the taxpayers' money goes,' said Rosalia, her face looking more pinched than usual.

'I like a man with a healthy appetite,' said Fausta. Her little dog struggled to escape from her bag, hoping to profit from a dropped crumb.

'You like a man with a pulse,' Rosalia replied, in a none-too-sotto voce.

Fausta frowned and held the dog's collar tightly.

'Hush, you two,' said Donatella. 'Let Agente Santoro enjoy his pastry.'

Carla finished filling the other cannolo tube and placed it on a saucer on the counter.

'Coffee?'

Gennaro could only nod.

'Honestly. If the police spent more time catching criminals, we'd all sleep safer in bed at night,' said Rosalia.

'You've nothing to fear on that account,' said Fausta. 'Your treasures are safe.'

Donatella tutted and rose to leave. 'I've had enough of you two. I'm going home.'

Gennaro mumbled through a mouthful of cannolo. 'Wait.'

He swallowed hard but too quickly, and a sharp piece of pastry shell stuck in his throat. He reached for his coffee, but Carla reacted instantly and passed him a glass of water.

He gulped it down and breathed again. 'Thanks, Carla.'

He wiped the sweet detritus from his mouth.

'Ladies, I wonder if you can help me. I'm looking for two women.'

Rosalia's eyebrows shot up.

'You should be out looking for that poor boy and his mother.'

'It is in connection to that investigation,' Gennaro said, joining them at their table. Fausta's dog poked its head forward to greet him. She let the dog lick his sticky fingers.

'What are the women called?' she asked. 'And what do they look like?'

'I'm afraid I don't have a description, only two names – Paola and Luisa.'

'How old are they?' asked Donatella.

'Again, I'm not sure, but I guess mid-twenties to early forties.'

Fausta sighed. 'That rules us out.'

'Let's be serious, ladies,' said Donatella. 'Who could it be?'

'I know two Paolas,' said Rosalia. 'The one who is married to the car mechanic, and the other who works in the shoe shop in town.'

'And there's the Paola at the medical practice,' said Fausta. 'As far as Luisa is concerned, there's widow Luisa, divorced Luisa, and slutty Luisa.'

Donatella covered her mouth with her hand. 'Fausta. That's dreadful.'

Fausta pouted her lips.

'It's the way I remember them.' She paused then added, 'The fact that it's true just makes it easier.'

Gennaro stopped scratching Fausta's dog and brought out his notebook.

'Ladies, let's start from the beginning. We'll begin with the Paolas.'

Thanks to the three gossips and a little help from Carla, Gennaro compiled a list of Paolas and Luisas, complete with some surnames, marital and moral status, sketchy descriptions, and a few addresses. He thanked them all and left for Bar Firenze where, over an Aperol spritz and some bar snacks, he filled in some more details and added three more candidates.

CHAPTER THIRTY

Giorgio Ricci removed the handmade straw hat as he entered the little trattoria. He put his sunglasses in the top pocket of his jacket and paused to let his eyes adjust to the light. A waiter approached and smiled.

'Signor Ricci?'

Ricci nodded and held out his hat.

The waiter took it with a slight bow. 'Follow me, please, signore.'

The waiter led the way to a table near the door, where a large man rose and stopped Ricci by placing a huge hand lightly on Ricci's chest.

'Please forgive the intrusion, signore,' he said in a thick Sicilian accent.

Ricci raised his arms straight out to the side while the bodyguard gave him a quick but thorough pat down.

He, too, gave a slight bow. 'Again, my apologies for the imposition, signore.'

He stood aside and sat back at his table.

The waiter smiled and set off again towards a table at the back of the otherwise empty trattoria.

The two men seated there stood to welcome Ricci. Both wore expensively tailored suits. The younger man held out his hand.

'Signor Ricci,' he said, pumping Ricci's hand. 'You found us then. I'm Signor Rossi and this is my colleague – also Signor Rossi.'

Ricci appreciated the man's wry humour. He was taller than them both, but the young man had a very strong handshake. The older man did not offer his hand.

'Please sit,' said the young man. 'We've already ordered for the table. I hope you don't mind.'

The three sat at the round table draped in a deep red pleated floor-length tablecloth, covered with a pressed white linen square.

The waiter appeared with a carafe of water and a bottle of wine. He set the wine on an adjacent table while he poured three glasses of water. He exchanged the carafe for the bottle of wine.

'Ninety-seven,' he said, showing them the label. 'An exceptional vintage from an exceptional producer.'

Ricci covered his glass. 'Not for me, thank you.'

The older Signor Rossi's eyebrows flicked up a fraction.

'You don't like the vintage, or don't you drink?'

'At one time I could have drunk for all of us,' replied Ricci. 'I never touch it now.'

The waiter hesitated.

'Pour for two, please,' said the younger Rossi.

The waiter nodded and produced a corkscrew from his pocket. He ran its blade around the foil and removed it, setting it down on the next table. Then he wiped the top of the cork with a clean napkin, inserted and twisted the corkscrew, and pulled the cork in a smooth movement. He placed the bottle on the adjacent table and sniffed the cork before passing it to the young man.

Using a clean part of the napkin, the waiter carefully wiped the open neck of the bottle then picked up a large wine glass. He poured about a tablespoon of wine into the glass, swirled it around the sides and examined both its colour and the tearing as it settled back into the glass. Then he sniffed it and, finally, tasted it. Satisfied, he poured another tablespoon of wine into another glass, swirled it around the sides, then emptied it into a second glass. When he had coated the sides of that glass, too, he emptied the wine into his tasting glass and poured two glasses of the precious vintage into the seasoned glasses and presented them to the Rossis.

They clinked glasses and sipped.

Younger Rossi nodded enthusiastically. 'Simply stunning,' he said to the waiter. 'We're ready now.'

The older Rossi studied Ricci closely.

'A wine producer who doesn't drink wine,' he said. 'Isn't that a bit of a contradiction, if you don't mind me saying so?'

Ricci smiled. 'Not at all. I know several producers who don't drink.'

'Are they all in recovery, like you?' asked older Rossi.

Ricci ignored the provocation.

'It may sound unusual, but for some, not drinking alcohol is merely a life choice,' he said, draping his napkin on his lap. 'Like not bribing public officials to win building contracts, if you don't mind me saying so.'

Both Rossis laughed and Ricci smiled.

'Well said,' replied younger Rossi. 'I'm going to like working with you. Ah, here is our starter.'

The waiter placed an oval *tagliere* of mixed salami and wedges of local cheeses in the centre of the table. They helped themselves to the selection.

Ricci turned to older Rossi. 'What line of work are you in exactly that you believe we can work together?'

'Oh, I think we have many mutual interests, Signor Ricci,' replied the older man.

'What makes you think that I'm looking for a partner then?'

The older man put down his cutlery.

'You're an ambitious man, Signor Ricci. You have plans to expand, and you've approached the bank for a loan. We like ambition, and we have access to funds which means that you could avoid the petty scrutiny that banks insist on.'

Ricci stopped and sipped his water.

'The bank's checks are a mere formality,' he said. 'The funds will be forthcoming, so I don't know what a partnership with you could bring to the deal.'

Older Rossi dabbed his mouth with his napkin and leaned back.

'We understand that there has been no planning approval, no plans submitted, no site inspection or report. Your ideas are at a very early stage, Signor Ricci, with many bureaucratic hurdles to negotiate. These can lose you time and money.'

Young Rossi now spoke.

'We have expertise and experience in bringing contracts to a close by assuaging the concerns of local interests. Many years of tried and tested ways of dealing with public officials. Our experts can draw up plans and have them approved in a very short timescale.'

The other Rossi continued.

'Not only can we supply a skilled workforce to do the building, but we can also provide peace of mind that when work starts, the site will be kept under constant surveillance until completion. It's like having an insurance policy without having to pay exorbitant policy fees.'

Ricci looked from one to the other.

'It sounds almost too good to be true. Where's the catch?'

The older Rossi picked up a piece of *pecorino*, popped it into his mouth, and chewed it before responding.

'We represent associates who from time to time find themselves cash rich. We constantly search for projects that they can support. Yours is one of those projects. There's no catch.'

Ricci placed his cutlery on his plate.

The two Rossis continued to eat, making little sounds of approval as they tasted each new offering.

Ricci turned and signalled to the waiter. 'Please pour me some more water.'

'Of course, signore. Sorry, signore.'

The Rossis sat back from the table.

'May I clear away, gentlemen?' asked the waiter.

Young Rossi nodded. 'Yes, thank you. It was all delicious.'

'Thank you. Pasta will be ready in a few minutes.'

Ricci waited until the waiter had cleared the table and gone.

'What do I have to do? If I want to accept your offer.'

Older Rossi replied, 'As I said, we represent associates who occasionally find themselves with funds to invest. This is one of those times. Withdraw your application for a bank loan. The appropriate funds will be sent to your account.'

'Hmm,' said Ricci. 'How long will that take?'

Young Rossi produced a phone from his jacket and placed it between his hands on the table in front of him.

'The funds can be transferred before our pasta arrives.'

Ricci shook his head. 'Just like that?'

Young Rossi turned his palms upwards. 'Just like that.'

Ricci stroked his throat.

'You know that I was a financier,' he said. 'I know that it's impossible to transfer such an amount of money without rigorous checks being made.'

Older Rossi took a sip of wine and held the glass up to eye level, swirling the wine to admire its colour.

'You know the bureaucracy and regulations governing the Italian wine industry are among the most Byzantine and complex in the world, yet every year Italy produces good wine.' He took another sip. 'And once in a while, despite the labyrinth of petty officialdom, a wine as stunning as this one is made.'

He put his glass on the table and turned to Ricci.

'And do you know why that is? It's because there are people who know how and when to prune, when to harvest, how to balance the fruit, the tannin, and the sugars, to have a perfect fermentation. Their passion and knowledge let them work within the rules and still achieve greatness. How passionate are you, Signor Ricci?'

Before Ricci could answer, the waiter appeared, skilfully balancing three bowls of *pici al ragù di Cinta Senese*. Young Rossi slid his phone to the side and the waiter served the pasta, topped up the wine and water, and left.

The three men all held their napkins to their chins and twisted forkfuls of the thick, uneven, handmade pasta into its delicious sauce made from a famous Tuscan breed of pig, and ate in silence for a while. Young Rossi finished first, dabbed his mouth, took a large mouthful of wine, and folded his napkin onto his lap. He jabbed his thumbs onto his phone and waited until it buzzed before putting it back into his jacket pocket.

'Please finish your pasta, Signor Ricci,' he said. 'Then if you would be so kind as to contact your bank, you'll see that we are serious about this project.'

Ricci looked startled. 'What have you done?'

'I've transferred a quarter of a million Euros to your account.'

Ricci swallowed hard. 'But I didn't agree. What if I were to say no?'

Young Rossi looked across the table to his older companion.

'You are free to do so but you would then bear all the risks of the project, all the petty niggles, all of the delays, yourself.'

Ricci was unable to speak.

Young Rossi continued, 'You would also not be able to achieve your other twin ambitions.'

Ricci held his breath. 'And what are those?'

Young Rossi laid his hand on Ricci's wrist and smiled.

'Signor Ricci, we know that you have plans for a housing development, so we'd like to help fund that, too.'

Ricci blanched but found his voice.

'But I've told no-one about those plans. How did you…?' Ricci snatched away his hand. 'Let's stop this charade,' he said angrily. 'Rossi and Rossi? Really? You're Mafia, and you want to use my legitimate projects to launder your dirty money.'

The huge man at the door began to rise to his feet, but the older Rossi raised a finger to stop him.

'Signor Ricci,' he said reassuringly, 'we and the people we represent are businessmen, like you. When we perceive an investment opportunity, we conduct due diligence – as you would do yourself – and we check not only the project but the person behind the project.'

He paused to sip his wine.

'So, we know that you were a financier, we know why you left, and we know where you found the money to buy your agriturismo. We know its annual turnover, who your guests have been, how many bottles of wine and oil you produce every year, even who you've slept with. Now, my colleague Signor Rossi said we could help you achieve your ambitions to have a housing development. This is how it will work. Your name will still appear on all the paperwork, and you will be the owner of the development – nominally at least – while we fund the entire project and use our labour and materials. You will get a percentage of the profits merely for letting us use your name. All of this will be detailed in a written and notarised contract that will satisfy any subsequent scrutiny.'

He placed his hand on Ricci's shoulder.

'We trust you, Signor Ricci, and we want you to trust us, too.'

Ricci twisted his shoulder free and faced young Rossi. 'You said my twin ambitions?'

The younger man smiled.

'Oh that.' He adjusted his napkin as the waiter approached. 'We're going to fund your candidacy for the position of sindaco.'

CHAPTER THIRTY-ONE

Cristina waited outside the chalet, listening until she was certain that the occupants were moving around. She knocked the door. A few moments later, it opened a little and Daniel Cooper, dressed in a fluffy white towelling robe, peeked out.

'Ispettore?'

'Signor Cooper, I'm so sorry to disturb you, but I wonder if I could come in for a moment.'

'Who is it, Daniel?' Asia called from inside.

Daniel replied over his shoulder. 'The ispettore. She wants to come in and ask more questions.'

'Now?'

Daniel looked at Cristina, and she nodded.

'Yes, now,' he replied. Then he added, 'Give us a moment, please.'

He closed the door and Cristina turned to face the pool area. Sabine and Jaap had returned and were stretched out on loungers. How could they all go about their normal lives when somewhere out there a child was missing – hurt, afraid, dead maybe?

Behind her the door opened.

'Come in,' said Daniel, now dressed in shorts and a loose shirt.

Asia Cooper wore a long sheer robe over her bikini, looking a little flushed as she sat on one of the couches, sipping a tall drink.

'Your timing stinks,' she said.

'Please sit,' said Daniel. 'May I offer you something?'

Cristina sat opposite Asia. 'No, nothing, thanks.'

Daniel sat beside his wife and placed his arm across her shoulders.

'This had better be important.'

'I believe it is important, Signora Cooper. I understand that you had an argument with your husband?'

Anger flashed in Asia's eyes. 'What the hell has that to do with you?'

Cristina held her gaze.

'And I believe that you have had trouble conceiving, even though you desperately want a child.'

Asia shrugged off Daniel's arm. 'You've crossed a line,' she raged.

'So desperate that you want to find a child from Asia or Africa.'

She held her hand out at Cristina. 'Stop it. Stop it now.'

'So desperate that you're prepared to break the law.'

She shook her head vigorously. 'Not true.'

'So desperate that you'd kidnap a little boy.'

Asia let out a scream that became a wail that ended in shoulder-heaving sobs. She doubled over, fists pushed into her face. Daniel placed a hand gently on her back, but she shrugged it off.

Cristina inhaled slowly and deeply and waited. Very slowly, Asia Cooper began to regain a modicum of composure. She reached out and grabbed a handful of tissues from the box on the table, dabbed and wiped her face, and blew her nose loudly in an extremely unladylike manner.

She sat upright and smoothed her hair away from her forehead and inhaled deeply, swallowing a sob.

'You think you've figured it out,' she said. 'Figured me out. Well, Miss Ticking Clock, we have a lot in common. You want a child as badly as I do. It's obvious the way you look at every man you meet – sizing them up as sperm donors. Well, me and Daniel, we have more than that. We have a stable, loving relationship. Sure, it ain't perfect, but it is what it is, and it works. And look at you. So desperate to solve this case that you look at us to be patsies? The foreigners so desperate to have a kid so they'll steal one? Well, your investigation has drawn a blank – like your love life. We had nothing to do with the boy's disappearance.'

CHAPTER THIRTY-TWO

It was late afternoon by the time Santoro reached the penultimate address on his list. None of the women that he'd interviewed were current or former girlfriends of Mancini, although he had unearthed two other illicit relationships.

Paola, the wife of the car mechanic, was having an affair with the owner of the dog training school whom she had met when she took her new puppy to obedience classes. After initial improvements, the lovers had conspired to train the dog in bad habits so that their liaison could continue.

He also discovered that while 'divorced Luisa' was having a scandalous relationship with a cleric from the nearby town, 'slutty Luisa' lived a life of almost monastic purity. Her only indiscretion – if it could indeed be called that, and the one for which Fausta had given her the title – was that she dressed to show off her cleavage and always wore vivid red lipstick.

Santoro stepped off the narrow street, down several stairs to a tiny, shady terrace lined on one side with large terracotta plant pots holding hydrangeas, jasmine, and oleander. Cooking aromas and music from a popular radio station diffused into the warm, scented air around him from the open shutters and windows above.

He rang the doorbell. A small dog barked and was scolded to silence by its owner. An attractive brunette with shoulder-length hair opened the door.

'Come in, Agente, I've been expecting you.'

'Oh?'

'You've already spoken with friends of mine.'

Santoro followed her through a cool, dark corridor that opened into a traditional living room with plain stucco walls and large wooden beams in the ceiling. The shutters were closed to a point on that side of the building, but enough light streamed through them to allow the agente to make out the dark wooden table, cabinets and sideboard, and the chintzy couches and armchairs. Santoro crouched to offer the back of his hand to the tiny Yorkshire terrier that scampered over to greet him. The little dog's dry, rough tongue licked the sweat from between his fingers and palm then lay on its back to be stroked.

Luisa laughed. 'I see you've neutralised the security system.'

Santoro looked up at her.

'Dogs like me,' he said, as the little Yorkie pushed its ear harder against his tickling fingers.

'It seems that you like them, too.' She clapped her hands. 'Bed, Schizzo.'

The little dog stood up, shook its head, gave a kind of snorting sneeze, then trotted out of the room.

'Come with me and I'll show you where you can wash your hands.'

Santoro followed Luisa into the kitchen and washed his hands under the running tap while she uncorked a bottle of wine.

'I was about to have some pasta,' she said. 'Would you care to join me?'

She wore a plain white t-shirt and shorts and stood, barefoot, tanned legs slightly apart, holding up the bottle.

'I'm not sure,' he said. 'I'm on duty.'

She put down the wine and tossed him a towel. 'As you wish. The pasta's ready. I'm going to eat.'

She drained the pasta and added it to a frying pan of *Ragù di Chianina*, tossing it to mix.

Santoro's resistance evaporated as the pasta took on an unctuous coating of slow-cooked minced beef. 'Yes, please,' he said. 'I'd love to.'

Luisa smiled and set out two bowls, some bread, and two glasses.

'Pour us some wine.'

Santoro gladly obeyed, and moments later he was nodding enthusiastically, mouth full of pasta.

They ate in silence, each studying the other.

With the last of the pasta gone, Santoro tore open a slice of bread, held it by the crust and used its open texture as a *scarpetta* to wipe up the last of the sauce. He sipped his wine and pushed his chair back from the table.

'Thank you, Signora…'

'Luisa's fine. And you're welcome. I'm glad of the company.'

'I'm sorry, Luisa, I have to ask you some questions.'

'Go ahead.'

Santoro brought out his notebook. 'I understand that you're a widow.'

Luisa collected the empty bowls and cutlery. 'Yes. I lost my husband four years ago.'

'I'm sorry to hear that. My wife died three years ago, and I still haven't got over it.'

She nodded.

'How old are you, Luisa?'

'Thirty-one.'

'Any children? Family?'

She finished clearing the table and wiped the oilskin tablecloth with a damp sponge.

'No children. My parents are still alive, and I have a sister and a brother.'

'And a dog.'

She laughed and filled the Moka with coffee and water. 'And a dog.'

'What can you tell me about Signor Mancini?'

Luisa placed two small coffee cups on the table. 'What do you want to know?'

Santoro scratched his head with his pencil.

'Oh, general stuff. His background, who his friends are.'

Luisa poured the coffee.

'Agente, we didn't have that kind of relationship. I'm a young widow. I miss male company, and there are too many in Cassiatorre ready to gossip, given the slightest encouragement. It suited me that Pino lives outside of town. I only saw him a couple of times and didn't go there to chat.'

Santoro put down his notepad and picked up his coffee cup.

'You must have formed an impression of what kind of person he is. He's quite a bit older than you.'

'Yes, he's older, but he's kind, polite, and unlike younger men…'

Luisa placed her hand on her chest and her fingers stroked the hollow at the base of her throat.

'Unlike younger men?'

'…very attentive.'

Santoro finished his coffee. 'Did you know he was a police officer?'

She picked up her cup and drained it.

'I knew Pino did something that had trained him to be very organised. His house is tidier than mine – even the things in his wardrobe are arranged by colour and season.'

'Apart from that, nothing out of the ordinary then?'

Luisa tidied away the cups.

'Nothing.' She frowned. 'Except there were no photographs anywhere. No photographs of family or friends. I thought that was unusual.'

Santoro looked up. 'Unusual how?'

'He's from the south, like you,' she replied. 'People there are even more obsessed with family than the rest of Italy. Do you have photographs at home?'

Santoro grinned. 'Lots.'

'Well, there you are then. It was like he had no family, no friends, no ties.' She shrugged. 'Like a spy, or something.'

CHAPTER THIRTY-THREE

Moretti knocked on the Vice Questore's open door and popped his head round.

His superior was standing, arms folded, at the window. 'Come in and close the door behind you.'

Moretti stood behind the chair.

'Take a seat,' said Innocenti.

Moretti sat and looked at the papers on the desk. On top of a tidy bundle was a sheet with the letterhead of the sindaco's office. As he leaned forward to get a better look, Innocenti turned round, and Moretti sat back quickly.

'What you're trying to read upside down is a letter from the sindaco. He's up for re-election this year. Did you know that?'

Moretti sighed. 'I think I did see a hundred or so posters of his face plastered on every possible surface.'

Innocenti stabbed the desk with his finger.

'That's exactly the tone that will block any further promotion for you, Moretti. I don't know how you got as far as you have.'

Moretti smoothed his moustache with his index finger. 'Being exceptionally good at my job, perhaps?'

Innocenti banged the desk with his fist.

'God knows it wasn't by respecting authority. To get on in this job these days you need to take account of politics. Understand?'

Moretti looked past him out the window. 'Politics, Vice Questore.'

'Everything is political nowadays. We've to meet targets, quotas, customer satisfaction ratings, performance milestones. Are you listening, Moretti?'

Moretti looked at his superior. 'Milestones, Vice Questore.'

Innocenti snatched up the sindaco's letter and tossed it to Moretti.

'Read this.'

Moretti scanned the letter and slid it back to Innocenti.

'Well?'

'He's completely missing the point.'

Innocenti picked up and reread the letter.

'How come? He's asking what we're doing about the drugs cache and the fact that the Mafia are trying to move into the area.'

Moretti shook his head.

'The point is that a week ago a young boy disappeared from a locked house. His mother is missing, and his father is dead – the funeral's tomorrow, by the way – and the sindaco is only concerned about a coked-up wild boar and a stash of prescription medicines. Mario and his mother are our priority.'

Innocenti pointed at Moretti.

'Let me make this clear for you. Your priority is to do what you're told. Exceptionally good at your job? It doesn't look like it from this side of the desk. The sindaco wants this, all of this, cleaned up before the election campaign starts in earnest. Find the boy and his mother and find out whose drugs smacked-out the boar.'

Moretti's phone buzzed in his pocket, and he stood.

'Coked-out, Vice Questore. Smacked-out is heroin, not cocaine.'

'Get it fixed, Moretti. Now get out.'

Moretti lifted his phone to his ear as he left the office. 'Yes?'

'Can you speak?'

Moretti closed the door behind him and began walking back to his office.

'I can now. What is it?'

'The person we were chatting about has withdrawn his application for a loan.'

Moretti quickened his pace. 'When?'

'This morning.'

CHAPTER THIRTY-FOUR

Carmela Perri stopped the car, pulled onto the verge and read Nicola Bartolini's text message. It was obvious that the young boy was upset, but she was unsure how she should proceed.

Please don't tell my parents.

She found Moretti's card in her purse and started to key in his number then hesitated, cancelled the call, and pressed her phone to her forehead. She sighed deeply, dropped the phone beside her, and drove into Cassiatorre.

As she made her way from the car park to the Questura, she saw the tall figure of the new detective approaching across Piazza Garibaldi.

She waved her hand in the air like a pupil with the answer.

'Excuse me,' she said. 'Good morning, I wonder if I could have a little of your time.'

Cristina looked over at the young woman wearing the dress with fitted bodice, skinny straps, and a full skirt. She was about to ignore her when the young woman smiled; her lipstick matched the colour of the huge red poppies printed on her dress.

Cristina smiled back. 'Good morning. I don't wish to be rude, but I'm in rather a hurry this morning. Who are you?'

Carmela looked up at Cristina.

'Sorry, I'm Carmela Perri – Mario's teacher. I appreciate that you are busy, but I've received a message from one of his classmates, and it might be important. Can we talk somewhere?'

Cristina looked at her watch. 'All right, come back to the Questura.'

Cristina walked back to the Questura, with Carmela almost trotting beside her.

'We can talk in my office. Please take a seat and tell me how I can help.'

Carmela tucked her skirt beneath her and showed Cristina the message.

Please help me.
I think Mario has disappeared because of me.
Please don't tell my parents.

Cristina passed the phone back. 'Who sent it, Maestra Perri?'

'Call me Carmela, please. It was a boy called Nicola Bartolini.'

Cristina switched on her phone and began to make notes. 'What is Nicola like?'

Carmela sat forward with her hands between her knees.

'He's a lovely boy, good looking. One of Mario's friends – or so I thought.'

'Could he have done something to upset Mario?'

Carmela shrugged. 'Nothing that children do surprises me, but I don't think so.'

Cristina pointed to Carmela's phone.

'Then why would he write that?'

'Children often feel guilty about things they haven't done.'

'If we had to speak to him, how do I get in touch with his parents, Carmela?'

Carmela picked up her phone and clicked to her contacts.

'His parents work in Maghicchio. His father owns an electrical contractor business, and his mother works in a care home.'

She passed over the phone. Cristina photographed the details and returned it.

'Does he have any brothers or sisters? Who looks after him?'

Carmela switched off her phone. 'He's an only child, and as far as I know, their cleaner comes in during the school holidays to look after him.'

Cristina swivelled in her chair.

'I'm sorry if I've upset your plans,' said Carmela.

Cristina picked up her phone.

'No, you did the right thing. This won't take long,' she said, as

143

she punched in a number. 'Hello, I'd like to speak with Signor Bartolini, please... Ispettore Furlan in Cassiatorre... No, nothing is wrong... All day? All right, I'll try his wife's number... No, really... That's fine... No, please reassure him... Thank you. Goodbye.'

Cristina keyed in his wife's number.

'Hello, Signora Bartolini? Ispettore Furlan at Cassiatorre... No, everything's all right... I wonder if I could speak with Nicola. I understand that he's at home with your cleaner, is that right? ...No, you don't have to be there... Look, I have Nicola's teacher, Maestra Perri, with me. I'll pass you to her.'

Cristina put her phone on speaker and handed it over.

'Signora Bartolini, it's Carmela Perri.'

'Maestra Perri, what's all this about?'

'Nicola sent me a text message, and I wasn't sure what to do about it...'

'So, you went to the police?'

'It was about Mario.'

'What about Mario? Does Nicola know something?'

'I don't know. The problem that I have is that he told me not to tell you or Signor Bartolini, but I felt I couldn't ignore it.'

'So what are you asking me?'

Carmela passed the phone back. 'Signora Bartolini, Furlan again. I'm sure that it's nothing, but I'd like a quick word with Nicola, if only to satisfy myself.'

'I can't get away from work until five.'

'It really won't take long, I'm certain. So if you'll allow it, I'll speak with Nicola, with either the cleaner or Maestra Perri present acting in loco parentis. What do you think?'

'I'm not comfortable with either of those ideas. Can't it wait?'

'Signora Bartolini, although I'm sure that Nicola can't help our investigation, we are looking for a missing boy, so every minute is valuable. I also want to reassure your son.'

'I'm not sure. Have you contacted my husband?'

'I tried him first, but his office said that he's out on site visits all day.'

The line went silent.

'All right, Ispettore, go and speak to Nicola, but with Maestra Perri and not the cleaner. We don't want our business broadcast through the entire town, understand?'

Cristina nodded. 'Perfectly. Thank you.'

'Let's go in my car,' said Carmela. 'Nicola knows it, and you won't attract attention.'

They set off together and drove to the other side of Cassiatorre.

Carmela pressed the button of the entry system.

'Yes?'

'It's Maestra Perri. Has Signora Bartolini called you?'

'Yes, come in.'

The buzzer sounded and the lock clicked. They pushed the metal gate open and walked to the house. The cleaner met them at the door, looked them both up and down, and let them in. She wore a sleeveless, button-through floral housecoat – the unofficial uniform of Italian housewives – and wiped her hands on a cloth.

Carmela shook hands first.

'This is Ispettore Furlan.'

'Uhuh, I'm Ilaria.'

Cristina shook hands. 'Where is Nicola?' she asked.

'You're from the north,' said Ilaria. 'That'll be why you're in such a hurry.' She nodded over her shoulder. 'He's outside, playing with my boy.'

'Sorry, that was rather direct,' said Cristina. 'We'd like to speak with Nicola on his own, please.'

'You can wait through there.'

Ilaria went out to the garden and spoke with the boys. Nicola came in but hesitated when he saw Cristina.

Carmela crouched down in front of him and smiled.

'Nicola, I got your message,' she said warmly. 'Now, I haven't said anything to your parents – like you asked – but I told this nice lady who would like to ask a couple of questions. Is that all right? She's a police officer.'

Nicola took a half step backwards.

Cristina sat on her haunches.

'Nicola, I'm Cristina Furlan. Can I start by saying that I think you are a very brave boy for sending the message to your teacher. It was a very short message, wasn't it?'

Nicola nodded.

Cristina continued, 'I need to ask you one or two things –to give us a bit more detail. Do you think you could manage that?'

Nicola nodded again.

'Let's all sit over here,' said Carmela.

They moved to a table. Cristina sat opposite Nicola, with Carmela between them at the head of the table.

'Nicola, you're one of Mario's friends, aren't you?' asked Cristina.

Nicola's head was down, and his hands were on the table in front of him. 'I suppose so.'

'And you play together?'

He traced his finger around bunch of grapes printed on the tablecloth. 'Sometimes.'

'At school or out of school?'

'A bit of both.'

'Is that here or at his place?'

'It's always here. He sometimes stays when his mum and dad are at work.'

'He must like coming here, don't you think?'

Nicola shrugged.

'Does he eat here?'

He nodded.

'What does he like?'

'He likes meat. He doesn't get much meat at home because his mum is a vegetarian.'

Carmela touched the back of his arm. 'You're doing really well, Nicola.'

He looked sideways up at her, and she smiled.

'Nicola, I don't understand why you think Mario disappeared because of you,' said Cristina. 'It sounds to me like you were a good friend to him.'

Nicola's chin touched his chest and he remained silent.

'I agree,' said Carmela. 'You always help him in class. I've seen you putting your arm around his shoulder and whispering.'

A large tear splashed on to the tablecloth. 'I bully him,' said Nicola. 'I say bad things and he gets upset.'

The two women exchanged a glance.

Cristina produced a packet of tissues and handed them to Nicola.

'What sort of things, Nicola?'

He opened the packet, removed a tissue, and blew his nose.

146

'What sort of things?' Cristina repeated softly.

He dabbed his eyes with another tissue. 'Things about him being poor.'

Carmela put her hand on his arm again.

'Tell me one of the things,' said Cristina.

Nicola's body shuddered with a sob. 'I said it would be better for him if his parents died, because then he'd get put in an orphanage.'

Carmela looked puzzled.

Cristina brought her head closer to his. 'Why would that be better?'

'I said that the orphanage would let him out to play and he'd have more friends.'

'Anything else?'

His lip quivered. 'That he has no playing out clothes and that's why his parents lock him up.'

He dug the heels of his hands into his eyes and began to cry.

Carmela rubbed his shoulder and they let him sob.

Ilaria looked in from the garden, but Cristina signalled her to stay outside. When he seemed to be stopping, Carmela opened out a couple of tissues and gave them to him. He dried his eyes and blew his nose loudly.

'Nicola,' said Cristina. 'I don't know why Mario disappeared, but I can guarantee it had nothing to do with what you said to him.'

He looked at her for the first time since they sat down. 'Are you sure?'

'I'm certain.' Now she reached out and rubbed the back of his hand. 'Can you tell us why you said those things?'

His head fell again. 'I found out that I'm adopted. It's me that should be in the orphanage.' He looked up quickly at them both. 'My parents don't know that I know. You can't tell them.'

Cristina and Carmela each held one of his hands.

'Your secret is safe with us,' said Carmela.

He looked at Cristina. 'Promise?'

'Promise.'

He sighed and squeezed their hands. 'Do you know what happened to Mario?'

'We don't yet, unfortunately, Nicola,' replied Cristina. 'But as soon as we find him, we'll let you know. We'll let everyone know.'

CHAPTER THIRTY-FIVE

The desk officer handed Moretti his mail as he passed. He nodded, still on his call.

'Any reason?'

'None. But yesterday there was an injection of funds, in the same amount, to his account.'

'Source?'

'Still checking, but it seems legitimate.'

Moretti reached his office and dropped his mail on the desk. 'Okay, keep me updated. And thanks.'

He pocketed his mobile and used the desk phone to first call Furlan and Santoro into his office, then to ask Alfiero, the desk officer, to bring him an espresso from the bar.

Furlan arrived ahead of Santoro.

'Good morning, Commissario.'

'Good morning, capo.'

'Good morning. Please take a seat and I'll fill you in on my meeting with the Vice Questore. The sindaco wants us to concentrate on finding who's behind the drugs cache that the wild boar dug up.'

Both officers gasped and opened their mouths to speak, but Moretti silenced them with a hand.

'I know. I told him that our priority was Mario and his mother, so let's share any new information. You start, Cristina.'

'Alicia from the agriturismo tipped me off that she'd heard the

148

American couple fighting about adopting a child. I checked with the Dutch couple, and they confirmed that there had been a fight, but not for that reason. They said that Asia Cooper, the lawyer, got drunk and said that she'd do almost anything to adopt a child.'

Moretti picked up his mail. 'Do you believe her?'

Cristina wrinkled her nose.

'I believe that she is desperate for a child. I'm not certain if she's so desperate that she would kidnap Mario.'

'Thoughts, Gennaro?'

Santoro rubbed his grey stubble.

'She's wealthy enough, and she's a lawyer. She also sounds very determined. I wouldn't rule her out at this stage. It might be an idea to find out what her plans are when she leaves Ricci's place.'

Moretti tapped the edges of his mail against the back of his hand.

'Good suggestion, but that would involve other agencies over which we have no control.' Moretti addressed Cristina again, 'What about the guests who've left the agriturismo?'

'They've all been checked out. Nothing to report.'

He sighed.

'Anything else, Cristina?'

'I had an odd meeting this morning. Mario's teacher stopped me in Piazza Garibaldi and told me that a classmate of Mario had messaged her thinking that his bullying had caused Mario to disappear.'

'Is that going anywhere?'

'Again, I don't think so, but I discovered that the boy's cleaner sometimes looks after both boys. I was wondering why not on this occasion.'

Moretti scanned one of the internal mail messages, crumpled it up and tossed it towards the bin, missing it by half a metre.

'Do you get these printed messages about changing your login password?'

Santoro smiled. 'No, capo, we respond to the email reminders.'

'How did you get on yesterday, Gennaro?'

'I set my diet back about a month, but I eventually found the two women – Paola and Luisa.'

'And?'

'Neither of them could give me anything to go on, except that

Luisa noticed something unusual. Mancini has no photographs of family or friends anywhere in his house.'

Moretti opened an envelope with his finger.

'She's right. I should have noticed.'

'And it fits with our information that he has a new identity. When I told her that he was a former cop, she didn't seem surprised.'

Moretti took out the folded paper. 'Anything else?'

'Yes. I discovered that both Paola and Luisa, and another two of the women that I interviewed, had slept with Ricci at some time.'

Moretti dropped the mail. 'Ricci. Is there anyone in Cassiatorre that he hasn't slept with?'

Cristina raised her hand.

'Well, you've only just arrived, Cristina, so give it time.'

She blushed.

'No, Commissario, I was going to say that Asia Cooper has slept with Ricci. That's what the argument was about.'

'And I've found out that his account has had an injection of a quarter of a million. Ricci's up to no good. Santoro, get your contacts to dig into his past.'

'Capo.'

Moretti picked up the folded note again.

'We need to make sure that we have full surveillance coverage at Domenico's funeral tomorrow. I've arranged for the whole thing to be filmed, from the church to the cemetery. We should capture everyone who attends, and we can study the footage and pick out anyone that seems out of place.'

'Fingers crossed Chiara and Mario turn up,' said Santoro.

'I doubt it,' replied Moretti.

He opened the note.

'It's another ransom demand.'

He held it up by the corners and read it out.

'One million Euro for Mario's safe return. Call this number at 8pm.'

He placed the paper carefully on its envelope.

'*Mannaggia*. This one looks genuine. Call Forensics, Gennaro.'

*

A little before eight o'clock, Moretti sat surrounded by the tech team and the other detectives ready to make the call.

'Is everyone ready? We might only get this one chance.'

The two officers from the tech team gave a thumbs up, while Furlan and Santoro nodded. Moretti punched in the number on the desk phone, pressed speaker, and waited until precisely 8pm to press call. The dial tone repeated four times then a recorded message began.

'Mario is still alive and unharmed. We have him. As proof, when you checked the contents of the waste basket in his house, you will have found a Kinder wrapper and a piece of paper torn from *La Gazetta dello Sport*. You have two days to raise one million euro. Your next instructions will be in a message on the phone that you will find in the litter bin outside the Questura.'

The message ended and Moretti looked at the tech officers.

'Nothing, Commissario,' said the one in front of the computer screen. 'The message was too short.'

'I'll go and get the phone,' said Santoro.

Cristina moved aside to let him pass.

Moretti folded his arms. 'At least we have a recording, right?'

The other tech officer nodded, slid his headphones to around his neck, and played the recording.

When it finished, Moretti circled his finger, and it was played again.

'Any thoughts?'

'Well, it definitely means that Chiara has disappeared without her son,' said Santoro. 'Where can she be?'

Cristina added. 'It's obviously a male voice, muffled as if through a scarf, speaking in an accent that's not from here – maybe Rome?'

'Definitely from Rome,' said the sound recordist.

'Any background sounds?'

The sound recordist put his headphones back on and listened again. 'No. My guess is that instead of talking through a scarf, the phone was wrapped in material, so it blocked out ambient sounds.'

'Clever,' said Moretti. 'Cristina, cross-check the call records from both Domenico and Chiara's phones, and make a list of those with the Rome area code. That might shake out a lead.'

'Yes, Commissario.'

Santoro reappeared with the phone wrapped in a handkerchief.

'Thanks, Gennaro,' said Moretti. 'Give it to them.'

The officer at the computer donned a pair of gloves and took the phone. He opened it, removed the SIM card, and inserted it into a reader.

'Completely clean.'

'Okay,' said Moretti. 'Put it back together, get it checked for prints and DNA, then bring it back to me. I think we've done all we can for tonight. Thanks, everyone.'

CHAPTER THIRTY-SIX

Moretti stood on the stage of the small theatre next door to the Questura. The Vice Questore sat behind him, while seated below him were Furlan, Santoro, all the town's uniformed and Municipal Police, and a squad of forensic photographers equipped with both still and video cameras. A large white screen was suspended from the ceiling at the back of the stage. He raised his hands for silence.

'Thank you all for getting here on time. I want to make sure that everyone knows their job today.'

He waited until the muttering ceased.

'Municipal officers, you are the inner ring in charge of crowd and traffic control. Even though Domenico Rosati did not involve himself very much in the life of Cassiatorre, the circumstances of the case mean that there will be people from out of town arriving to gawp. After the funeral Mass, the cortege – led by the parish priest on foot – will take its usual route to the cemetery. I can't predict if the visitors will follow, so you must be prepared to make last minute tweaks to your normal plans in terms of closing or opening side roads.'

A hand went up.

'Please bear with me and let me finish. I'll take questions at the end. Next, I want to talk to the State Police.'

He signalled to the back of the theatre, and a technician projected a map of the town centre onto the screen. Moretti used a laser pen to point out details.

'You are the outer ring, and you need to position your cars here, here, here, and here, to control traffic movement into and out of Cassiatorre. You must be ready to block off access or escape if that proves necessary, so you must stay in your vehicles the whole time until the operation stands down.'

Several comments about being stuck in hot cars made it to the stage, but Moretti ignored them.

'Dog teams. There is a parallel investigation of the drugs cache. I want you to mingle with the crowds to see if your dogs can identify any suspects.'

One of the canine officers unleashed his dog and it wandered to the front of the theatre, to the great amusement of all the police and the great annoyance of the Vice Questore.

Moretti smiled. 'If it stops at your feet, you'll be suspended pending investigation.'

The crowd laughed and the dog's handler called it back.

'Photographers. You have the most difficult but perhaps the most important job today. We need to photograph everybody who turns up today, whether they are at the service or in the crowd. Now, I know that you'll have met to organise yourselves into zones, but can I emphasise that I'd prefer ten shots of everyone present rather than anyone is missed. All right, questions.'

The Municipal officer who had raised her hand spoke first. 'Do we issue parking fines as usual?'

Some of the others groaned.

Moretti's outstretched arms, palms down, silenced them.

'Use your discretion and common sense. If someone is causing an obstruction, fine, issue a ticket. If they are over the time they've paid for or are parking at the roadside, don't bother. You have enough to do today.'

Moretti scanned the theatre for other hands. There were none. He half turned to Innocenti.

'Did you want to add anything, Vice Questore? Milestones, maybe?'

Innocenti rose to his feet and moved to the front of the stage.

'This is the biggest combined law enforcement group ever assembled in this province. It shows how serious we are about this. The drugs cache points to an escalation of the scale of crime in this area that suggests organised, outside influences, probably with

Mafia connections. Remember that the sindaco wants results, and quickly, so let's get the best out of the manpower we're deploying today. That's all.'

The officers began to get to their feet. Moretti signalled to the back, and two large photographs appeared behind him on the screen.

'This is Mario and Chiara Rosati, his mother. If you see anyone that looks even remotely like them, don't hesitate, act. Thank you.'

As the theatre cleared, Moretti joined Furlan and Santoro.

'All we can do is mingle in the crowd and be ready to respond,' said Moretti. 'I've had a message to say that the phone has been checked, so I'm going next door to pick it up.'

They walked outside together to find Piazza Garibaldi much busier than usual. Moretti thought about a coffee but the throng outside Bar Italia changed his mind.

'Okay, I'll meet you two at the church shortly.'

He stopped at the desk. 'You have a package for me?'

Alfiero, the desk officer, handed over two items and two reports.

'Thanks.'

Moretti first took the phone from its bag and checked it – no communication. He placed it on his desk then leafed through the report. Two pages that told him there was neither DNA nor fingerprints.

He sighed and picked up the report on the ransom note – only a seven percent correlation of probable origin with the first note and, as with the phone, no DNA, or prints. Tight-lipped, he sent the other two a text message.

Looks like ransom note is genuine. Waiting for call. See you soon.

He popped the phone into his shirt pocket and left to find them.

*

Something about the movement outside Bar Italia caught Moretti's attention. He walked quickly over. Carla's son, Gigi, was struggling to get back inside with a tray of glasses and crockery, but the customers had spilled outside and no-one was moving.

'Police. Clear the way!' he shouted, using both arms like a swimmer doing the breaststroke to roughly clear a path towards Gigi.

'Get behind me, Gigi,' he said. 'Out of the way, please.'

He continued through the bar as far as the counter. Carla's face was flushed as she struggled to serve the crush.

'Are you on your own today?'

'Yes, the girl who was supposed to come in didn't arrive.'

Moretti stationed himself at the till. 'Okay, you serve, I'll collect the cash and, Gigi, you continue clearing the tables and loading the dishwasher.'

Gigi nodded and set off again with his tray under his arm as Carla managed half a smile.

'You've done this before.'

'A long time ago, but it's like riding a bike. Next.'

Working together, the three dealt with the customers, and the bar emptied enough to free up Moretti.

'I'll take a coffee when you have a minute,' he said, moving to the other side of the counter.

'Right away.'

Gigi stood red-faced amid a cloud of steam as he emptied a load from the dishwasher. Moretti tousled his hair as he passed, and the boy gave him his lopsided grin.

Moretti stood at the door to catch the breeze. Piazza Garibaldi was emptying as people made their way to the church.

Carla arrived with his coffee. 'Here you are, no charge,' she said, placing it on the table next to him.

Moretti leaned forward to pick it up when Carla stood on tiptoes, put her hands on either side of his face, and kissed him full on the lips.

'Thanks, Dino,' she said. 'That was getting really scary.'

Moretti had no words as he watched her slim figure return behind the counter. She stuck out her lower lip and blew the hair off her forehead, smoothing it to the side with a finger. Moretti, too, suddenly felt hot. He downed his coffee in three sips, waved, and left.

CHAPTER THIRTY-SEVEN

Cristina was taller than most of those entering the church, and Moretti joined her.

'Gennaro is already inside, Commissario.'

'It's even busier than I thought,' said Moretti.

'The local radio and TV were here but I moved them on. They've set up inside the church.'

'Good, we don't want this to be more of a circus than it already is. Who's inside?'

'Mainly locals, but a fair number of strangers from out of town. I recognised some of Signora Rosati's workmates, and Gennaro said that quite a few of Domenico's workmates are here, too.'

Moretti scanned Piazza Garibaldi as the last few stragglers hurried to the church, looking like sheep being rounded up by the Municipal Police.

'Anyone out of the ordinary?'

Cristina gazed into the distance. 'Your wife is inside, Commissario.'

Moretti tsked and saw the answer on Cristina's face before he asked the question.

'You know, then?'

She nodded without looking at him. 'Commissario, it's a small town.'

He rubbed the nape of his neck.

'Thanks for letting me know. Let's go inside.'

As the two detectives positioned themselves on either side of the open doors at the back of the church, Moretti scanned the congregation. Maria was sitting at the front of the church next to three pallbearers and the sindaco, who was wearing his tricolour sash. Domenico's cousin shared the front row on the other side with another three pallbearers and the three busybodies. Domenico's coffin sat on trestles between them.

Santoro was stationed halfway down, right beside the central aisle, level with where the film crew of the local TV station had set up their tripod. Other officers, both uniformed and plain clothes, were scattered through the congregation. When he saw Ricci in the second last row, Moretti's stomach knotted slightly. His aching doubt returned, and he briefly glanced at Maria at the far end of the church, then back to Ricci, but the feeling in his stomach disappeared, replaced by a jolt of excitement when he noticed the two impeccably suited men wearing black sunglasses sitting in the back row of the church, immediately behind Ricci. A third, huge man sat beside them. Moretti took out his phone, checked it was on silent, and took several photographs of different combinations of the group.

The chat in the church stopped with the appearance of the priest and altar servers. Everyone stood and the service began. The pattern of prayers, hymns, readings, and blessings proceeded until the point where Domenico's cousin rose to say a few words.

'Thank you all for coming here today. I'm Davide, Domenico's cousin – the only one of his relatives young and well enough to travel. I have only been to Cassiatorre twice before, but I know how much Domenico loved living and working here. I know that he will have done work for many of you here, and although he didn't really integrate into the social life, he always felt part of the community. He and Chiara were a very private couple who worked hard to buy their property outside the town. Owning that land, that house, was, after the birth of his son, Mario, his greatest source of pride.'

Davide's voice faltered, and he dabbed his eyes with a tissue.

'Domenico was proud of his family and his work, but where is his family now?' His voice quickened and crescendoed. 'Where is his wife and son? It's over a week since his accident. What's been done in that time?'

Davide pointed his finger at the uniformed officers spread through the church. 'What have the police done about finding Mario and Chiara? There they all are, look at them – spying on everyone, with their cameras. You should be ashamed, all of you. Why are you here? Why aren't you out looking for Mario and Chiara?' The hand holding the tissue became a fist and he shook it at them all. 'You're all in it together. All part of the cover up. All part of the plan to steal Domenico's land and rob the family of our inheritance. I know all about it. Domenico told me everything, how he refused to sell—'

The ransom phone in Moretti's shirt pocket rang loudly, stopping Domenico mid-sentence. The entire congregation turned around and looked at him as he struggled to take it out of the pocket and silence it. He raised an apologetic hand and hurried out of the church, into the crowded vestibule, holding the phone to his ear. Cristina followed him.

'Hello,' he said, squeezing out of the vestibule and into the overspill outside the church. 'Moretti here.'

'Have I called at a bad time?'

Moretti instantly recognised the voice from the recorded message. He pushed out to the open and walked past the hearse towards Piazza Garibaldi.

'It hasn't been two days, why are you calling?'

'To check that you had the phone and that you were on track to get the money. That's all.'

'Look, I—'

The call ended.

'*Mannaggia.*'

Cristina caught up with him. 'Is everything all right?'

Moretti tucked the ransom phone back into his shirt pocket and surveyed Piazza Garibaldi. 'It was the voice from last night's message. He couldn't have picked a worse time to call.'

Cristina also looked all around.

'Do you think he knew you were in the church?'

'I don't know, maybe. Who can say?' He held up his phone. 'Look, these three behind Ricci – they have to be Mafia.'

Cristina flicked through the series of photos. 'What are they doing here?'

'I don't know, but I'm going to find out who they are and why

159

they're behind Ricci.'

She handed back his phone. 'What do you want me to do?'

'Call the roadblock team and have them stand by. I'll message Gennaro and get him to keep eyes on Ricci and the Mafia guys. We can both move to the door and apprehend them when they come out.'

'Won't they use the crowd as cover?'

'Hmm, yes, you're right. Okay, we'll stand off a bit, but tell the Municipal Police over at the overspill to make sure nobody hangs around chatting when they come out. They must disperse everyone immediately and quickly.'

'Yes, Commissario.'

She turned and strode off, already calling the mobile squad.

Moretti messaged Santoro.

Ricci at very back of church sitting in front of three Mafiosi. Two suits and a gorilla. Get help from uniformed officers. Follow Ricci and the three Mafiosi. Cristina and I will pick them up outside.

The overspill crowd parted as the priest and altar servers appeared, followed by the pallbearers carrying the coffin. The funeral director opened the door of the hearse and supervised the sliding of the coffin inside. Davide waited until his cousin's coffin was in place and declined the offer of riding in the hearse. As the crowd began to push out from the church, the Municipal Police ushered everyone to the sides to leave the area directly in front of the entrance clear.

The cortege set off following the priest, and those who wanted to go to the cemetery were allowed to fall in behind in an orderly fashion; the others were dispersed – brusquely if necessary – away from the church. Moretti was alert, waiting for the appearance of the Mafiosi, and heedless of the glares and muttering from some of the congregation.

The photographers took position and carefully captured everyone who left the church. The Municipal Police either walked slowly alongside the cortege, or moved quickly ahead to control traffic, their role of crowd control being taken over by the officers leaving the church. Moretti and Cristina told them of the plan.

Bar Italia became busy again, and little knots of people clustered in random groups in Piazza Garibaldi. As the last of the congregation reached the back of the church, Santoro sent Moretti a message.

Targets entering vestibule.

Moretti signalled to Cristina and the other officers, and they all readied their pistols. Some stragglers, the three gossips, the sindaco, and Maria came out of the church. The stragglers wandered away. Maria noticed him, then turned immediately away and began chatting to the sindaco. The three gossips glowered at him as they passed on the way to Bar Italia.

Moretti cursed under his breath but maintained his concentration. Moments later Santoro appeared.

Moretti's voice was little more than a dry croak. 'Where are they, Gennaro?'

Santoro opened his arms in a shrug.

'I don't know. I saw them enter the vestibule and thought that they came right out.'

Moretti holstered his gun. 'Is there another way out?'

Santoro pointed. 'That door there leads to the cloisters, but it's always locked.'

Moretti and Cristina ran past the agente towards the door.

Cristina reached it first.

'It's open.'

The two men followed her into the cloisters and through the open door at the far end. The overflow carpark was full, but a settling cloud of dust told them everything.

Moretti stopped, gasping for breath, and pulled out his phone.

'All units on maximum alert.' He gulped in air. 'Suspects on the move.' Another breath. 'Apprehend.'

He leaned over, hands on knees, recovering. Cristina, gun still drawn, walked up and down checking inside the rows of parked cars. Santoro arrived, half walking, half running.

'Sorry, capo. I don't know how I missed them.'

Moretti straightened up and put a hand on Santoro's shoulder.

'We missed them, Gennaro, all of us.'

'Before they left, Ricci turned and said something to the others. I think he organised their escape.'

'Well, if we were missing a motive before, I think we have one now. Contact the Questura, Gennaro, and put out an all-points search for them, then catch up with the cortege and go with it to the cemetery.'

Cristina returned. 'All empty. They've escaped.'

'Stay here, Cristina, and let no-one shift their cars until I send some uniformed officers to relieve you. I'll also get a video team round and we'll record all the number plates. There's a chance that we have the missing car on film.'

'What about Ricci, capo?'

'I'll organise Cristina's relief, then I'm going to Bar Italia,' replied Moretti. 'I've an idea I need to check out. Cristina, meet me there and we'll go together to the agriturismo.'

Cristina holstered her pistol. 'Yes, Commissario.'

CHAPTER THIRTY-EIGHT

Moretti ignored the snub of the three gossips as he entered a quieter Bar Italia. Carla's helper had arrived, and things were running smoothly again.

Carla smiled over at him, and he tilted his head back. She wiped her hands on a towel and came over to meet him.

'Do you have a minute?'

She turned to check the queue.

'Yes, if it's only a minute.'

Conscious of the attuned eavesdropping antennae of the gossips, Moretti suggested they talk outside.

They stood in the shade near the bar's side entrance. Carla stretched her arms above her, looked across the road to the small park, and sighed.

'It's good to breathe fresh air. It was crazy in there earlier. Thanks again for helping.'

Moretti faced the same way so that his lips could not be read by anyone inside.

'Glad to help. Can I ask about your customers today?'

She placed her hands on her hips and twisted her torso slowly from side to side while still looking straight ahead.

'You can ask, Dino, but I can't guarantee to remember.'

'It's when everyone had left for the funeral. Can you remember who was in the bar?'

She stopped her stretches and cocked her head to the side.

'The two funeral guys arrived, parked the hearse, and came in for a quick coffee. There were three young mums, regulars, with their toddlers in strollers. They stayed longer, chatting, and left when the first few arrived from the church at the end of the funeral. There was a man who's become a regular who sat reading his paper – he'd been there during the rush and left about halfway through the service – and a couple of the police officers. Again, they came in, had a quick coffee, and left.'

Moretti's pulse quickened a little.

'The man who left during the service, does he have a Roman accent?'

Carla looked through the glass door back into the bar.

'Dino, you know what it's like here. The regulars always ask for the same thing. I learn what that is after a few days and have it ready when I see them come in. That's why people come back. I haven't heard him speak for ages. He leaves the money on the counter and goes.'

Dino tutted.

'But think, Carla. When he did speak, right at the beginning, did he sound as if he came from Rome?'

Carla paused, her hand reaching for the door.

'He's not from here and not from Rome either. I'd say he was from Abruzzo, over towards the coast – Pescara, maybe.'

Moretti opened his mouth to ask another question.

'Sorry, I have to go.'

He opened the door for her. 'Thanks, Carla.'

'Are you ready, Commissario? Or are you having a coffee?'

Cristina's long stride quickly closed the gap between them.

'I'm ready, let's go in my car.'

They crossed the road to the side street where Moretti had parked.

Cristina had to push the passenger seat all the way back.

'It's my legs,' she apologised. 'I have to do this in most cars.'

Moretti stared ahead. 'Hmph.'

Cristina smiled and brightened her voice.

'Couldn't you find a place any closer to the Questura?'

Moretti started the car.

'It's a long story,' he replied, and drove off.

She tried again.

'The photography team were doing a thorough job of photographing the number plates when I left.'

'Good.'

They drove in silence for a while.

'Commissario, are you okay? Excuse me for asking, but is it because of how your wife was?'

He sighed.

'No, it's not that.'

Moretti slowed as they circled a roundabout and crunched the gears as he accelerated.

'I had a hunch about who made the call, but I was wrong.'

They remained silent until they arrived at the agriturismo's security barrier.

Moretti lowered the window and pressed the button. At the first crackle from the speaker, he spoke. 'Commissario Moretti, open up.'

There was no reply, only a click, but the barrier lifted and they sped down the long, cypress-lined drive to the main buildings, Moretti undoing his seat belt as he drove.

'That's Ricci's car,' said Cristina. 'I recognise it from before.'

Moretti stopped the car with a skid on the gravel surface. 'And covered with dust from a country road. Let's go.'

Cristina took longer to extricate herself but soon caught up and reached the entrance first.

They burst in, and Alicia jumped back, mouth agape.

'We need to see Signor Ricci,' said Cristina.

'Now,' said Moretti.

Ricci heard the raised voices and came out from his office, still dressed in his black suit and tie.

'Officers,' he said calmly and smoothly. 'Please join me and tell me how I can be of assistance. Alicia, bring us some cold water and coffee, please.'

He stood aside, ushered the astonished detectives into his office, and insisted that Moretti and Furlan sat.

He took his seat behind his desk and leaned back with his fingers crossed and hands resting on his middle with his thumbs tucked into his belt.

'What can I help you with today?'

'You can start by telling us who you were talking to in church a short time ago, Signor Ricci,' said Moretti. 'And why you drove off with them in such a hurry.'

Ricci grinned.

'I'm afraid you are conflating two entirely separate events, Commissario. I overheard the gentlemen behind me saying that they wanted to avoid the crowds at the front. I merely informed them that there was another way out of the church, and they followed me.'

Moretti leaned forward.

'You and they both disappeared. How do you explain that?'

'Speaking for myself, I got into my car and drove straight here. I don't know what anyone else did.'

'How did you avoid the roadblocks?'

'Were there roadblocks?' Ricci raised his eyebrows. 'I didn't see any, but then I came back to the estate from the service road near the town.'

'And the other three men?'

'Commissario, as I have already said, I came home by myself. I don't know what more to tell you about anyone else.'

'So you won't mind if we search the chalets and the rest of the property?'

Ricci leant forward and steepled his hands.

'Not at all, Commissario. You can start as soon as you show me your search warrant.'

Moretti was about to speak when his phone rang. He held up a hand to Ricci as he rose to his feet.

'This had better be important, whoever you are, I'm interviewing someone.'

The desk officer at the Questura apologised.

'Commissario, it's Alfiero, it might be better if you were alone.'

Moretti left Ricci's office, strode through reception, slamming the door open, and stopped outside. Several of the guests around the pool looked up.

'All right, Alfiero, this better be good.'

'I'm afraid it's bad, Commissario,' replied the desk officer. 'Very bad. The immigrants have escaped.'

Moretti's free hand grabbed the wiry hair at the side of his head.

'Escaped? How the hell did that happen? Where were you? Where was everybody?'

'Commissario, everyone was outside at the funeral. I slipped out for a coffee. I couldn't have been away more than a couple of minutes.'

'When I get back there, I'll see from the CCTV exactly how long you were away.'

There was a short pause at the other end.

'I'm afraid you won't. Whoever let them out switched the camera off and took the disk out of the machine.'

Moretti swore and turned and kicked the wall of the agriturismo office as Cristina appeared.

'I've told Ricci we'll be back with a w—' She stopped abruptly. 'What's wrong?'

Moretti stuffed his phone back into his jacket.

'Somebody has freed the illegal immigrants. We need to get back to the Questura.'

CHAPTER THIRTY-NINE

Alfiero took a step back as Moretti burst into the Questura.

'A couple of minutes? Really?'

The officer could not look at Moretti.

'Commissario, before you check, I was about ten minutes. I went to Bar Italia for a coffee, and then I had a cigarette.'

'Have you been down there?'

'Not since I called you.'

'Stay here. Cristina, come with me.'

He led the way to the cells where the immigrants had been held. They checked the locks.

Moretti shook his head.

'Nothing – not a scrape, not a scratch. Check the door at the end of the corridor, Cristina.'

She turned the corner.

'Open. This is how they left.'

Moretti joined her. The door had been pulled to. He kicked it.

'*Mannaggia.* This was planned, Cristina, and by someone who had a key.'

They returned to the officer's side of the front desk.

'Where is the key to the cells?'

Alfiero took a key from a chain on his belt and unlocked a key safe under the desk, opened the door and stood back. The cells key was in its usual position.

'Who else has a key for that safe?'

'No-one, Commissario, it's passed by hand when the shift changes.'

Moretti rubbed the back of his neck.

'Who else has keys for the cells?'

'Apart from the one in the safe, there's one in Innocenti's office, and I think you have one, Commissario.'

Instinctively, Moretti thrust his hand into a trouser pocket and produced the key.

'Is Innocenti in?'

'No. He had a meeting with the sindaco.'

'Where does he keep his copy of the key?'

'Commissario?'

'Never mind. If he comes back, stall him. Cristina, you stay, too, and call me if he appears.'

Moretti hurried to Innocenti's office and closed the door behind him. He started with the desk drawers, carefully moving the contents but finding nothing. He cursed quietly, then removed each drawer in turn to check the sides and the back. Still nothing. He replaced the drawers then crouched under the desk. There, taped to the underside of the kneehole, was a key. He left it in place but checked it against his copy. His phone rang and he almost bumped his head.

'Innocenti's on his way.'

Moretti scrambled to his feet and, making sure that the chair was as he found it, left Innocenti's office. They met in the corridor.

'Ah, Vice Questore,' he said. 'I was looking for you. There's a problem.'

Innocenti's face told Moretti that the news had already reached him.

'Come into my office.'

Moretti followed him inside.

Innocenti sat at his desk, leaned over, reached under it, and produced the cells key.

'Do you have your key to the cells, Moretti?'

Moretti retrieved it from his pocket and held it out for Innocenti to compare them.

'The third copy was locked in the key safe.' He tossed Moretti's key back. 'How in heaven's name could they escape?'

Moretti dropped the key into his pocket.

'We'll investigate it, Vice Questore, but why were they still here? We notified Immigration ages ago.'

Innocenti placed his hands on his desk, palms open.

'The Immigration Service is busy throughout the whole peninsula, and since we already had the immigrants in custody, they were the lowest priority. They're dealing with the ones who are crossing the Mediterranean.'

'As I said, we'll look into it – along with everything else.'

He turned to go.

'Moretti, wait. I had a call from Signor Ricci. He said that he wasn't making a formal complaint of harassment – not yet – but that he's considering it. What the hell are you playing at?'

Moretti looked down, shaking his head.

'He was at the funeral. We saw him talking to three strangers from out of town. We're sure they're Mafia, and we're sure that he helped them escape. They could be linked to the drugs cache, Mario, and his mother's disappearance. Who knows, maybe even the escape of the immigrants.'

Innocenti folded his arms.

'These so-called Mafia, do you have any evidence tying them to any of the things you said?'

'Not yet.'

'Not yet. I thought so. And do you really think that you can persuade a judge to issue a search warrant based on wild guesses?'

Moretti stood, arms at his sides, clenching and unclenching his fists. 'I know that Ricci is involved with the Mafia.'

Innocenti slapped the desk.

'That's the point, Moretti, you don't know. You haven't a shred of evidence. I'm just back from a meeting with the sindaco. This is election year, and he's found out that the self-same Signor Ricci is standing as a candidate against him. If you go stomping about his business, we'll face all sorts of wrongful accusation charges, and on top of those we'll be charged with political interference in the election. Do you understand?'

'Yes, Vice Questore.'

Innocenti pointed his finger at Moretti.

'Let me make this perfectly clear. I don't care if Ricci throws a party and invites every Mafia family in Sicily. Unless you have hard evidence of any crime, as far as you are concerned, he is fireproof until the election is over. You have not to contact him, question him, or harass him. Now repeat that.'

Moretti winced.

'I have not to contact, question, or harass Signor Ricci until the election is over, unless I have hard evidence.'

'Good. Now concentrate on finding the boy and his mother and find the damn immigrants. It shouldn't be too difficult – there are nine of them, and they're black.'

'Yes, Vice Questore.'

Innocenti shooed Moretti away with his hands and picked up his phone.

*

Moretti found Cristina waiting in his office.

'How did it go, Commissario?'

Moretti stood in the doorway and sighed.

'The short version is that Innocenti's key was in his office, we've to find Mario, his mother, and the immigrants, and I've to have no contact with Ricci until after the election unless I have hard evidence. He made me repeat it so that I understood.'

'So we can't put cars at the roads out of the agriturismo?'

He sat at his desk and leaned on his elbows.

'No point, Cristina. By now they'll have been driven off the property.'

She folded her arms and reddened.

'He can't do that.' Her voice was loud and shrill.

Moretti sat up.

'Sorry, Commissario, but he can't tie our hands like that.'

Moretti's finger smoothed his moustache, first left side then right, and his eyes twinkled.

'Ah,' he said, with the hint of a smile. 'But when he said, "You've to have no contact with Ricci" and made me repeat it, I did, saying I, not we.'

Cristina beamed. 'So what are we going to do?'

'Let me text Gennaro,' said Moretti, digging out his phone. He punched in a message and sent it. His phone pinged almost immediately.

'The service at the cemetery is finishing,' he said, pressing more keys. 'Cristina, you call the State Police and tell them that they can stop blocking the roads, and that they've to do perimeter sweeps including on the dirt roads to look for the immigrants. Oh, excuse me. Gennaro? Dino. The immigrants have escaped… Long story. Listen, I need you to speak to the Municipal cops and have them redeploy through the town… Not all of them; they can leave one or two for traffic control and use the rest… On my orders… No, right now… Yes, my office. I'll fill you in here… Right, see you.'

Cristina was finishing her call.

'…Immediately… Yes, on Commissario Moretti's orders… Thank you.'

'Right, Cristina, let's make a start before Gennaro gets back.'

Moretti counted on his fingers.

'I have a key for the cells; there's one in the key safe at the desk, and the duty officer has the key to the safe; and Innocenti has a key. Three keys, all accounted for, so how did the immigrants escape?'

Cristina closed her eyes before responding.

'There are five possibilities.'

'Go on.'

Now she counted on her fingers.

'Alfiero opened the key safe, took out the key and used it, or gave it to someone and went out for a coffee and a smoke as an alibi. Someone used Innocenti's key and put it back, again while Alfiero was out of the Questura. Someone previously made a copy of Innocenti's key, or someone previously made a copy of the safe key.'

Moretti reached into the top pocket of his linen jacket and found a small cigar. He held it under his nose, rolled it between his fingers, and sniffed.

'I think we can discount Alfiero as having personally let them out. Did he give someone else the cells key? That's a possibility, but we then have the problem of who that was and what Alfiero's motive might be. We can rule out someone using Innocenti's key and putting it back. It was taped to the underside of his desk, and when I felt it, the tape was smooth – it hadn't been touched. We can forget about someone making a copy of his key, too, for the same reason. And anyway, why would an unknown party at some unknown time in the past make a copy of his cells key so that at some unknown time in the future they would be able to set prisoners free? It's too far-fetched.'

Moretti put the unlit cigar between his lips and sucked air through it to get the tobacco flavour.

'There's a sixth possibility that you've imagined,' he said. 'Why don't you say it now?'

Cristina swallowed and looked directly at Moretti.

'It was your key that was copied.'

Moretti nodded almost imperceptibly.

'And who do you imagine would be in a position to do that, Ispettore Furlan?'

'Signora Maria De Luca. Your wife,' she replied quietly. 'The immigrants' lawyer.'

CHAPTER FORTY

As soon as they were out of the Questura, the immigrants split into four pairs, with Yusuf heading off on his own. They scattered in different directions, through the narrow, empty streets of the town centre, casting wary glances up at the shuttered windows lest anyone should see and report them. Hugging the walls, they moved as quickly as they could, covering their heads with their scarves and keeping their hands in their pockets or inside their sleeves to hide their colour.

In a few minutes, two of the Somalis found themselves on a dirt road at the edge of the town and ran, shoulder-to-shoulder, heads now uncovered, at a steady pace that most professional athletes would have been pleased with.

Another pair of Somalis had their progress impeded by encountering a series of dead ends. They retraced their steps before at last sprinting across a road and reaching open countryside where they, too, put a considerable distance between them and the town.

The last pair of Somalis were less fortunate. They chose to run off in a direction that led them to the cemetery, where they were immediately recaptured by the Municipal Police, assisted by the mourners.

The two Ethiopians kept Yusuf in sight for a while until he led them to the edge of town, where they headed off downhill in the direction of Maghicchio, keeping to the dirt roads parallel to the main road.

Yusuf turned uphill as soon as he was sure that the following Ethiopians were safely out of the town. He headed for his shelter to pick up his few possessions as planned.

*

The noise at the Questura entrance brought Moretti and Cristina to the front desk where two Somalis, each handcuffed to a Municipal Police officer, were shouting and struggling to get free. Santoro was helping to subdue the one who was lashing out at the officers, but he only came under control with the assistance of Moretti and Cristina.

Alfiero held out the fingerprint scanner.

'That's pointless, Alfiero,' said Moretti. 'They've burned off their prints, remember.'

With great difficulty the two men were bundled back to a cell.

Moretti thanked the Municipal officers then returned to his office with the two detectives. He flopped into his chair and half waved the others to sit.

'Well, Gennaro, how did the service at the cemetery go?'

Gennaro, for once, did not refer to his notebook.

'Not everyone who was in church went, but there was still a crowd. Domenico's cousin Davide had another outburst. Two of the female Municipal cops calmed him down and stayed at his side so that he didn't start off again.'

Moretti pulled out the cigar from his jacket pocket.

'*Mannaggia*,' he said. It was broken in two. 'What set him off?'

'I don't know. He pointed at the surrounding landscape and started ranting about how his cousin was never accepted by his neighbours – and something about being cheated. I don't know, it was all a bit incoherent. And as I said, the two female officers did a great job in calming him down.'

Moretti studied the two bits of his cigar, threw the smaller piece in the bin, and pocketed the larger part.

'Do you think we should interview him? Find out what's on his mind?'

Gennaro nodded.

'I think that would be a very good idea. I don't know if it will help with anything we're doing, but it might prevent a complaint against us, the authorities, who knows.'

'What else?'

'Well, there was the excitement when the two Somali guys turned up. The service had finished, and people were leaving the cemetery. No-one was really talking, so there wasn't much noise for such a crowd. The two immigrants came running round the corner and, well, collided into the people at the front. About a dozen fell over or tripped, including the Somalis. Again, the Municipal cops did a great job and grabbed them right away. Some of the men from the crowd helped, too. You saw yourselves how one was struggling and fighting back, so they cuffed them.'

Moretti groaned.

'Did my wife see all that? We'll need witness statements from anyone who laid hands on them, otherwise she'll have a field day with us for police brutality.'

'I'm sure she didn't. She wasn't there.'

Moretti and Cristina exchanged a glance.

'At the cemetery or in the cortege?'

Santoro looked puzzled. 'Neither. When the sindaco joined the cortege in Piazza Garibaldi, she left.'

Moretti rubbed the nape of his neck.

Santoro looked from Moretti to Cristina.

'Am I missing something?'

'The detainees were released while Alfiero was out for a coffee and a smoke. Whoever did it had a key.'

Cristina looked at the floor.

Santoro's eyes widened. 'No, capo, you can't be thinking that.'

Moretti half shrugged.

'Until I speak with her, I can't rule it out.'

Moretti sensed the awkwardness starting to grow in the office. He slapped his thigh.

'All right, let's see how our list is growing.'

He spun his chair to face the chart on the wall.

'Mario, his mother, whoever is behind the ransom note, Domenico's cousin, the drugs cache, the escaped immigrants, the Mafia – have I missed anything?' Moretti turned to face the two detectives. They shook their heads.

'Innocenti's told me that he wants us to find Mario, his mother, and the immigrants.'

'Are we going through with handing over the ransom cash?' Santoro asked.

'If it gives us a lead to Mario, then I think we've no choice. Innocenti has agreed, and the bank is organising the money. We need to wait for the phone call.'

Cristina looked relieved that the tension in the room was broken.

'What I don't understand, Commissario, is how Chiara has disappeared. Why didn't she try to get help for Mario and her husband? Why didn't she report the accident?'

'We've been over this, Cristina,' replied Moretti.

'I know leaving Mario at home alone was breaking the law, but surely at a certain point a mother would prioritise the safety of her child over any consequences for her.'

'That's irrelevant now that we know Mario's been kidnapped.' said Santoro.

'As for Chiara's disappearance,' added Moretti, 'with no identity card, no credit or bank cards, no phone, nothing that will register anywhere, she becomes invisible unless someone reports seeing her.'

'But what if she had help?' Cristina doggedly continued. 'What if someone helped her get Mario and they're sheltering them both?'

'Not without keys,' Santoro repeated. 'You didn't see that place. It was locked up tighter than—'

'Our police cells,' Moretti interrupted, dryly. 'All right, Cristina, I'll admit it's a possibility, but if you're right it would have to be someone local, and you found out yourself that she doesn't mix. Do you believe that she knows someone that well? Well enough to depend on? And even if it was true, do you think that she would stay hidden, knowing how much media attention there's been, how many people are looking for them? Would she have missed Domenico's funeral? It doesn't add up.'

'And there's the ransom demand,' Santoro piled in. 'What's all that about if she's hiding somewhere with Mario?'

'At least you're speaking about her in the present tense,' said Cristina, buckling slightly under their questions. 'So that means you think she's still alive.'

'I do, I think they're both still alive,' Moretti replied gently, seeing how his ispettore had sagged. 'And until there's evidence to the contrary, she and Mario are missing persons, that's all.'

'So, do you want us to focus on the immigrants?' Santoro asked.

'They were Innocenti's priority, not ours,' said Moretti, smoothing his moustache left and right. 'We'll let the local cops get on with chasing after them, and we'll park the drugs cache to one side, too, for the moment. We can't do much about Mario or his mother until tomorrow when we get the call about dropping off the ransom cash, so let's concentrate today on interviewing Domenico's cousin Davide and my wife. Cristina, you're the only one of us who doesn't know Maria, so I want you to find her and discover what she knows about the escape. Gennaro, we'll find Davide. We'll meet back here this afternoon. Clear?'

The two nodded, and they all stood. Moretti reached into his pocket for the broken cigar.

'Cristina, you might want to try my house first, in case Maria has gone home.'

'Yes, Commissario.'

'Gennaro, I want you to speak to the cops who restrained Davide at the cemetery and get an address for him, then meet me at the smokers' bin in Piazza Garibaldi.' He held up the remains of his cigar. 'I'm going to smoke this beauty,' he said ironically, as he headed out.

Moretti paused under the loggia to light the cigar and surveyed the square. The crowds had gone, and the town had returned to normal. He stepped out into the sunlight and sauntered to the smokers' bin. Carla waved at him from Bar Italia. He smiled and waved back. She frowned and changed her wave to a beckon, but he shook his head, pointed at his watch, and shrugged.

Now she pointed at his car. He smiled. He'd left it parked there for some time, and with so many of the local police on duty for the funeral, Carla was probably worried that he'd get a parking ticket. He dismissed her concern with a patting wave and another smile. She shook her head and stabbed her finger at his car then resumed clearing the outside tables.

Santoro appeared behind him.

'Ready, capo? I know where Davide's staying.'

Moretti turned and took a final puff of his cigar.

'Look, Gennaro,' he said with a grin. 'Carla's worried that I get a parking ticket.'

'Maybe she's telling you that you already have one,' said Santoro. 'There were cops here today who might not recognise your car.'

Moretti stubbed out the cigar on the perforated lid of the bin. 'Okay, we'll move it to humour her.'

They strolled down to the car. Santoro saw it first.

'*Minchia.*'

'You worthless piece of scum,' Moretti raged impotently at the unseen pest who had left a large prawn under the wiper.

CHAPTER FORTY-ONE

The first pair of Somalis had taken a wide clockwise route on dirt roads and animal tracks, only slowing their pace as they neared their destination. They crouched warily into the tall grasses, bringing their breathing quickly under silent control, moving stealthily from shrub to shrub towards the massive, sprawling juniper bush. Each retrieved his own long stick from its hiding place and squatted in the shade of a low bush to give their surroundings a final sweep through slitted eyes. When they were certain, they crawled forward together, close to the short green grass, to the prickly extremity of the juniper. Using their sticks to carefully lever up its low, grey, gnarled and twisted branches, they moved aside an old jute sack and, first one then the other, disappeared underneath and slid on their bellies down the long, gentle slope they had dug under and between its roots.

The dark, narrow slope opened out into a large funeral chamber with corridors leading off that had been carved out of the tufa by the Etruscans. And when they lit a tealight from a box on the dry, almost level floor, their shadows flickered beside the polychromatic figures painted on the walls above a grey-green frieze. Fragments of pottery and figures, both human and mythical, lay neatly arranged on the floor near a collection of bone and glinting metal ornaments, toilet articles, and jewellery. Incongruously placed on top of a large rectangular cinerary urn, set against one wall, were several bottles of mineral water, a few plastic cups, a packet of breakfast biscuits, and two unopened trays of dates. The two men sat cross-legged on the floor, poured some water, and waited in silence for the others.

The second pair of Somalis, after losing time in the labyrinthine *vicoli* of Cassiatorre, arrived unobserved at the scrubby hillside where the juniper bush grew, and soon were seated beside their companions.

The Ethiopian pair, although led to the edge of the town by Yusuf and closer to the hidden tomb, had to stop and hide frequently when their dirt road took them too close to the main road and passing traffic. The fields around them were laid out to a mixture of grain, young sunflowers and fallow grazing, where two tall black men crossing would attract attention. Instead, they slunk along the wooded field margins until they could break into a run between the vines. So successful was their creeping that they startled, and almost stood on, a male pheasant sheltering in the shade. It rose with noisy wings whirring and its call raucous like a strangled cockerel.

The men froze and their attention turned immediately to the road only sixty metres away. But there was no traffic except for a red faced, Lycra-clad cyclist struggling with the steep incline. They stood motionless for a full five minutes before warily setting off again. When the juniper was in sight, they remained hidden for another twenty minutes to make sure they hadn't been followed, before joining the others underground.

*

Yusuf followed a long zigzag route to his shelter on the hills overlooking Cassiatorre. The structure was crudely set into the slope, its walls and the floor were bare earth. Yusuf had made a roof that sloped back into the hill from corrugated metal supported by old pallet timber. He had placed large stones from the hillside's plentiful supply to keep the roof sheets in place and covered the metal surface with soil and brush to keep off the sun's rays.

Lifting the flat stone he had placed two metres from the shelter, he retrieved the hunting knife that he had hidden under it. Then he slid the pallet, covered on the inside with a threadbare bedsheet that was the shelter's door, and ducked inside, crouching under its low ceiling. A rolled-up sleeping mat and a rucksack containing a few clothes were tucked into one corner. An upturned wooden fruit tray that once contained peaches held three tealights, a lighter, a bottle of water, a wafer of soap, a toothbrush and paste. He put everything into the rucksack and moved the fruit tray, then, kneeling, attacked the hard packed soil beneath it with the hunting knife until he reached the thin stone that protected the Illy coffee tin buried there.

Carefully scraping away the earth, he freed the tin, brushed and blew the dirt off it, unscrewed the lid, and pulled out the plastic bags. From one he took out and counted the banknotes before returning them to the plastic bag and tucking it in his pocket. The other he opened gingerly and shook it over the fruit tray. The bright yellow gold tumbled out. A pair of earrings, intricately worked in the shape of vine leaves, and two necklaces – one with gold vine leaves beaten from the thinnest gold, shaped and arranged in order of size; the other made of short cylindrical segments, each exquisitely tooled like scales that gave the piece the impression of a snake's body.

Even in the dim light of Yusuf's shelter, the pieces radiated beauty, power, and the artistry of the craftsman who had made them twenty-four centuries ago. Yusuf collected them carefully back into the plastic bag, returned it to the coffee tin, and hid it under some clothes in his rucksack.

He spent a minute or two filling in and tamping the hole in the floor then left his shelter, shouldered the rucksack, slid the knife under his belt, and made his way cautiously past Signor Giusti's flock of grazing sheep and down the hillside.

He recalled how he'd met the Somali and Ethiopian immigrants. Signor Erpicone was a demanding and unfair taskmaster who, when they were discovered on his property, paid them nothing, provided them with a broken-down shed to stay in, and supplied them with little in terms of food and drink. Terrified of being reported to the authorities and transported back to their native countries, they had accepted their hardship without complaint. When darkness came, they'd go out foraging for food in the surrounding countryside, and that is when they had met Yusuf. He returned with them to their shack and shared a meal with them. They explained that Erpicone had them dig narrow, dangerously narrow, test holes deep into his land.

Only one man could dig at a time, the earth and stone being

hauled up in a bucket attached to a rope. The first time the unshuttered walls of the holes collapsed, the digger was trapped and almost died before being rescued by his frantic companions. From then, the digger always wore a rope tied around his waist. The men thought they were searching for water, but Erpicone was, in fact, searching for Etruscan remains. He had them backfill every empty hole before beginning again in a different spot.

When they excavated some pottery fragments from a test hole at the boundary between his place and the Rosati property, Erpicone instructed them to work only on his neighbour's land. Their workday was shortened to fit with that of the Rosatis, but was equally laborious because they had to carry the excavated earth off the property so that their trespass would go unnoticed. On their second attempt, they discovered the tomb when the soft rock they were digging through gave way and the digger dropped into the burial chamber. He was rescued when the others pulled him out. Curious, another descended and felt around in the darkness. He brought up a small figure carved in *pietra fetida* – a soft limestone full of sulphur particles that has a characteristic bad smell when its surface is scratched. When they gave it to Erpicone, even with his poor eyesight he immediately knew what the figure was.

Erpicone sent their leader down with a torch to investigate and report back, and from his account they were able to make a rough sketch of the layout that included the tomb's entrance tunnel. They blocked off the bottom of their shaft and backfilled it, restoring the surface to match the surrounding bare earth. A new tunnel was begun, starting under the juniper bush, and angled towards the tomb.

Yusuf remembered how excited the others were when they told him about discovering the entrance to the tomb, and the feeling of wonder and astonishment they shared with him at finding such treasure intact. They agreed that the stone and base metal artefacts would be given, a few at a time, to Erpicone, and that they'd keep the gold for themselves.

Yusuf visited them often, bringing food, fresh milk, and news. With some of the money that he made selling the occasional lamb, he bought clothes and cooking utensils for them from a Chinese man who'd recently opened a stall that seemed to sell everything at the weekly market. In time, the others trusted Yusuf to keep the gold jewellery safe. He was now returning with it to put into operation the plan that they'd been talking about for months.

He slid on his belly down the slope and into the tomb chamber. Six grim expressions met his smile as he discovered that their leader and another had been taken by the police.

CHAPTER FORTY-TWO

Having disposed of the prawn, Moretti drove Santoro to the other side of Cassiatorre to Hotel Miravalle – a small family hotel where Domenico's cousin was staying. The receptionist called up to the room and Davide came down. They held up their badges.

'This is Agente Santoro and I'm Commissario Moretti, can we have a word with you, please?'

Domenico's cousin had changed from the suit he had worn to church into camouflage cargo trousers and a green t-shirt. He looked like his cousin – short, thick set, dark skinned, with workers' hands. He nodded and walked past them.

'Come with me, we can talk out here.'

They followed him out to a small, tidy, walled courtyard garden fringed with fruit trees. Three sets of dark green plastic garden tables and chairs were laid out in three of the corners. A child's swing and plastic slide occupied the remaining corner.

The man sat and glowered at Moretti. 'Like the beer,' he said flatly.

Moretti sighed.

'Like the beer, Signore…'

'Parodi. Davide Parodi.'

'I understand that you were upset at the burial today.'

Parodi dropped his head and rolled it from side to side slowly.

'You understand that I was upset?' He slammed his hand violently on the table and glared at Moretti. 'Furious would be closer,' he shouted. 'And I want something done about it.'

The thump brought the receptionist to the door. Moretti signalled him over.

'Make a note of Signor Parodi's complaint, Agente,' Moretti said to Santoro. Santoro pulled out his notepad.

Moretti turned to look up at the nervous receptionist.

'Bring us three small beers and some nibbles, please.'

The young man nodded and hurried inside.

'Now, what is it you want to tell us?'

'They're trying to cheat Domenico – all of them. They're all in it.'

Moretti held up his hand like a traffic policeman.

'Signor Parodi, it's clear inside your head, but we can't see inside it. So, start from the beginning, speak slowly so that my colleague can write it down, and tell us everything. You are Signor Rosati's cousin. Where did he come from, and how did he end up in Cassiatorre?'

Parodi inhaled deeply and dropped his shoulders.

'He trained as a builder and worked for a time at the naval base in La Spezia, then he worked for a small firm doing work on houses and agricultural buildings before he started working for himself.'

The receptionist appeared with the drinks and snacks on a tray, which he left on the table and returned indoors.

Moretti sipped his beer. 'Was he successful?'

Parodi nodded and heaped two spoonfuls of peanuts into his cupped hand.

'He was doing really well for a while and managed to earn a ton of money.' He stopped to throw some peanuts into his mouth.

'A young, single guy with a good job and lots of money. He must have been popular with the ladies,' Moretti suggested.

Parodi crunched the peanuts.

'Too popular,' he said, revealing teeth covered in chopped nuts. He swigged his beer. 'He still used to go to the same clubs and bars that he visited when he worked at the naval base. The difference was that he now had much more money and could splash it around. The girls loved him but the sailors, and the guys he used to work alongside at the base, hated him.'

'Did he get into fights?'

Parodi raised his eyebrows and pushed out his bottom lip.

'Nothing serious, but let's say he was advised to leave the area for his own good.'

'So, he had to give up a successful business.'

'Not right away.' Parodi picked up a small sandwich. 'He decided to move, sure enough, but he got his head down and did a whole bunch of jobs, kept away from La Spezia, and saved hard. When he reckoned he had enough, he finished up and moved.' He bit into the triangle of bread.

'To Cassiatorre?'

'No,' he replied, still chewing. 'To the port of Bari. He had all the building skills to walk into a good job there, and he'd learned enough to keep himself out of trouble.'

'Is that where he met Chiara?'

'Indirectly. He worked Monday to Friday at the port but did some private work at weekends. He was doing a job for the father of Chiara's boyfriend. That's how they met.'

'But that doesn't explain how he ended up here.'

Parodi speared an olive on a cocktail stick. 'The boyfriend's father was connected to some low-level gangsters.' He wagged the cocktail stick for emphasis. 'Chiara was afraid that there'd be reprisals.'

'So they came here?'

'So they came here.' He popped the olive in his mouth.

'But why here?'

'They reckoned that it was far away enough from Bari for safety and close enough to visit family in Liguria.'

Moretti took another sip and wiped the froth from his moustache. 'Does Chiara have family?

Parodi shrugged. 'Maybe. Probably. I don't know.'

'Were they happy here?'

'Happy enough. They had jobs. They had a nice place.'

'Did you know that they left Mario alone, locked in the house?'

Parodi looked shocked. 'No.'

'Can you think why?'

He took a long gulp of beer. 'I know Domenico sunk every cent he had into the place. He hoped to be able to start his own business again and thought that the land would be good for storing materials and equipment. He bought it at the top of the market and probably overpaid. He told me he found the mortgage payments tough, and such a big place has lots of local taxes.' He stabbed another olive. 'I guess the simple reason is they couldn't afford a babysitter.'

'Who exactly was trying to cheat him?'

Parodi offered the plate of sandwiches to Santoro, who refused with a curt shake of his head, before helping himself to another.

'He was approached by a neighbour who wanted to buy his property, but like I already said, Domenico had bought at the top of the market.' He bit the sandwich, his replies punctuated by chews. 'The price the neighbour was offering was much less. Domenico would have been out of pocket after he paid off the mortgage, so he refused. Then the neighbour came back with another offer, this time for the land only. Domenico asked why he wanted it, and the neighbour skirted around the answer. He said that he wanted to grow vines, but Domenico didn't trust him, so he refused again.'

'Do you know which neighbour?'

'I heard the name but I'm not sure.'

'Could it be Giusti... Erpicone... Mancini... Di Vittorio... Ricci?'

'It was Ricci.'

Moretti and Santoro shared a glance. 'Are you sure?'

'Certain. It was Ricci.'

'And would you be happy to sign a statement once Agente Santoro gets it typed up?'

'Yes. Absolutely.'

Santoro put down his notebook, took a long deep gulp of beer, and picked up a sandwich.

Moretti leaned back as far as the plastic chair would safely permit.

'How often did you see your cousin, Signor Parodi?'

Parodi wiped his mouth and hands with a paper napkin, screwed it up, and studied it.

'I'm ashamed to admit that I didn't keep in touch as I should have.' He twisted the napkin. 'Domenico and I were very close as children and right up to the time when he left for Bari. Since they moved here, I visited a couple of times although we spoke on the phone and he told me about Ricci.' The napkin tore, and Parodi dropped the pieces on the table in front of him. 'That's why I want to make sure that Chiara and Mario are found, and that they get a

188

fair price for the property if they want to sell up.'

Moretti reached over and patted the back of Parodi's hand.

'That's what we all want. You've been a great help, Signor Parodi. We'll find Mario and his mother.'

Moretti's gut twisted as he masked his doubts and fears. 'And I'm sorry for your loss.' Moretti left his card on the table.

The two detectives left and paid for the drinks at reception. As they drove back to the Questura in silence, Moretti pondered Parodi's revelation and Santoro pondered the prawn.

CHAPTER FORTY-THREE

Moretti dropped Gennaro off then parked in a side street. Gennaro and Cristina were already seated in his office when he got there.

Moretti stood behind his desk. 'Well, Cristina, what did Signora De Luca have to say?'

Cristina stretched her lips wide, making the tendons on her neck stand out.

'I didn't speak to her.'

Moretti frowned. 'How do you mean?'

'I went first to your home, like you said, but she wasn't there. So I came back to the town and asked around. The sindaco was the last person she was seen talking to. I called him and asked if he knew where she had gone.'

Moretti cringed.

'He said that she left right after the funeral service,' Cristina continued. 'She was travelling back south.'

Moretti dropped into his chair, pulled out his phone, and called his wife's mobile. It went straight to voicemail.

'Maria, when you get this, call me right away. Thanks.'

Moretti returned the phone to his pocket. The desk phone rang, and he grabbed it. The others leaned forward.

'Yes?' Moretti sagged. 'Fine, yes it's all right, bring them in.'

He dropped the handset on to its base.

'Alfiero,' he said dismally. 'There have been some reports of a boy answering Mario's description since the funeral was broadcast.'

Alfiero knocked the door and came in with a folder.

'Give it to Gennaro, please.'

Alfiero did so and left. Santoro flicked through the pages in the folder. Cristina watched Moretti rubbing the heels of his hands in his eyes.

'How did it go with Domenico's cousin?' she asked.

Moretti straightened up.

'Well, he thinks Ricci was trying to buy their podere at a knockdown price, and Domenico was having none of it.'

'That must have been what the bank loan was for,' said Cristina, leaning in. 'What did the bank manager say?'

'He didn't,' Moretti replied. 'All he would tell me was that it was for a major expansion. Then Ricci withdrew the loan request at the same time as a quarter of a million just happened to arrive in his bank account.'

'So, he didn't drop the idea after Domenico refused?'

'No, he got the money from a different source. I think the Mafia guys got to him, and they want to use the agriturismo or the major expansion as a conduit for money laundering.'

'That makes sense,' said Cristina. 'But I've been thinking about another possibility.'

'Oh? Tell us.'

Santoro looked up from the folder.

Cristina's hands were at her knees, fingers interlaced.

'I have to say that I haven't fully thought it through, and it might sound a little far-fetched.'

'As far-fetched as a prawn?' offered Santoro.

Cristina looked puzzled.

Moretti glowered at Santoro. 'Ignore him, Cristina. Go on.'

'Well, the Americans, the Coopers, are desperate for a child. They're also rich. What if they paid Ricci to find them a child? What if they paid Ricci to have Mario kidnapped? What if it's their money that's in his bank account?'

Moretti gaped.

'That's not only far-fetched,' said Santoro, 'it's crazy. What about the ransom demand?'

Cristina's face brightened and she spoke more quickly.

'That's the clever part,' she said with the widest smile. 'The ransom note does two things. First, it deflects our attention to

191

some mysterious third party. We lose control of the timeline because we're waiting for the phone call. If the pickup doesn't go ahead, we never see Mario again, and we blame ourselves forever for losing the chance. If the money is picked up, either it goes back to Ricci or maybe even the Coopers, and we still never see Mario again. Either way, we look like chumps.'

Moretti leaned back and grabbed the hair on the nape of his neck with both hands.

'That's ingenious,' he said. 'Far-fetched, but ingenious. Gennaro, tell me why it can't work.'

Santoro closed the folder.

'First,' he turned to Cristina and clapped his hands gently together, 'I have to applaud the ispettore for some very clever deduction.' She blushed a little. 'Second, I have to halt the celebrations and remind everyone that the Rosati house was locked from the outside. Neither Ricci, the Coopers, nor anyone else could get in there to take Mario.'

Cristina's shoulders sagged and her head dropped onto her chest.

Santoro reached over and placed his hand on her shoulder. 'Sorry.'

'Good work, Cristina,' Moretti said. 'And good work, Gennaro, for keeping us right. So, we can't connect Ricci to Mario's disappearance, but we can look for connections to Domenico Rosati and the Mafia. I'd like to be able to pull Ricci's phone records, but as Cristina already knows, I've been officially banned from any contact with Ricci. However, Davide Parodi's statement gives us – not me personally – another route to establishing the proof we need about his involvement with the Mafia.'

Cristina perked up. 'We're already checking Domenico's phone record.'

'Good. If we establish a link between Rosati and Ricci, it at least will give us a timeframe to work with. Can you take that forward, Cristina?'

'Yes, Commissario.' She began punching into her phone with her thumbs.

Santoro slid the folder onto Moretti's desk.

'You might want to chase some of these up,' he said. 'Reports of sightings of Mario from Tuscany and Umbria coming from the

TV transmission, but social media has prompted other reports from Rome, Bologna, and Taranto.'

Moretti slid the folder back without looking at it.

'You do it, Gennaro. I trust your judgement to winnow out the chaff.'

Santoro reached for the folder and placed it under his seat. 'Are you okay, capo?'

'What?'

Santoro hesitated.

'Are you okay?' he repeated. 'You seem a bit subdued.'

Cristina looked up from her phone briefly then concentrated on it again, head down.

Moretti rubbed the back of his neck.

'I keep thinking about Maria,' he said quietly. 'I can't believe that she had anything to do with the immigrants escaping.' His hand slid to his cheek and then to his chin, rubbing the stubble. 'It's not just the headlines that would be on every newsstand; it's the fact that I didn't see it coming.' His voice faded. 'It's the loss of trust, the betrayal.'

Silence hung in the room like a shroud.

Cristina jumped when the phone on her lap buzzed at the same time as the desk phone rang.

Moretti grabbed the handset. 'Yes?' He shook his head as he listened. 'I see. Bring me the details.'

He put the phone back. 'A body's been discovered. Suspected drugs overdose. That's all we need.'

Cristina held up her phone.

'Good news here, Commissario,' she smiled awkwardly. 'The tech guys have recovered phone records and texts from Signor Rosati's phone. They've pinged the file to you.'

Moretti and Santoro shifted in their seats to a more upright posture.

Moretti clicked on the mouse and brought his computer back to life. A double click brought the file to his screen. He scanned the document.

'Thanks, Cristina, the tech guys have done a good job,' he said animatedly. 'They've annotated the calls list with numbers they've identified. There are calls to and from his wife's phone, his work, and from Ricci. So that proves they were in contact, and from the looks of it the times correspond with Ricci's request for a bank loan.'

'That's something to go on at least,' Santoro said encouragingly.

'There's also a couple of calls from an unknown number at the same time.'

'That could be anything,' Cristina explained. 'A cold call from a business, an individual who is withholding their number. It probably isn't anything sinister.'

'But it could be. Can the tech guys can trace it?'

Cristina frowned.

'Not really. Criminals use prepaid SIM cards and throw them away after a single use.'

Moretti's attention was on the screen. He scrolled down.

'Ah, they've also listed messages recovered from the phone.' He turned the screen towards them. 'Look, here are communications between Rosati and his cousin. They confirm what Parodi told us.'

The three detectives craned forward to read the screen.

'He mentions Ricci by name,' said Santoro.

'But he was clearly spooked by something,' Cristina added. 'Look how his language changes here – less chat, no salutations, just facts – and he refers to "the thing" and "the offer". Scroll up, Commissario, and check the phone call dates.'

Moretti found the calls list.

'You're right, Cristina,' said Moretti, pointing to the screen. 'Here. That's the first anonymous call. That's when his message language changed.'

Moretti turned the screen back and stood.

'Gennaro, get Parodi's statement typed up. Cristina, sit here and print out the phone records, then cross-reference them with Parodi's statement, and let's see if we can build enough of a case to take to Innocenti.' He changed places with Cristina. 'While you're doing that, I'll check out the drugs overdose. I'll meet you both back here later.'

CHAPTER FORTY-FOUR

A ten-minute drive on the winding roads into the hills above Cassiatorre brought Moretti to a run-down farmhouse. Forensics officers had already begun their investigations. He recognised many of the team who had worked on the Rosati case. He approached one of the white-suited officers.

'What do we have?'

The officer pulled down his mask.

'Seems straightforward. The deceased was found lying on the sofa. On the table in front of him there were two lines of cocaine and traces of another two. No marks on the body, no signs of anyone else being there. Looks like he was alone and overdosed.'

'Did you find any more cocaine? I'm interested in whether they could be from the same cache that the boar dug up.'

'Yes, two small bags. Our analysis should show if they are of the same purity or are cut with the same agents.'

'Thanks.'

Instead of going straight back to the Questura, Moretti drove to the hill where Gennaro and Cristina had picked up Yusuf, parked, and made his way to the Somali's shelter. It was bare except for an empty fruit tray. Moretti slid it over with his foot. The earth beneath it had been disturbed and packed back down, but it was not as compact as the rest of the dirt floor. A small piece of stone, half buried in the dirt, caught his eye. He knelt on one knee and picked it out with a finger, rubbed it clean, and took it out to the light to examine its odd shape more closely. As he headed back down to his car, he wondered what Yusuf had hidden there.

*

Now back at her own computer, Cristina worked in silence on the spreadsheet, carefully organising the different phone numbers by name and assigning each a different colour for quicker cross-referencing. Gennaro knocked the jamb of her office door and entered carrying a thin sheaf of papers.

She looked up from the screen and rolled her chair back. 'Finished?'

The agente dropped the papers on her desk.

'Finished,' he said with a sigh. 'And so should you be. That can wait until the morning.'

Cristina smiled, picked up the papers, and leafed through them. Gennaro's notes seemed like a verbatim record.

'Great work, Gennaro.'

'I've sent you an electronic copy, too.'

Cristina pulled her seat back to the desk. She found it in a couple of mouse clicks.

'Wonderful, that'll save me hours.'

Gennaro folded his arms and frowned a little.

'Cristina, I mean it,' he said softly. 'You'll ruin your eyes. The commissario has gone for the night. Finish up now.'

Cristina nodded.

'Look, I will,' she said, attention already focused on the screen, fingers clicking the mouse. 'I'm going to cut and paste extracts against the phone records on my spreadsheet. Then I'll stop.'

When Gennaro didn't budge, she shot him a glance and grinned.

'Honest.'

He unfolded his arms, shrugged, and left, muttering to himself in his southern dialect.

Cristina shook her head and pressed on, energised by the text of Parodi's statement. In the next half hour, she could see the beginnings of a case growing against Ricci.

CHAPTER FORTY-FIVE

Moretti leant against the wall, puffed on the little cigar, and looked at his garden. The grass needed cut, the terracotta pots of herbs needed watered, the roses needed pruning, and an empty plastic bag had blown in from somewhere. Maria would have organised them both to get the work done, but he didn't have the energy. He hadn't slept well the night before; in fact, he'd hardly slept at all.

It began when he arrived home and emptied the mailbox. As usual, he took it all through to the kitchen counter to sort out, his and hers, expecting to add to the growing bundle of Maria's mail. But it was gone. She'd been home. His instinct made him go to the bedroom. A suitcase was missing from on top of the wardrobe, and he knew. He knew but checked anyway. Her wardrobe rail was missing several garments, about as many as would have fitted in the suitcase.

He tried to remember. Yes, he was sure. She'd taken summery clothes, casual clothes, dining-out-with-friends clothes, to add to the business clothes she'd already taken only two days before. He lifted the lid of the antique school desk that she used as a dressing table. The spaces inside told him that she had taken some jewellery, too.

Back in the kitchen, Moretti opened the fridge, looking inside for inspiration until its alarm beeped. He closed it and looked in the freezer, rummaging around until his fingers started to numb. Excavating a frosty box of frozen fish, he thought for a moment about how he would cook it, then put it back. He had no appetite, neither for food nor solitude.

He tried phoning Maria again, but the call still went straight to voicemail. The perpetual demon of his guilt was now joined by another two-headed demon of her betrayal of both his working life – if it was indeed Maria who had set free the captives – and his married life, if her wardrobe meant that she was planning to dress for other than work. The demons were joined by a lesser imp representing the anonymous vandal who left fish under the wiper. As his torment continued, he fidgeted with the stone that he had picked up at Yusuf's shelter.

He went early to bed, but his only company were the thoughts and questions his demons placed inside his head. The room felt warm and stuffy; he was listless, hungry, and something didn't smell good. Sometime after midnight, he rose again and showered, hoping to cleanse mind and body. Under the battering spray, he reached blindly for a bottle and began to lather his hair. The fragrance of Maria's shampoo filled the shower cabinet, and he leaned forward, placing both hands on the tiles, letting the warm water wash away the traces.

Dressed in a hooded towelling robe, Moretti made a coffee and sipped it at the open window to feel the cooling breeze. A large moth, eyes cinnabar red, shed its scales flapping against the insect screen, compelled by the ceiling light behind him. Outside, in an irrigation pond, frogs rasped a chorus. Further down the valley, a dog scented a passing fox, and its warning bark set off its neighbours in a baying and yapping cacophony that quickly crescendoed and slowly died.

Moretti pondered going to the Questura to escape reminders of Maria but sat at the table instead and finished his coffee. A cock crowed and the breeze changed, sliding the shutters on their latches. He went to bed again, only to have his mind filled with thoughts of Mario and Chiara. *How could a boy vanish from a locked house? How could he and his mother simply disappear?* Memories of his own daughter's disappearance floated like wraiths in his consciousness. He prayed Mario would not suffer the same fate and eventually fell asleep.

CHAPTER FORTY-SIX

Carla's broad smile welcomed Moretti as he entered Bar Italia carrying a large holdall that he'd stuffed with empty boxes. His *Good morning* was met by three tuts from the gossips, a glance over the top of their newspapers from two men, and a lopsided grin from Carla's son Gigi.

By the time he reached the counter and dropped the bag at his feet, his cappuccino was poured and ready, and Carla was holding out his cornetto. He bit into it hungrily and, mouth full and chewing, circled his index finger to order another.

Carla picked up another cornetto in a serviette, placed it on a saucer, and slid it onto the counter in front of him.

'Thanks again for your help yesterday, Dino,' she said warmly.

The three busybodies picked up on her tone. They stopped chatting and leaned perceptibly closer to eavesdrop.

Moretti swallowed and gulped some coffee.

'I couldn't believe how busy the town was yesterday. It must have been good for business.'

Carla shrugged and began emptying the circular dishwasher.

'I prefer it like this,' she said over the clatter. 'It was out of control yesterday.'

Moretti finished the first pastry and nibbled the second less frantically.

'Yes,' he said, turning to the three ladies who all immediately straightened up. 'It was quite an eventful day.'

Fausta produced and flicked open her fan, waving it vigorously. Rosalia looked outside at nothing in particular, and Donatella merely smiled.

'Let's hope that today is less exciting, eh, ladies?' Moretti said, before turning back to his coffee, draining it, putting some money on the counter, and picking up his bag.

'I'll finish this on the way to the Questura,' he said, walking off with his pastry. He nodded and raised it as he passed their table. 'Ladies.'

As Moretti walked across Piazza Garibaldi to the Questura, he felt a vibration in his shirt pocket. He stuffed the rest of the pastry into his mouth and pulled out the burner phone to read the message.

Expect instructions at noon.

He cast hopefully across Piazza Garibaldi but there was nothing out of the ordinary. He hurried into the Questura. Alfiero avoided his glance.

Moretti stopped at the man's desk. 'Alfiero, anyone can make a mistake. Let's forget it and move on.'

Alfiero smiled and nodded energetically. '*Sissignore*, Commissario.'

'Good. Now, which uniforms are on duty today?'

Alfiero reeled off a list of names.

'Great, tell Riccardo to meet me in my office right away.'

Alfiero was picking up the phone even as Moretti walked off.

Moretti tucked the holdall under his desk, picked up the office phone, and called the bank.

'Put me though to Dante, please. It's Moretti.'

While he waited, he smoothed his moustache. A few flakes of pastry fell onto his desk, and he collected them absentmindedly with a pinkie and dropped them on the floor.

'Hello?'

'Dante? Dino. Is everything ready?'

'Good morning, Dino. Yes, all in order here. I'll need the written authorisation and a signature.'

'Fine. I'll come over personally.'

'Do you have a time?'

'I'll be with you before noon.'

'See you then. Ask to come straight through to my office.'

'Good. See you then.'

He hung up as a policeman appeared at the door and saluted. Moretti waved him in.

'Riccardo, were you on duty at the funeral yesterday?'

'Yes, Commissario.'

'Did you see the disturbance when the Somalis arrived?'

Riccardo grinned. 'I was in the middle of it.'

Moretti clapped his hands together.

'Perfect. Take four or five men, tape off the area where it happened, and do a fingertip search.'

'What are we looking for, Commissario?'

'Anything that doesn't belong there.'

Riccardo frowned. 'Can you be a bit more specific, Commissario?'

Moretti shrugged, palms up. 'Bring me everything that doesn't belong there – and hurry.'

Riccardo saluted, turned on his heel and left, almost colliding with Gennaro and Cristina in the corridor.

'Come in, you two,' Moretti said brightly. 'We have to plan our strategy for the handover of the ransom money.'

The two detectives sat, each carrying a folder.

'So, you had a call about the drop off?' said Gennaro.

Moretti nodded.

'It was a text message. They're going to call back with further instructions at noon.' He bent forward and pulled the holdall from under his desk. 'I brought this to put the money in.'

'How many are you taking to the bank with you, Commissario?' asked Cristina.

Moretti dropped the bag at his feet and slid it under the desk again.

'I'm going alone,' he replied. 'Less conspicuous that way.'

Gennaro and Cristina both shifted in their seats.

'At least let us watch your route,' said Gennaro anxiously. 'If I sat in my car in the bank's car park, I could see all the way down to Piazza Garibaldi. And if Cristina was outside Bar Italia, she could see almost as far as the car park and clear across the square back to the Questura.'

Moretti looked at his colleagues in gratitude.

'Fine,' he acquiesced. 'We'll do it your way. Now, let's see what's in those folders you're both holding. Gennaro first.'

Santoro opened the manila folder and took out the top sheet.

'Nothing about Chiara, but this is a list of reported sightings of a boy fitting Mario's description,' he said, placing the sheet on the desk and turning it so that Moretti could read it. 'I'm still waiting for the local cops in each area to confirm and send photographs if possible. Call me cynical, but my guess would be that none of them are genuine. This is the sort of situation that opportunist thieves hoping for a reward look for. I gave it a Priority 1, so replies should start to arrive this morning.'

Moretti studied the list.

'All but one sighting is in the south.'

Gennaro shrugged.

'Capo, they know a thing or two about kidnapping and ransoms down there. Take your pick – Mafia, 'Ndrangheta, Camorra, Sacra Corona Unità – and they're the big guys. Then factor in smaller gangs or rogue individuals, or even some of the Albanian gangs trying to get a foothold in the peninsula. You know, some of them would even kidnap a boy resembling Mario to pass him off as the real thing if they thought they could get a reward.'

Moretti shook his head and slid the sheet back.

'Keep me posted, Gennaro. Cristina, how did you get on?'

Cristina opened her folder and fished out stapled copies for each of them.

'As you can see, I've drawn up a spreadsheet of the phone calls and messages sorted by number, date, and time. I've assigned each number a colour to make it easier to follow the sequence, and I cut and pasted extracts from Gennaro's notes to fit.'

She paused to let the men scan the spreadsheet.

Moretti's finger and thumb splayed his moustache.

'So, there's a definite link to Ricci,' he said. 'But not nearly enough to talk to him. What I'd like to get my hands on is his phone record. Any ideas about the unknown number?'

Cristina cleared her throat and placed her copy on her lap.

'Well, we probably will never know for certain who the caller, or callers were, but we can infer quite a lot from the sequence.'

'Go on.'

'Well, if you look at the responses to calls and messages, a pattern begins to emerge.'

Gennaro scratched his head. 'Nothing is emerging on my copy.

Care to explain?'

She smiled.

'Look at what happens after a call from or to his wife – the ones blocked in yellow.'

Gennaro studied the chart. 'I don't see anything happening.'

'That's exactly right,' said Cristina excitedly. 'Now look at the calls from his work – the blue ones.'

'Again, nothing.'

'Now look at what happens when he gets or makes a call to Ricci – orange.'

'Ah,' said Santoro, smiling. 'I see it. He calls or messages his wife. But wait, not always.'

Cristina leaned forward in her seat.

'Exactly,' she exclaimed. 'And that's where the pattern appears.'

'I see it,' Moretti blurted out. 'He always calls his wife if the unknown caller – that you've marked in red – contacts him right before or after Ricci does.'

'And the contacts get more frantic in the days leading up to his death,' said Santoro. 'And that's when he contacts his cousin, Parodi – the green ones.'

Cristina beamed and sat back in her seat.

'This is what I think went on,' she began. 'Ricci wanted to buy Domenico's land, but he refused. He doesn't bother to call his wife about that. Ricci calls again several days later, maybe upping his price. Domenico refuses again. This time he does call his wife, but he waits until his lunch break. Then, after another few days, we see the first red call. He calls his wife immediately after that one and, look, he calls Ricci right after speaking to her.'

'This is a wonderful piece of deduction, Cristina,' said Moretti. 'Absolutely first class. If you're right, then we can see the pressure increasing.' He folded his arms. 'Gennaro, tell me how it can't work.'

Gennaro slowly shook his head.

'I can't,' he said in admiration. 'It reads right. I can't fault it. It's a plausible explanation.'

'The only problem,' said Cristina, 'is that it's not enough to be able to pin anything on Ricci.'

'That's it,' said Moretti. 'We need Ricci's phone record.'

'Commissario, the Vice Questore will never sanction that

request.'

The desk phone rang.

'Yes?' Moretti looked at his watch and stood. 'We'll be right through.'

He hung up and put Cristina's spreadsheet in a drawer.

'Gennaro, see if you can speed up the identification of those sightings and get Parodi to come in and sign his statement. Cristina, come with me.'

CHAPTER FORTY-SEVEN

The pair hurried to the front desk where Riccardo waited with a large cardboard box.

'Bring it through here, Riccardo,' Moretti said, leading to a back office. 'Cristina, help me clear this desk.'

They moved the papers and folders off the surface.

'Empty it there, Riccardo.'

As Riccardo tipped out the contents of the box, Moretti bent over the desk and used a pen to sort out the collection of objects. He looked up at the young policeman.

'Is this all of it?'

'Yes, Commissario.'

Spread out in front of them was an odd assortment – a hair bobble, a pebble, a ring pull, several cigarette butts, a few pieces of broken glass, two small pieces of terracotta, a metal screw, an empty ball pen refill, and the leg from a pair of sunglasses.

'Aha. That's what I'm looking for.'

Moretti separated the pebble and the pieces of terracotta from the rest and popped them into an evidence bag.

'Great work, Riccardo. You can bin the rest of this stuff.'

The officer looked baffled. Moretti patted his shoulder. 'Really, you've given me exactly what I wanted.'

'And what was that, Commissario?' he asked, as he slid the rejected debris back into the box.

Moretti held up the plastic bag.

'An invitation to Erpicone's place. Come on, Cristina.'

Cristina gave Riccardo a puzzled look as she followed Moretti out into Piazza Garibaldi. They both immediately stopped and gaped.

Posters of Ricci were attached to railings, lamp posts, and street signs, and a trestle table was set up at one side with Ricci's campaign workers handing out leaflets. Down on the main street, a van with loudspeakers on its roof was cruising slowly along as one of the occupants announced that Ricci was contesting the election for sindaco.

'Shit!' Moretti swore. 'This is all we need. Where's your car?'

'At the back of Bar Italia.'

'We'll go in that,' said Moretti, whose own car was hidden several streets away.

Several minutes later they were driving along the dirt track to Erpicone's farm. The farm dogs came out to meet the car with their usual barking and yapping that changed to tail wagging as Moretti got out.

'You've the same knack with dogs as Gennaro,' said Cristina enviously.

Moretti used both hands to stroke the heads pushing into him. A guilty memory prevented him from replying.

A squat, dungareed figure threw open the farmhouse door.

'Clear off!' Erpicone shouted. 'Or I'll have the law on you.'

'We are the law,' shouted Moretti in reply. 'It's Commissario Moretti and Ispettore Furlan.'

Erpicone's face twisted into a sneer.

'Moretti, good,' he snarled. 'You've saved me the bother of having to come to the Questura to complain about that butter-fingered bitch.'

'Now, now,' Moretti cut him off sternly. 'That language will get you into even more trouble than you already are.'

Erpicone spat on the dust at his feet as they approached.

'Trouble? Me? What bloody trouble?' he fumed. 'I never leave this damn house. It's your foul-mouthed pet giraffe that should be in trouble.'

'Signor Erpicone, we need to talk with you about the immigrants you had working on your farm,' explained Moretti. 'Now, we can all go inside and talk there, or we can take you right now to the Questura, but I don't know how long it'll take, and your dogs might go hungry.'

Erpicone screwed up his face and broke wind loudly.

'You better come in then,' he said, turning back inside.

The two detectives looked at each other. Cristina shook her head and followed Moretti into the gloomy but near spotless interior. Erpicone was already seated.

'May we take a seat? Moretti asked.

'Go ahead,' snapped Erpicone. 'You didn't bloody ask when you took my workers, did you?'

Moretti ignored him. He and Cristina sat on a sagging sofa.

'What work do they actually do?'

'This is a farm. Everything here is work: sowing, planting, weeding, pruning, harvesting.'

'I'm no farmer,' said Moretti. 'But I imagine the seed stock, fertilisers, and supplies are very expensive.'

Erpicone growled his agreement.

'And I guess that paying wages to eight workers is a major expense,' Moretti continued. 'What do you think, Ispettore?'

Cristina followed his lead.

'It sounds like the kind of expense that could get somebody into debt,' she agreed. 'The kind that would probably need a bank loan.'

Erpicone looked blindly from one to the other.

'I clear my debts and pay my way, you parasites,' he snapped, pointing in their direction. 'I even pay your wages. Go and check at the bank if you don't believe me.'

'We did, Signor Erpicone,' replied Moretti. 'And we found that you had a loan for thirty thousand Euros.'

'I'll pay it back,' insisted the farmer angrily. 'The harvest will more than cover it. It always does.'

'We noticed that there were some big money transfers into your account recently, Signor Erpicone,' Cristina said. 'Where did that money come from?'

'What are you, the *Guardia di Finanza* now?'

'It would help if you answered the question,' Moretti pressed.

'I don't know what you're talking about,' seethed Erpicone. 'The only movement of money has been out of my account, and that was to pay the pruning squad.'

'Do you expect us to believe that large amounts of money have arrived in your account, and you know nothing about it?'

Erpicone folded his arms. 'You can believe what you like.'

'I see,' Moretti said. 'Do you know the law about excavating ancient artefacts, Signor Erpicone?'

'Everybody around here knows,' he raged, waving his hands in the air. 'But go ahead and search, dig anywhere you like. There are no tombs on my land.'

Moretti fished out the evidence bag and removed the small stone. He handed it to Erpicone.

'What do you think this is?'

Erpicone rolled the stone through his fingers.

'It's a stone. My fields are full of them. Take as many as you want.'

'Smell it,' Moretti said sharply.

Erpicone's eyes widened, revealing the extent of his cataracts.

'Smell it?' he yelled. 'Are you crazy or just sick?' He held it out for Moretti.

Cristina looked askance at the commissario.

Moretti pushed back Erpicone's hand. 'Rub the stone between your fingers and smell it,' he insisted.

The grizzled old farmer obeyed, held the pebble to his nose and immediately screwed up his face.

'It stinks,' he spat, throwing the stone towards the sofa. 'Where have you had this, you stinking pervert?'

Moretti picked up the stone and returned it to the evidence bag.

'I think one of your workers had it,' replied Moretti. 'And I think he dug it up on your land.'

He turned to Cristina.

'It's called *pietra fetida*, or stink stone,' he explained. 'It's a kind of limestone local to this area that has been formed from thermal waters, so it contains a large amount of sulphur particles. It smells of rotten eggs when you work it or rub it. The ancient Etruscans used it extensively because it is easy to carve.' He turned back to the farmer. 'So, Signor Erpicone, how did one of your workers happen to have a piece of Etruscan stone on him?'

The old man's mouth sagged at the corners then hardened into a grimace.

'How the hell should I know what these heathens do when

they're supposed to be working?' he railed. 'For all I know, he found it. Maybe he never had it in the first place. That's it – you planted it. Where's your proof?'

Moretti nudged Cristina and tilted his head towards the door.

'All right, Signor Erpicone,' he said, as they both stood. 'We'll leave it there for the moment. We have other business to deal with. Don't bother to get up, we'll see ourselves out.'

Erpicone got to his feet.

'That's it, clear off and take your shit stone with you before I set the dogs on you.'

Moretti and Cristina left him mumbling and cursing behind them as they headed back to her car.

The farm dogs stood, tails wagging, to see them off the premises.

As they drove along the dirt track back to the main road, Cristina asked, 'What was all that about, Commissario?'

Moretti smiled and held up the evidence bag.

'The stone I gave him was found by Riccardo and his men this morning, at the spot where the Somalis ran into the funeral party.' He leaned over and fetched another stone from his pocket. 'I found this piece half buried in Yusuf's shelter. I think Signor Erpicone has been searching for buried treasure, and I think I know who has been buying his finds.'

Cristina turned to glance at the second stone.

'Do you mean Ricci? Maybe we can check his bank records.'

Moretti sighed.

'Not now, we can't,' he said gloomily. 'Not now that the election campaign has begun and Ricci's face is plastered everywhere. Let's head back to the Questura, and I'll pick up the cash from the bank.'

CHAPTER FORTY-EIGHT

On opposite sides of Piazza Garibaldi, the supporters of the two rival candidates set up trestle tables. Giorgio Ricci's supporters had seized the early initiative and covered every possible surface with his face, including pasting over Mayor Donati's posters. Although he was a wealthy wine producer and owner of an agriturismo, Ricci had two disadvantages – he was relatively unknown in the small town, and even after all the time he had been there he was still an incomer. His campaign sought to use both facts to his advantage.

As a newcomer, he had none of the loyalties and expectations of his rival and none of the baggage. Ricci knew that background checks would show him in nothing but a good light – he had paid enough for that to be the case. His campaign was centred around the need for change. He presented himself as a successful businessman whose fresh ideas would benefit the town and bring in the tourists, now so vital for its economy. Background checks would also show his healthy bank balance, thanks to the Rossis, whose experience in supporting winning political candidates had meant that his candidature was announced only ten minutes before the deadline and the first of his posters were in place ten minutes after the deadline.

Skilled organisers had quickly recruited local youths, all wearing t-shirts sporting his face and name, to hand out leaflets, badges, car stickers, and balloons with his campaign slogan, *Giorgio Ricci – The Face of Change.*

Although the incumbent running for his fourth term in office, neither Achille Donati nor his party machinery were complacent. Indeed, his tenure had, up until the appearance of Giorgio Ricci, been guaranteed by the dedication and hard work of his extended team who, through informal chats in bars, or Piazza Garibaldi, or in private homes, busied themselves with seeking out what the good people of Cassiatorre wanted and needed so that they could access regional and state funding to secure it.

The children's play park, the new roof for the primary school, the town's roads and pavements, a capping of business rates, the summer concert season that brought in tourists, the winter film evenings that afforded a chance to meet neighbours in the little theatre, the football, volleyball, and basketball teams, and the buses for the two old folks' homes, all benefited from external funding secured by Donati's established team. But most of all, Donati's organisation was without paragon in ensuring that every contract for all work done in Cassiatorre and the surrounding area went to local contractors, who in turn used local suppliers and employed local people. Under his administration, regional, state, and even EU funding had found its way into the pockets of almost every inhabitant of Cassiatorre.

At six thirty, half an hour after close of nominations, Donati's core team had arrived at his home to plan an election strategy. On their way to the meeting, they had seen Ricci's posters already plastered everywhere, so it was obvious that Ricci was a credible, well-prepared contender that they needed to take seriously.

Donati convened the meeting in the cantina under his house. Well-lit and comfortable, it was more than a wine, oil, and preserves store; it was the place where Donati entertained various groups seated at the long refectory table that dominated the space. He sat at one end of it and went round the table, quickly collecting information from his team.

'How are our finances, Fabrizio?'

'We have a very healthy surplus, as we haven't had to use any campaign funding for years. The funds are in a ring-fenced immutable account and are ready to be used.'

'Michele, Anna, who can we call on to work for us?'

'Ricci has recruited much of the youth, but despite their enthusiasm they don't really know much about the issues and the way local politics works,' Anna said. 'We can call on their parents and grandparents to canvas for us.'

'Older people are also more likely to vote, and they all owe us for past favours,' added Michele.

'Paolo, which party is behind Ricci?'

'None. He's standing as an independent, so he won't have the benefits of a known quantity.'

Achille frowned.

'Ricci's campaign is all about change,' he said. 'What's our response to that, Paolo? We can't be seen to be stagnant.'

Paolo shook his head.

'We're not going to respond to his campaign. That lets him always have the initiative. We're going to show how, under your administration, this whole area has done well, and standards of living have risen.'

Achille shook his head. 'Not good enough. The electorate have heard it all before.'

'So, what do you have in mind?' quizzed Paolo.

'We're going to take a radical approach and show that we can support those whom society has forgotten. We're going to fight for the underdog.'

'The underdog?'

'We'll show that Cassiatorre is an open, caring, and welcoming place,' he exclaimed. 'So, we're going to fight to keep the immigrants here and absorb them into Cassiatorre as useful members of society.'

There were gasps all around the table.

'But, Achille, they arrived here in rubber dinghies,' exclaimed Michele. 'They've been working illegally.'

'Exactly,' Donati continued. 'And we can strike a chord with all those who have family who emigrated to America in the past, or whose youngsters can't find work in Italy today and have left for Germany, Sweden, and England.'

Paolo, the campaign manager, saw the possibilities immediately.

Everyone tried to speak at once, so Achille banged his hand on the table for silence.

'You know I'll run your campaign any way you want, so I need to know, are you serious, Achille?' Paolo said evenly. 'You do know that they're classed as illegal, and at the moment are either in custody or on the run, but either way they're supposed to be handed over to Immigration for processing.'

'I'm deadly serious,' Achille replied. 'The whole immigration agenda is one that plays well for the party nationally, so I'm certain that if we made this the central focus of our campaign, we'd be able to pull in some national figures for the hustings.'

Achille looked around.

'What do the rest of you think?'

There was a muttered agreement from the group.

'That's decided, then,' Achille declared. 'I'll run a campaign championing human rights, referencing the Italian diaspora and their migration for food and work. How quickly can we get some publicity out?'

'Settimo and I could start to write some copy and have a release ready to go to the printers within an hour,' Antonietta said excitedly. 'We can get them posted up overnight so that they're in place for people waking up tomorrow.'

'Ah, about that,' said Settimo hesitantly. 'I've had a text message from the printers. There's been a small fire on their premises, and the sprinkler system came on and ruined all their stock. They'll be out of business for a couple of days. We'll have to look elsewhere for our printing.'

CHAPTER FORTY-NINE

Maria De Luca took the last garment out of her suitcase, shook it, put it on a hanger, slid an anti-moth card over the hook, and hung it up carefully in the huge old-fashioned wardrobe. The case that had drawn her here was complex and would succeed or fail entirely on her knowledge of the law and her ability to persuade the tribunal. She performed better in front of her peers – she could speak in the jargon of the law without having to translate it, with all the imprecision that that permitted, for a jury of lay people. There would be no place for nuance in her argument. For her to win – for her clients to win – absolute clarity and meticulous attention to detail was essential, because despite the proclamation displayed in every Italian court, the law was not equal for everyone.

She had already begun to rehearse the legal arguments on the journey down, speaking into her recording device – memos to herself to refer to previous cases and judgements that supported her case. In six hours' time, she would meet with her co-counsel and his staff, who would play devil's advocate as she presented the skeleton of her argument. The more severe and rigorous their shredding, the stronger would be the case that she presented in court. The thought of what was to come made her stomach lurch, sending burning reflux into her gullet. She paused and sipped some water. She hated this feeling – the anticipation, the dread – knowing how personal, direct, unfair, and dirty their questioning would be. It felt like her Gethsemane, but she had to endure it or be crucified in court.

She closed the suitcase, slid it under the large metal-framed bed, and stood up. She placed her fists in the small of her back and pressed, arching backwards at the same time until she could see the wall behind her. Then she straightened up, shook her arms, sat at the ancient dressing table, put in her earphones, and began to transcribe her notes onto her laptop.

She felt her phone's vibration through the wood of the dressing table and glanced at the message on its screen.

Man injured. Serious. In hiding. Please advise. Battery low.
Yusuf.

Her determination instantly split in two. Part was urging her to continue the preparation for what could prove to be a career-defining case; part was compelling her to return to Cassiatorre to help a group of men she had barely met. Her head said stay, her heart said go. She picked up her phone and punched in a number.

'It's Maria. Look, something's come up and I must get back.' As the voice on the other end began to speak, she interrupted. 'No, I'm not backing out. I need you to bring everything forward. Have your people ready in fifteen minutes.'

That was the easy bit. Now came the hard bit. She sent a reply, grabbed a few things for an overnight stay, packed up her laptop, and headed to Gethsemane.

CHAPTER FIFTY

Moretti waited until Cristina and Gennaro were in position then left for the bank to collect the ransom money. His trip was uneventful, except that on his return to Piazza Garibaldi he was accosted by a youth with lank hair and a nose piercing who grinned and tried to thrust one of Ricci's election leaflets into his hand.

'Sorry,' he said, waving it away. 'I have to remain impartial.'

Ricci's face was everywhere. In one poster, he was in profile as if looking over his vineyards; in another, he was full face with the bokeh effect blurring the landscape and sky behind him. In yet another, he was photographed with one foot on the floor, sitting one buttock on the corner of his desk, arms folded and smiling, in front of the wall covered in the competition certificates his wines had won.

Moretti fought the urge to tear all the posters down and entered the Questura. Cristina and Gennaro followed shortly after, and while the three waited in Moretti's office for the handover instructions, Alfiero appeared at the office door carrying a supermarket shopping bag.

'This came for you, Commissario,' he said.

'Who brought it in?' Moretti asked.

'A kid, about seven years old. I didn't recognise him.'

Cristina jumped to her feet. 'Will I go and try to catch him?'

Moretti waved her back down and looked in the shopper.

'No point, Cristina. He won't know anything. Let's see what's in here.'

There was a red holdall, like the black one that Moretti had used, and a printed note.

Put cash in here.

Gennaro held the red bag open while the others transferred the cash.

'Are you sure about this, capo?' he asked.

Moretti paused.

'No, Gennaro, I'm not sure,' he snapped. 'In fact, I'm very unsure. I think this could be a complete waste of time and public money, and the end of my career. But what alternative do I have? If there's a chance that we can get Mario back safely, then I think we need to take it. If either of you have any better ideas, now's the time to let me know.'

'Well, Innocenti wouldn't have authorised it if he didn't think it had a chance of success,' Gennaro offered.

Moretti glared at him. 'He didn't.'

Cristina stopped too now, and the silence coagulated around them. Moretti shook his head, and they continued to fill the bag without further comment.

At noon precisely, a message arrived on the burner phone.

Take cash to bus stop outside Bar Italia. You have five minutes. Go alone. Keep phone in your hand.

'*Boia.* Five minutes,' Moretti hissed. 'We're about to get shafted.'

He looked at the others and grabbed the holdall.

'Wait here,' he said. 'But keep an eye on me out of the window.'

They nodded.

He walked quickly down the gentle slope of Piazza Garibaldi and stood at the bus stop. The square was busy with canvassers, and behind him he could feel the eyes of the three gossips scanning him.

Another message.

Throw bag in blue pick-up truck. Don't miss.

He looked along the road. Approaching at speed was a light blue truck with almost-black tinted windows. It showed no signs of slowing, so Moretti readied himself and tossed the bag into the open cargo bed as it screeched around the corner. He ran after it to try to get its number plate, but the truck disappeared round the back of Bar Italia. He followed, but by the time he arrived, it had been abandoned, engine still running. The driver and the money had vanished. Cristina arrived minutes later while Moretti was still doubled over, hands on knees, catching his breath.

'It's gone,' he gasped. 'All of it. I think I've committed career suicide.'

'What are you going to do now, Commissario?'

He stood up, mopped his brow, and said, 'I'm going to buy a beer, then I'm going back to the office to pack up my things.'

They met Gennaro coming towards them as they headed back to Bar Italia and walked three abreast, with Moretti in the middle.

'Maybe they'll be in touch once they're safely away and have checked the money,' said Gennaro.

Moretti patted him on the back and smiled ruefully. 'I'm sure that's what'll happen, Gennaro.'

They turned the corner and sat at a table outside. Carla came out, smiling as usual, to take their order.

'Three beers and something to eat, please, Carla,' said Moretti, without asking the others.

She nodded and went back inside.

Fausta's voice drifted out to their table.

'See, this is where the taxpayers' money goes, keeping our police in beer and sandwiches. I wonder how much today is going to cost us?'

The three detectives looked at each other then, first Moretti, then all three burst into laughter.

'Disgraceful,' came Fausta's comment from within.

Carla brought the drinks on a tray and served first Cristina, then Gennaro, with Moretti last.

'The food will be coming in a moment,' she said.

'Thank you,' they chorused. They clinked their glasses together and each took a long pull of the cold beer. Moretti wiped the froth from his moustache.

'Uh oh,' he said. 'This could be trouble.'

They turned to watch the figure crossing Piazza Garibaldi towards them.

Moretti put some notes on the table.

'In case I have to go,' he said, 'enjoy your lunch and get the Forensics team to check the truck.'

He stood and stretched out a hand to greet the new arrival.

'Sindaco Donati, how good to see you,' he said, as the politician pumped his hand. 'Would you care to join us?'

Donati nodded to the other two detectives.

'Thank you, Dino,' he said quickly, his expression unreadable. 'But I rather urgently need a word with you.'

Moretti's stomach dropped. 'Of course, Sindaco.'

'Please excuse us,' said the politician, with the merest bow. He extended his left arm and gathered Moretti with his right. 'Let's walk together.'

CHAPTER FIFTY-ONE

Moretti decided to say nothing until he knew what the sindaco wanted to talk to him about. So they headed off on the road towards Maghicchio in silence until they were well out of earshot of the bar.

'How are you, Dino?' began Achille. 'How are things?'

Moretti was uncertain how much Donati knew.

'Oh, busy as usual,' he replied blandly.

'And how is your wife?'

Why is he asking this? thought Moretti. *He spoke with her at the funeral only a few days ago.*

'She's actually working on a case away from home for a few days.'

They walked in silence for what seemed like ages.

'How's your search for the missing boy and his mother going?'

Moretti's stomach lurched again. This was it.

'Oh, you know,' he said, trying to brighten his voice and keen not to reveal too much. 'We're making progress.'

Donati's hands were clasped behind his back, and he stared into the distance.

'Good, good.'

They walked a few metres in silence.

'You'll have seen the hubbub in Piazza Garibaldi this morning.'

'Yes,' Moretti said, frantically trying to work out where the conversation was going. 'Very busy.' Then he added quickly, 'But you must be sure of winning. I mean, you've brought an enormous benefit to the community.'

Donati looked heavenwards now.

'I've learned that in this life one's past record stands for nothing, Dino. Popularity is transient. The public are fickle and unforgiving of errors. They don't always see the necessity to bend the rules, not even by a little.'

Moretti found it difficult to swallow. Donati was building to a climax.

They stopped, and Donati faced him and fixed his gaze. Moretti held his breath.

'How well do you know my opponent, Giorgio Ricci?'

The gasp escaped Moretti before he could control it.

Donati winced. 'I'm sorry, Dino,' he said. 'It's most unprofessional and unreasonable of me to ask, I know, but I think that I'm facing someone who is unscrupulous and has maybe already acted illegally in this election.'

Thinking fast, Moretti clenched his fists against his sides to hide the shaking. He licked his lips and found his breath.

'Sindaco,' his voice warbled, and he coughed. 'Sindaco, I don't know if I'm able to help you. I have been expressly forbidden by Vice Questore Innocenti from continuing my investigations into Signor Ricci.'

Donati's eyes slitted.

'Continuing,' he repeated. 'You said continuing, that means there is something. What is it, Dino?'

Moretti looked at the ground.

'Signor Donati, I'm sorry,' he said hastily. 'I misspoke. You must forget that I said that.'

Donati grabbed his arm.

'Dino, keep this between you and me,' he barely whispered. 'Someone set fire to the printworks that we always use for our publicity. They have all my stock photographs on file so can churn stuff out quickly. I think it was Ricci or someone acting for him. You leave Vice Questore Innocenti to me. Why are you investigating Ricci?'

Moretti checked both ways along the road.

'Achille, I can't answer that question,' he said quietly and firmly. 'But if you were to ask me what investigations I have ongoing, then

I'd say that I'm investigating the disappearance of Mario Rosati and his mother. I'd add that I'm also investigating the circumstances around Domenico Rosati's death, and allegations that someone was trying to cheat him by buying his land at below market value. I'm investigating another allegation that Domenico, a neighbour of Signor Ricci, was being pressurised from somewhere to sell his land. I'm also investigating two people of interest who appeared at Domenico's funeral but, with the assistance of Signor Ricci, managed to escape before we could identify and speak with them. And finally, I'm investigating the whereabouts of the immigrants whom we had in custody but escaped with the help of a person or persons unknown. But let me make it unambiguously clear that I am not currently investigating Signor Giorgio Ricci, because I am following Vice Questore Innocenti's orders not to do so.'

Donati released his grip on Moretti's arm and smiled, revealing teeth straightened and whitened at the taxpayers' expense.

'I see,' he said, turning back and setting off. 'Well, Commissario Moretti, I understand your position entirely. It certainly sounds like you have a busy schedule.'

Moretti fell in step with the sindaco.

'It's an anxious time – and for you, too. How are you going to run a campaign without publicity?'

'I'm focussing on the plight of the immigrants.'

'The immigrants?'

Donati looked to the horizon.

'Poor, frightened men escaping from war or famine, doing whatever it takes to make a life for themselves and send money home, asking for nothing except a chance to work and be allowed to live here in peace as free men until the law changes. They should be celebrated, not hidden away. That's what I'm campaigning for.'

Moretti shot him a sideways glance.

'You'll still need posters.'

'I wonder then, if I were to make a formal report, if you or your team could find time to investigate the circumstances of the fire at the print shop?'

Moretti tutted and wagged his finger.

'No, Sindaco, not if you made the report,' he said. 'If, on the other hand, the proprietor was to file a report, then time would be found immediately.'

Donati stopped to grab and shake Moretti's hand while holding his shoulder.

'I enjoyed our talk, Dino, but if you'll excuse me now, I have a call to make and an election to win.'

He turned to make his call and Moretti headed back to Bar Italia.

CHAPTER FIFTY-TWO

As Moretti approached Bar Italia, he noticed the anxious expressions on his colleagues' faces and that they had almost finished their beer and eaten most of the food.

'Is everything okay, Commissario?' asked Cristina.

'For the moment, yes,' Moretti replied, reaching for a sandwich. 'The sindaco wants us to investigate last night's mysterious fire at the printworks he uses for his campaign leaflets.'

Gennaro's was a reflex response. 'Mafia.'

Moretti chewed and nodded at the same time.

'I asked him to get the owner to report it and we'd look at it,' he said, mouth half full.

Gennaro made an entry in his notebook.

'I can tell you now what the report will say,' he said cynically. 'A fire was started using a small volume of accelerant that was squirted through the letterbox, or maybe under the door. The fire was enough to set off the sprinklers, which extinguished the fire. No serious damage, but they can't fill orders for a couple of days until everything dries out and they get in more stock. The only other damage was to the security camera which coincidentally went offline before the fire.'

Cristina shook her head.

Moretti nodded, sipped his beer, and said, 'You're probably right, Gennaro, but it gives us a possible way to get to Ricci. Get the Forensics guys down there after they've finished with the truck, then both of you interview the printer, take the details, and speak to Ricci. Make it clear that it's part of our general inquiries and not an accusation.'

Gennaro put his notebook back in his pocket. 'You mean a fishing exercise.'

'Exactly.'

A phone buzzed in Moretti's pocket. Gennaro and Cristina looked with anticipation that it was news about Mario, but Moretti pulled out his own phone.

'A message from an unknown sender,' he said. 'Shit! Whose car is nearest?'

Cristina looked at Gennaro. 'Probably mine. What is it?'

Moretti grabbed another sandwich and overturned his chair as he leapt to his feet.

'It's from Yusuf. One of the escaped immigrants is hurt. They're on a dirt road at the far end of Ricci's agriturismo. Gennaro, call an ambulance and tell them that we'll update them with the location, then deal with Forensics and the printer. Come on, Cristina, where's your car?'

They zigzagged at speed downhill towards Maghicchio, past the main entrance to the agriturismo until they reached a dirt road that defined the eastern perimeter of Ricci's property.

'Turn here,' barked Moretti.

Cristina barely slowed as she threw her car onto the dusty track. White dust flew up behind them as they raced along.

Moretti pointed ahead of them.

'There,' he called, as he dialled 911 to give their exact location.

'Got them,' Cristina replied.

She skidded to a halt beside the two men and dived out, leaving the door ajar.

The injured man lay on the ground; his leg was clearly broken and held between two long sticks bound with some t-shirt material.

Cristina crouched to help him.

'What happened, Yusuf?' asked Moretti.

'He tripped and fell,' Yusuf lied.

Cristina returned to her car and fetched a bottle of water. She cradled the injured man's head and dripped some water between his lips until he held up his fingers. She offered the bottle to Yusuf who gladly drank a little, too.

'Give him some more,' he said, motioning towards his groaning companion.

Cristina continued to give the injured man sips of water until the ambulance arrived a few minutes later. The paramedics assessed the scene, gave him something for the pain, secured his leg in an emergency splint, then lifted him onto a stretcher and up into the ambulance.

'Yusuf and I will go with him, Cristina. You go back to the Questura and help Gennaro. I'll make my own way back from the hospital.'

'Yes, Commissario.'

Moretti climbed up and sat beside Yusuf in the back of the ambulance, both rocking gently as it drove off more slowly than it had arrived over the uneven surface.

Moretti shifted slightly so that he could watch Yusuf's profile.

'Do you remember me, Yusuf?'

'You are Moretti – the husband of our lawyer.'

'That's right. Yusuf, how did the accident really happen? A young, fit man doesn't break his leg like that by falling over.'

Yusuf sat leaning forward, watching the patient, elbows on his knees, palms together. He replied without looking up.

'I don't know. Maybe something fell on it.'

'I see.' Moretti smoothed his moustache. 'That sounds more likely.'

The ambulance reached the asphalt road and sped up.

'I was wondering about your escape yesterday.' He noticed a tiny flicker in Yusuf's eyes.

Yusuf turned his head towards Moretti.

'Is this going to be one of your cosy chats, Commissario?' he asked, catching Moretti completely off guard. 'Our lawyer says that you are famous for them, and that we should say nothing to you without legal representation present.'

Moretti threw his head back and laughed, taking Yusuf by surprise.

'That's very good advice.' He wiped a tear away. 'Very well, Yusuf,' he continued, 'in that case you can listen while I talk.'

Yusuf turned back to watch his friend.

'You had help to break out of custody yesterday. We don't know exactly who, yet, but we'll find out. That's nothing to do with you, though.'

No reaction from Yusuf.

'You were clearly following a plan – and it was a good one – because you all disappeared completely. In fact, if your friend hadn't broken his leg, we'd probably never have found you.'

Still nothing from Yusuf.

'So, I was thinking. If I was on the run, what would I need? I'd need somewhere to hide, there would have to be provisions there – maybe a change of clothes. I'd need to have a job that paid well so that I could save money for travel and for bribing people. But you've already had a bad experience of that Yusuf, haven't you?'

He noticed the Somali swallow.

'I'd need documents and papers to let me travel. I'd have to have a destination in mind – probably not Italy. Maybe Sweden or England. How am I doing so far, Yusuf?'

No reaction, but Yusuf's almost black skin was beginning to glisten.

'I'd be travelling on my own, ideally, because it's easier for one person to hide than nine. So that's a problem for you, Yusuf.'

Yusuf's head tilted down a fraction.

'And most importantly, I wouldn't let myself get caught again. Now, that's where the real problem is for you, Yusuf. Your friend here is injured, another two are back in custody, and there are still five – none of whom can speak Italian – hidden somewhere, probably with not much in the way of food or water, judging by how thirsty you two were.'

The injured man groaned, and Yusuf laid a hand on his arm.

'On the positive side, you have a very good lawyer, although I must tell you that she's not here now. But the best news is that I spoke with the sindaco a little while ago. He is making you and your friends the centre of his election campaign.'

Now Yusuf turned his head.

'Yes, that's right. He's going to campaign for you all to be set free. He wants to find you all jobs and legal status in Cassiatorre. Now, whether you want to stay there is another matter, but at least if you have legal status you will be able to work, earn money, send cash home to your family and, if you want, travel to anywhere in Europe with all the proper documents. Now, how's that for a cosy chat?'

227

Yusuf slid his hands onto his knees, turned his shoulder towards Moretti, and studied his face.

'Do you mean this, Commissario? Is it true?'

'Absolutely true. No tricks.'

'And what do we have to give in return?'

'You have to give me your trust, Yusuf.'

CHAPTER FIFTY-THREE

By the time Cristina arrived back at the Questura, Gennaro had already contacted the printer and taken a statement. She found him in his office looking at the collection of photographs purporting to be of Mario.

'How is it going, Gennaro?'

He puffed.

'I can't do this,' he said. 'I'm trying to match this photograph of Mario to all these other kids. For a start, it's not a recent photograph, and second, some of these other photographs are blurred, quarter profiles, pictures of the back of the head, or the kid is in the distance. They could all be Mario, or none of them could.'

He slid back his chair and leaned back, hands behind his head.

Cristina turned some photos to have a look.

'I see what you mean.' She frowned. 'Wait, I have an idea.'

She retrieved a number from her phone contacts and called it.

'Carmela? Cristina Furlan. I wonder if you could help us. We've been sent a bunch of photographs of boys who look like Mario, and we don't know him well enough to decide. But you've taught him for six months, so I'm sure it will be simple for you. Can you come in and have look at them?'

She signalled to Gennaro to collect the photographs together.

'No, that's fine, I'll come to you. See you shortly. Bye.'

Gennaro filed all the photographs and details of the boys in a folder and slid it to Cristina.

'Well?'

Cristina picked up the folder.

'She's in the middle of baking at the moment and can't leave the house, so I'll take the photos there.'

'In that case, I'll type up the printer's statement. I don't want to interview Ricci without another witness present.'

Cristina nodded. 'I agree. I shouldn't be too long.'

*

Shortly after, Cristina arrived at Carmela Perri's house where she was greeted by the smell of baking.

She rang the bell, and Carmela came to the door barefooted, dressed in shorts and a t-shirt, with her thick black hair caught back off her face in a large hair claw.

'Hi, Cristina, come in,' she said, smiling widely and holding up hands covered in dough and flour. 'I won't shake hands, but you've arrived at the perfect time. The first batch are only this minute out of the oven. Follow me.' She turned and almost skipped along the short corridor.

Cristina closed the door and followed her into a small, messy kitchen, where a jumble of jars, packets, and plastic storage boxes cluttered the worktop, while the two cooling racks of fresh cookies on the table gave off delicious aromas of lemon and amaretto. Carmela filled the Moka pot and put it on the stove then turned round, wiping her hands on a towel.

'Now we can shake hands,' she said, thrusting her arm out at shoulder height. 'Have a seat, you make me feel tiny.'

Cristina laughed and sat, standing the manila folder against a chair leg on the floor while Carmela laid plates, small cups, saucers, and napkins on the table.

'The cookies look wonderful, Carmela. I see there are two types.'

'Thank you. The ones with the lemon glaze are *uncinetti* – Calabrian Easter cookies. The plain ones are traditional Sicilian soft amaretti cookies – made with real Sicilian ground almonds. I use my great-grandmother's recipes.'

Carmela used tongs to place two of each type of biscuit onto their plates as the Moka finished bubbling and hissing. She grabbed a patchwork potholder, picked up the Moka, and poured the strong black coffee into the cups.

'There,' she said with a huge smile, finally sitting. 'Tell me what you think.'

Cristina bit into one of the round amaretti.

'Mmm. Delicious. I bet you loved visiting your great-grandmother.'

Carmela nodded.

'My mother moved to Calabria when she married, and I was born and brought up there, but when we visited great-granny, or when she visited us, she spent almost the whole day in the kitchen preparing food.'

She pointed to Cristina's lip.

'You have icing sugar… That's it.' Carmela moved the cooling racks and wiped the table. 'Now, you wanted me to look at some photographs.'

Cristina picked up the folder and splayed the photographs.

Carmela sorted them quickly, rejecting all but two.

'This one could be Mario,' she said, squinting. 'It's difficult to make the features out.' She picked up the last photo and held it to face Cristina. 'But this one is definitely him.'

Cristina's eyebrows arched.

'Wow!' she gasped. 'Are you sure?'

'Absolutely certain. That's Mario Rosati,' Carmela said emphatically, then unexpectedly she began to weep, her slender body heaving.

Cristina moved quickly to kneel beside her to comfort her. 'What is it?'

Carmela threw her arms around Cristina's neck and buried her head under her chin.

'I suddenly thought of Mario and wondered how you had his picture,' she sobbed. 'I'm afraid to ask where it came from.'

Cristina wrapped one arm around her and stroked her head.

'It's all right, Carmela,' she said softly. 'These are photos sent in after Mario's description was broadcast. Most of them will be people looking for the reward, but you've helped us a lot today. Please don't be upset.'

Carmela leaned back a little; her eyes were red, and her face was wet. She pulled Cristina's face towards her and kissed her on the lips.

A jolt went through Cristina, but she didn't pull away. Carmela moved her mouth against Cristina's, and her tongue touched Cristina's lips.

Cristina gently, but firmly, broke the kiss.

'Carmela, I'm sorry,' she said. 'If I gave you the impression…'

'No, it's me,' she said. 'I'm attracted to you.'

Cristina felt awkward but did not break their embrace.

'Not to men?'

'Yes, but also to you. I don't know.'

Cristina thought to ease the situation.

'Because I'm so mannish, you mean?'

Carmela snorted.

'No, I admire your strength and your physicality.' She smiled a soggy smile. 'But also your softer side, like when we went to speak with Mario's friend Nicola. I see you as a woman first, Cristina.'

Cristina gave her a peck on the forehead then freed an arm, reached over to the table, and picked up a napkin. 'Here. Clean up, and let's eat these delicious biscuits.' Cristina returned to her chair and sampled the other biscuit while Carmela excused herself.

Cristina heard water running, and moments later her host returned with a fresher face. She was about to speak, but Cristina held up a finger and said, 'Nothing happened here. Two friends met for coffee and cookies.'

Carmela smiled.

'Thank you. In that case, let me top up your coffee.'

'Carmela, it's me, or rather we – the police – who ought to thank you. We could never have sorted through that sheaf of pictures. Certainly not in that time.'

Carmela picked up one of the uncinetti.

'I like all the children in my class, Cristina,' she said, poised to bite it. 'But perhaps Mario most of all.'

'I remember you told me before that he brings you presents.'

Carmela stood up excitedly and put the biscuit back on her plate.

'Oh yes, come and look.'

Without waiting, she hurried off to the next room. Cristina picked up the folder of photographs and followed. This room was as tidy and ordered as the kitchen was messy. A pair of comfortable-looking sofas faced each other, with a low table between them. A narrow gate-legged table stood under the window with a collection of small ceramics, and the walls were covered in family photographs and framed children's paintings. A tall, overstocked bookcase filled a niche beside the large open fireplace where Carmela stood, beckoning her.

'This is my Mario gallery,' she said, indicating the wide mantle shelf. 'Treasures from his imaginary travels.'

Cristina looked at the odd collection and smiled.

'Where does he travel to?' she asked, hoping for a clue into his whereabouts.

'The dried grasses and poppy seed heads in the posy vase came from The Haunted Meadow, a field belonging to one of their neighbours. The bat wing skeleton came from Vampire Valley, that's on Signor Erpicone's property. The snail shell came from Lizard Rock, somewhere on the agriturismo, and the odd-shaped pebble came from the Poison Pit on his own farm.'

The two women laughed.

'What an imagination,' exclaimed Cristina.

'He spends a lot of time on his own.'

Cristina pointed to the pebble. 'May I?'

'Of course, but be careful, it's poisonous.'

They laughed again.

Cristina picked it up, turned it in her hand, scratched the surface gently with her thumbnail, and held it to her nose.

'Oh,' she recoiled. 'It is poisonous. It stinks. Where did he find this?'

'On his podere somewhere. I don't know.'

Cristina replaced it carefully and pointed at the snail shell.

'And this came from Signor Ricci's property, you said. Does he go there often?'

Carmela picked up the shell and shrugged.

'I couldn't say,' she said, looking at it fondly. 'I know that he has particular games that he plays in each place, with a cast of imaginary characters located in each one.' She placed it back.

'Fascinating,' Cristina said. 'Do you know the last time he played in the agriturismo?'

Carmela looked up at her, and her eyes began to glisten.

'I met him a couple of days before he disappeared. He'd been playing somewhere in the agriturismo.'

'Lizard Rock,' interjected Cristina.

Carmela laughed. 'Probably, and he was worried.'

'Worried why?'

'Partly because he wants his playing places to remain secret, and partly because he broke one of his mother's golden rules.'

'What happened?'

'Well, he was seen by two of the guests and, worse still, he spoke with them despite knowing that he should never speak to strangers.'

Cristina looked puzzled.

'He seems such a conscientious boy and one who has his own set way of doing things. I wonder why he spoke with them. Do you know what they talked about?'

'They asked him what he was doing there and where he lived. Of course, that's why he was worried. He thought that they'd report him to his parents. As for why, I'm not sure, but it might have been the first time he'd spoken with a black woman.'

A thought that Cristina had dismissed returned. She placed a hand gently on Carmela's arm.

'Carmela, I'm sorry but I must go. I wish I'd come to you sooner. I'm sure our investigation would have been further ahead.'

Carmela smiled and nodded. 'And I must get back to my baking. Thank you for coming. I hope that I haven't put you off visiting again.'

'I'll be back. You have a lovely house, and I'm sure we'll be great friends. Your baking is great – and your kissing is too. Your future partner is lucky.'

After the short journey back to the Questura, Cristina stayed in her car and called Moretti.

'Moretti.'

'Cristina, Commissario. How's the immigrant?'

'His leg has been set, pinned, and cased in plaster. He's had a lot of painkillers, so he's been talking non-stop. Yusuf has been translating everything.'

'I've picked up a couple of useful snippets of information from Mario's teacher, too, so I was wondering…'

'About delaying Ricci's interview? Yes. Let's regroup back at the Questura. We're almost finished here. Transport is already on its way here for the three of us.'

CHAPTER FIFTY-FOUR

With Yusuf and the injured man locked up again with the two Somalis, the three detectives met in Moretti's office. Moretti had ordered coffee from Bar Italia, and Gigi now appeared with a little tray holding three small, lidded plastic cups and a few sachets of sugar that he transferred to Moretti's desk.

Moretti placed a note on the tray. 'Thank you, Gigi. Keep the change.'

Gigi handed him a folded piece of paper.

'My mother said I should give you this,' he said awkwardly.

Moretti read it. 'Thank you.'

The coffee was gone in an instant.

'Gennaro, did you get Parodi to sign his statement?'

Santoro slid a copy to Moretti.

'He said that he's heading back home tomorrow, so if we want to speak to him, it has to be today.'

'Thanks. Cristina, how did you get on with Maestra Perri?'

Moretti's choice of expression made Cristina blush.

'I have to confess I stayed rather longer than necessary because I sampled her home baking,' she said, hoping that her little confession would explain her red face. 'She's clearly very fond of all her students, and Mario in particular. Here are the important things I discovered.' She counted on her fingers. 'There's pietra fetida on the Rosati property; Mario had been on the agriturismo in the days prior to his disappearance; and Asia Cooper saw and spoke with him.'

Moretti and Santoro glanced at each other.

'So, Asia Cooper was lying,' Moretti said.

'About not seeing Mario, and about not walking about on the estate, unless Mario came right over to the poolside.'

'I wonder what else she's been lying about?' mused Moretti. 'Any luck with the photographs?'

Cristina beamed and pulled out the image that Carmela had identified.

'This one,' she said, planting it on the desk. 'This one is Mario.'

Gennaro leaned over to see it. 'Where was it taken?'

Cristina checked the details in the folder.

'A small village in the south. Borgo di Monte Groppone.'

Gennaro shrugged. 'Never heard of it. How about you, how did you get on?'

Moretti smoothed his moustache with finger and thumb and inhaled deeply.

'Well, I told Yusuf that the sindaco was making the immigrants central to his campaign, and that it would help them and the sindaco if I could find a reason for them to stay. Yusuf asked if finding out about corruption was a good enough reason. You can imagine my answer. He told me that the Somalis and Ethiopians working for Erpicone don't do any farm work, or at least a minimal amount. Their real job is to dig for Etruscan tombs. They dug scores of test shafts all over Erpicone's property and turned up nothing until, at the boundary of his farm, they found an intact tomb.'

The two detectives gasped.

'They brought out a number of treasures and handed them over to Erpicone.'

Gennaro slapped his leg. 'He sold them! That's how the money got into his account.'

Moretti nodded. 'And I'm guessing that Ricci's behind it.'

'What about the other immigrants?' asked Cristina.

'Yusuf said that he'll tell them to give themselves up if the sindaco signs a statement saying they are to be treated as free men and that he'll campaign for their rights.'

Cristina frowned. 'Do you think the sindaco will agree?'

'He already has. I called him from the hospital. He jumped at the chance.'

Gennaro looked puzzled.

'I'm sorry, I know it's very laudable, capo, but I don't see what Donati has to gain from supporting their cause.'

Moretti laughed.

'That's why you're an agente and not a politician,' he said. 'Think of the headlines in both local and national press. These men have made an important archaeological discovery – one that will boost tourism and the local economy.'

'Are we going to interview Erpicone?'

'No, Gennaro. He's a cantankerous old goat. I've already sent two uniformed officers to bring him here to see if he's a bit more cooperative and less aggressive out of his home territory.'

CHAPTER FIFTY-FIVE

The three detectives stood behind the two-way mirror of the interview room, watching Erpicone's shaky hands fiddle with the straps of his dungarees.

'I'll go,' said Moretti. 'You two watch, and if I miss anything, come in.'

Moretti entered and sat opposite the farmer.

'Good day, Signor Erpicone, it's Commissario Moretti.'

Erpicone's cloudy eyes turned in the direction of the voice.

'I know who you are,' he growled. 'I'm not blind.'

Moretti smiled.

'Can I get you anything? Water, coffee?'

'You can get a car to take me back home. If my family turn up and leave because I'm not there, I'll have your job. I might have your job anyway, because you've arrested me with no reason.'

'Please let me reassure you, Signor Erpicone, that you are here helping us with our enquiries,' Moretti soothed. 'You're not under arrest – at the moment.'

Erpicone slapped the table.

'What do you mean at the moment, you walrus-faced incompetent?' he fumed. 'Are you threatening me?'

Moretti looked towards the mirror, knowing that Gennaro at least would be smiling at the insult.

'As I said, you are here helping with our enquiries,' he repeated calmly.

Erpicone folded his arms.

'Well, this won't take long,' he grumped. 'I haven't done anything, I haven't seen anything, and I don't know anything.'

'Who paid you for the treasures removed from the Etruscan tomb by your workers?'

The directness of the question hit Erpicone like a slap, and his head jerked back involuntarily.

'What workers? What tomb? I don't know anything about treasure.'

'Oh, but I think you do, Signor Erpicone,' Moretti continued. 'We've interviewed one of the men, and he has given us full details of what he and the others have done, as well as the number, type, and appearance of the objects that they brought to you, including a bracelet, pottery, and a comb.'

Erpicone jabbed his forefinger into the table as his voice got louder.

'So, it's the word of an illegal immigrant against mine, a well-respected and honest member of the community. Nobody will believe him.'

Moretti deliberately lowered his voice.

'We are going to be taking statements from the other workers, and if I were to guess, I'd say that all of their statements will corroborate his.'

'Still their word against mine. You have no proof,' Erpicone replied defiantly.

Moretti ignored him and continued. 'One of the interesting things that our witness could remember were the dates when they handed you the different treasures.'

Erpicone folded his arms again and turned away, unseeing, from Moretti.

'I don't find that interesting at all, and neither will anyone else.'

'The dates coincide with money that was paid into your bank account.'

The cranky old man shrugged, arms open. 'I'm a farmer. I grow things. I sell things. You clearly don't know that's how farming works.'

Moretti persisted in a controlled, measured tone.

'Yet, when we interviewed you before, you told us that your bank loan would be paid off after the harvest. Tell me, Signor

Erpicone, what crops have you harvested and sold since you took out the bank loan?'

'I can't remember. Olives and hay.'

'Farming must be more lucrative than I thought, because your olives and hay brought in almost ten thousand Euros.'

'Well, there you are then. We're agreed,' he said smugly. 'You know nothing.'

'What I do know, Signor Erpicone,' said Moretti, smoothly, 'is that you'll have a record for the transactions and will have issued receipts and kept a copy for yourself so that the correct amount of tax can be levied.'

'I leave all of that side of things to my accountant.'

'And can you give me their contact details?'

Erpicone leaned across the table. 'No,' he snapped.

Moretti sighed. 'Signor Erpicone, I'm a policeman. I ask questions. You answer them. You clearly don't know that's how helping the police with their enquiries works. Maybe we should stop this interview.'

'Good, the sooner I'm out of here the better.'

'Oh, I'm sorry, Signor Erpicone, if I've given you the wrong impression,' Moretti said good-naturedly, sliding back his chair and getting to his feet. 'You won't be leaving here until either you answer my questions honestly and fully, or until we get a search warrant from the judge and bring in a squad of officers to do a thorough search in your house, outbuildings, and all your farm. That ought to take about four days. Goodbye.' He slid his chair under the table and left Erpicone alone in the room.

Moretti joined the two detectives in the viewing room, and the three watched as Erpicone stood up yelling and cursing, tossed his chair to the corner of the room, kicked the table – hurting his toes – then sat on the table, first rubbing his toes and muttering to himself then, arms folded, sat in silence.

'He's scared,' said Cristina. 'That's why he's acting out.'

Moretti nodded. 'Do you want to have a try?'

'Yes, but he hates me.'

'He hates all of us,' Gennaro said.

Cristina entered the room with a bottle of water that she placed on the table. Without speaking, she picked up the tossed chair and repositioned it in front of Erpicone at the table before sitting down on the other side with Erpicone's back to her. Still in silence, Erpicone slid off the table and sat down, peering at her blurry image. He was first to break the silence.

'I know what you're doing, lightning rod,' he said.

Cristina could smell traces of alcohol from his breath. She didn't respond.

'You're playing good cop, bad cop.'

Still Cristina said nothing.

He fidgeted anxiously with the bib of his dungarees.

'Cat got your tongue?'

Cristina sat in silence until the tension in the room pressed in on them like an avalanche.

'I haven't seen my parents for a year,' she said softly. 'And I miss them every day.'

Erpicone opened his mouth to give an unkind retort but stopped himself, and they both sat in silence again.

'A year is a long time,' he said quietly. 'Why so long?'

Cristina sighed.

'I guess it's my fault. I got caught up in my job, my career, and work took me away. I don't think there's any one reason; it just happened. I got into a bad habit.'

He leaned forward and put his hands on the table. 'You should visit them.'

Cristina nodded.

'I know. I will. After we've found the missing boy.' She held out the bottle. 'I brought you some water.'

Erpicone took it and unscrewed the cap. 'How do you get on with them?'

She smiled, and in the quiet room the edges of her lips made a tiny smacking sound.

'My mother is very proud of me, but I'm a disappointment to my father. He wanted me to become a lawyer then a judge, like him. He couldn't understand that I had different ambitions.'

Erpicone sipped some water.

'I want the podere to stay in the family,' he said. 'But it's not the sort of job that young people want these days – it's hard work, long hours, and you're always fighting the weather. Money's easier to come by in the city.'

'Signor Erpicone, I can hear how important your podere is to you,' Cristina said thoughtfully. 'I'm going to arrange personally for someone to look after the dogs and the animals while you're here. Someone will be there this afternoon, and they'll stay there in case any of your children return to pay a surprise visit.'

Erpicone nodded and raised the bottle to his lips. Then he aimed it at Cristina and squeezed hard with both hands. She inhaled sharply as the cold water hit her.

'There's a surprise visit, bitch!' he yelled, as he got to his feet. 'Did you think I was going to fall for your sob story? I know that you and Ricci are all in this together. Well, it won't work. I'm not selling.'

Cristina was on her feet, soaked from head to waist, as Moretti and Gennaro burst into the interview room followed immediately by a uniformed officer. The three restrained and cuffed Erpicone before the uniformed officer led him, still cursing and yelling, to the cells.

Cristina leaned forwards, arms outstretched.

'Are you all right, Cristina?' Moretti asked.

She looked at the expressions on the men's faces and she burst into laughter.

'What a twisted old sod he is,' she said. 'He had me completely fooled.'

Moretti and Gennaro laughed, too.

'But he's given us a lead, Cristina,' Moretti said. 'We now know that Ricci wanted to buy his land. Dry yourself, change your clothes, and come back to the office.'

*

Cristina returned wearing a spare shirt borrowed from one of the uniformed officers.

'Have a seat, and I'll update you,' Moretti said, as he welcomed her back into his office.

'Erpicone is now in the cell next to Yusuf and the injured man. There is a uniformed officer down there, and Yusuf is pretending to give him a statement so that Erpicone can hear how much we know.'

'How is he reacting to that?'

Moretti grinned. 'With no water to throw around, he has to content himself with saying that everything is bullshit and lies.'

242

Cristina shook her head and smiled. 'Do you think he'll cooperate?'

Moretti shrugged. 'We'll work on the basis that he won't. I called the bank and put a bit of pressure on Dante. I asked him to cross-check the dates when the cash appeared in Erpicone's account with withdrawals from Ricci's account.'

Cristina raised her eyebrows. 'And?'

'They correspond,' Moretti said triumphantly. 'The figures are not exact, but they are close enough.'

Cristina's expression changed to one of concern. 'Close enough for what, Commissario?'

Gennaro folded his arms.

'Close enough that the commissario now wants to interview Ricci himself, here.'

'Commissario, you can't,' Cristina gasped. 'Vice Questore Innocenti gave you a direct order.'

Moretti nodded and raised his hands in mock surrender. 'Which the current sindaco countermanded.'

Cristina looked at Gennaro, who rolled his eyes.

'But, Commissario, Signor Donati is not the current sindaco,' she pleaded. 'He is only a candidate. He could lose, and you'd be censured, maybe sacked.'

Moretti shook his head.

'I'm sorry, but my mind's made up,' he said firmly.

'In that case, don't embarrass Ricci by bringing him here. Let's go to his place, and we can interview Asia Cooper at the same time.'

Moretti looked at her distraught expression then at Gennaro, who pursed his lips and nodded.

'Very well,' he conceded. 'We'll go to his place. Gennaro and I will interview Ricci, you can speak with Asia Cooper, Cristina.'

CHAPTER FIFTY-SIX

Moretti pressed the buzzer at the barrier.

'Commissario Moretti for Signor Ricci. I have a few questions as part of an ongoing enquiry.'

There was a long pause then a voice spoke.

'Please direct all questions to Mr Ricci's legal representation.'

Moretti held the button down again.

'We are trying to do this discreetly, but if Signor Ricci would prefer, we can formally arrest him and lead him through the main square in handcuffs.'

A short pause and then the barrier lifted.

The three detectives made their way to reception. Cristina scanned the pool area looking for the Coopers, but all the guests were new arrivals.

Moretti addressed Alicia the receptionist.

'We're here to speak with Signor Ricci and the guest Asia Cooper.'

Alicia glanced at Cristina then back to Moretti.

'Signor Ricci will see you momentarily. Signora Cooper is in her chalet with Signor Cooper, I believe.' She blushed.

Cristina understood.

'I'll wait outside for them, Commissario.'

'And we'll wait here for Signor Ricci.'

After a few minutes, the desk phone rang.

'Signor Ricci will see you now.'

Alicia knocked then opened the door to Ricci's office and showed the detectives in.

Ricci was behind his desk. Stacked on the floor beside it were cardboard boxes of campaign material.

'I have just reported you to Vice Questore Innocenti, Commissario Moretti,' Ricci said sullenly. 'I fully expect that you will be hearing from him very shortly. Now, I'm very busy with my election campaign. Take a seat and ask your questions.'

Moretti and Gennaro both sat. Gennaro took out his notebook.

'Thank you for seeing us, Signor Ricci,' said Moretti smoothly. 'This won't take long. We have been checking various phone records in relation to the death of Domenico Rosati, and your number came up on several occasions before his fatal accident. Would you care to say why?'

Ricci steepled his fingers.

'Signor Rosati is a builder that I have used at various times in the past. There are several projects that I am planning, as well as the ongoing maintenance of the agriturismo, so our conversations were about that.'

'There were also calls from unknown numbers in the days before his death.'

Ricci sneered. 'Commissario, how can I answer that?'

Moretti nodded.

'I see. We interviewed Signor Rosati's cousin, a Signor Parodi, and he told us that you had approached Domenico about buying his property.'

'Not true.'

'Signor Parodi told us that you had made an offer but that it was under market value.'

'Not true.'

'We also discovered that you had applied for a bank loan for approximately the same sum as you had offered Signor Rosati.'

Ricci hesitated a fraction then recovered. 'I didn't offer to buy his property.'

'Then your application for a loan was withdrawn on the same day that a similar sum was credited to your account.' Moretti looked closely at Ricci. 'Where did those funds come from, Signor Ricci?'

'That's confidential business information,' Ricci said testily. 'I don't have to answer unless you are arresting and charging me.'

'It also appears that you approached Signor Erpicone about buying his property, too.'

'That is true, but he refused to sell.'

'And we notice that three sums of money left your account, and three corresponding sums of money appeared in Signor Erpicone's account within twenty-four hours.'

'How did you gain access to my bank details?'

'It's part of a wider investigation.'

Ricci's eyes narrowed. 'Your career is over, Moretti, do you know that?'

'Answer the question, Signor Ricci, unless you want to be charged with impeding our investigation.'

Ricci dismissed the remark with a wave. 'Coincidence. What is your point?'

'We suspect Signor Erpicone of selling Etruscan tomb artefacts. Would you know anything about that?'

Ricci placed his palms on the table. 'Has Erpicone admitted this?'

'Is that a yes, Signor Ricci?'

'You know better than that,' he chided.

'Returning to the phone records, we checked and discovered that you were also in touch with Chiara Rosati, Domenico's wife.'

Gennaro shifted in his chair.

Ricci looked past Moretti to the door. 'That was ages ago.'

'And was that to do with building work, too?'

He now returned his gaze to Moretti and smiled.

'If you must know,' he said indelicately, 'we were arranging a weekend away together, and if you check more thoroughly, you'll find that it was she who contacted me.'

Moretti struggled to hide his growing hatred.

'We did check thoroughly, and we discovered that you've had calls with several women. Were these of a romantic nature?'

Ricci folded his arms and looked away towards the certificate wall. Moretti noticed sweat marks on the table where his hands had been.

'There was nothing romantic about it. I'm a single, wealthy man, whom women find attractive. There's no law against casual sex, is there?'

'Did you have casual sex with Asia Cooper?'

Ricci leaned forward and leered. 'You'd be surprised at who I've had casual sex with.'

Moretti dismissed the name that screamed inside his head.

'With Asia Cooper?'

'Yes, at her request.'

'And what did she want in return?'

Ricci sat back and shrugged.

'I think the experience was its own reward,' he said smugly.

'Well, it's no secret that she wanted to adopt a child. Did you agree to find one for her?'

Ricci leaned across the table, stabbing his finger at Moretti.

'You've crossed a line, Moretti,' he raged. 'Asia Cooper wanted to give birth to a child in the usual way. Her husband clearly isn't up to the job, so I agreed to sleep with her to father one, not to kidnap one.'

Moretti knew himself that he had gone too far.

Ricci looked up at a noise behind Moretti in the reception area. The door burst open and Innocenti entered.

'Signor Ricci, I must apologise for this intrusion.' He turned to Moretti. 'Commissario, get up and leave. Say nothing. As of now, you are suspended from duty pending a disciplinary enquiry and possible criminal charges. Agente Santoro, you and Ispettore Furlan are to return immediately to the Questura.'

Innocenti turned to Ricci.

'Signor Ricci, if I may have a word.'

Moretti and Gennaro left them to it.

'Capo, what the hell were you doing in there? How did you get Ricci's phone records?'

'I didn't, Gennaro.'

'But I thought…'

'And so did Ricci. It was a bluff.'

In vain, they looked outside for Cristina. Moretti returned to the car while Gennaro went back inside.

'Alicia, where is my colleague, Ispettore Furlan?'

'She is in the Cooper chalet, Agente.'

'Thanks.'

He waited with Moretti in the car until Cristina arrived, smiling, ten minutes later.

She opened the door, about to speak, but Moretti spoke first.

'I'm off the case. I'm suspended pending an enquiry.'

'What are you going to do, Commissario?'

'You're going to drive us back to the Questura, I'll collect my things, then I'm going out to dinner. What about you? What did you get from Asia Cooper?'

Cristina started the car and drove off along the dusty track towards the main road.

'Asia Cooper now admits she did see Mario, but she denies having any intention to have him kidnapped.'

'Cristina, Gennaro, I won't be in touch after I leave the Questura. I don't want to compromise the investigation, but there is something connecting Ricci to the Rosati's. He admitted sleeping with Chiara but denied making a bid for their land. You need to work on Erpicone. I think he's the key to the whole thing.'

CHAPTER FIFTY-SEVEN

Moretti switched off his phone, rang the doorbell, and stood back. The peach stucco walls of the front of the house were covered in climbing plants whose colour matched the flaking dark green of the shutters. A lizard's pointed head poked out of the foliage high enough to be unconcerned by his presence. In an untended vegetable garden, zucchini and tomato seedlings, salad plants and herbs competed fiercely with the weeds growing through them. The laurel hedge badly needed trimmed. It straggled upwards and into the garden, encroaching space that could be used for crops, fruit trees, or a flower border – clearly not a priority for the busy single parent.

'Coming.'

He could hear her smile in the cadence of that single word, and his spirits lifted in reply.

Carla opened the door. Now he saw her smile, and his burdens dropped to the ground.

'Come in, Dino,' she said, and he hesitated for a fraction, bathing in the happiness that radiated from her. She wore a loose, powder pink-coloured t-shirt with diamante rhinestones swirling from shoulder to shoulder, cropped jeans, and little canvas shoes.

He held out the wine and the polystyrene container of gelato.

'I brought these,' he said sheepishly. 'I wasn't sure what flavour you liked, so I bought a selection.'

She took the container lifted the lid and peeked inside.

'*Pistacchio, nocciola, fiordilatte.* Thank you, that really wasn't necessary,' she said. 'You bring in the wine. I'll pop this in the freezer for later.'

She turned and headed inside, leaving him in the wake of her light, but musky, perfume. He followed her into what would have been an ordinary kitchen except for the large French doors, open but protected by insect screens, allowing the evening light to flood in. Dressers and open shelves held glasses, crockery, pots, pans, and utensils in an orderliness that was absent outside. This is where her priorities were.

Carla dropped to her haunches to take a terracotta *cocotte* out of the oven. She called over her shoulder. 'Dino, you'll find a corkscrew in the top middle drawer of the dresser. Open the wine you brought, and we'll have it with the *stufato di cinghiale.*'

He opened the bottle and watched like a tongue-tied adolescent as she tasted and seasoned the wild boar stew before returning it to the oven. She stood, turned, smiled, and wiped her hands in what to him seemed a graceful choreography.

'You're very quiet. I bet you've had a hard day. Reach over and bring down a couple of glasses and I'll pour us some white wine.'

Moretto placed the glasses on the counter, and she half-filled them with a straw-coloured wine that frosted the sides.

'CinCin,' she said, as they clinked glasses. 'I'm so glad you agreed to come.'

'Thank you for the invitation,' he replied. 'It couldn't have come at a better time.' He sipped the fruity, pleasantly tart wine. 'Is it just the two of us tonight?'

'Yes. Gigi's visiting a friend. He's been working so hard in the bar, and when I said that you were coming to dinner, he asked if he could stay over.' She laughed. 'That means that he'll be having pizza, fizzy drinks, and playing on a games console until midnight.'

Her smile, her laugh, the wine, and the cooking aromas combined to relax him.

'Who's looking after the bar?' he asked. 'Oh, sorry, even I thought that sounded like a policeman.'

They both laughed.

'The girl who was supposed to be on duty the day of the funeral, remember? When you stepped in to help. She was keen to make it up to me, so I thought rather than spend the evening alone...'

'You'd arrange for some police protection,' he said, surprising himself.

Carla laughed and doubled over a little, resting her hand on his wrist. Her touch was warm, and he missed it when she took it away. She removed a sheet of foil from a large *tagliere* covered with crostini, cold cuts, and cheeses.

'Let's take this next door; the table is laid.'

Moretti didn't want to break the spell of this magical place.

'Carla, if it's all the same to you, I'd like to stay here in the light and warmth.' It was her light and warmth he meant.

She looked at him quizzically.

'Are you sure?' She shrugged. 'You're the guest. Bring over those stools.'

He put down his glass and picked up the two rush seat stools from the side and brought them to the counter. They sat, knees almost touching, and sampled the starters.

'Did you want to talk about your day, or do you need to leave your work outside?'

Moretti wiped his lips on a napkin. Her expression was so open, caring, reassuring.

'You'll find out tomorrow anyway,' he said. 'Everyone will. I've been suspended.'

Her jaw dropped open and she gasped. Her hand reached out in a reflex and touched his knee.

'Oh, Dino. I'm so sorry. Do you want to tell me about it?'

'The short version is that I disobeyed a direct order from Innocenti.'

Carla's eyebrows knitted.

'I'm sure the long version justifies your action completely, Dino,' she said, patting his knee. 'But I guess you're not at liberty to discuss the details.'

Dino took another, longer, sip of his wine then put the glass on the counter.

'Technically, I'm no longer a serving police officer so I think I probably can,' he said mutinously. 'I was told not to investigate Ricci because he's standing for sindaco, but I did. I went today, and Innocenti arrived and suspended me on the spot.'

Carla withdrew her hand from his knee and sipped her wine.

'What was it you were investigating?' she asked softly.

'Oh, it was a whole jumble of stuff, and I knew that I couldn't do it properly because of what the Vice Questore had said, but I felt I had to.' He rested one arm on the counter and reached behind his head and grabbed the hairs at the nape of his neck with the other. 'It was to do with Mario and Chiara's disappearance, Domenico's death, land deals – a whole bunch of things.'

Carla looked down. 'I see,' she said quietly.

'Do you know, he's slept with God knows how many women,' Moretti continued. 'Said that they come seeking him out. Would you believe the arrogance of the man?'

Carla took the hand on the counter in hers.

'Yes, Dino,' she said sadly. 'I would. I'm one of those women.'

Dino closed her hand in both of his and watched as a tear ran down Carla's face.

'Oh God, Carla, I'm so sorry. Sorry and stupid.'

She squeezed his hand.

'No, it was me who was stupid.' She stood up, broke free, and crossed to a box of tissues, wiped her eyes, and blew her nose. She sat back down and took his hands in hers again.

'My husband had left me, and my self-esteem had plummeted off the scale. I met him at an open evening that he hosted for local businesses, and one thing led to another. It was a big mistake.'

'I don't need to hear any more, Carla,' Moretti said tenderly.

'Yes, Dino, you do,' she insisted. 'One thing more, then we'll go next door and eat.'

'What is it?'

'The morning after we'd slept together, he appeared from the bathroom with a pair of scissors – small ones – and he cut off a piece of my hair from just behind my ear.' She freed one hand that went to the spot and rubbed it. 'He does that to every woman he sleeps with – he keeps them like trophies.'

Moretti felt sick and anger in equal measure.

He brought Carla's hand to his lips and kissed it. She slid off her stool, threw her arms round his neck, and kissed him until the tickling of his moustache made her giggle and she stopped. Moretti's arms were round her back, holding her loosely.

'I've often wondered what a proper kiss would be like,' she said, her arms still round his neck.

'And now you know, what do you think?'

She released her hold and stroked his moustache with the forefinger of each hand.

'I could get used to it.' She slid her hands down and broke his embrace. 'But the *pappardelle* are nearly ready, and I insist that we eat at the table next door.'

Moretti sighed. 'I'll take the wine through. What else can I do?'

'Pour two glasses of your wine, then come back for the parmesan and my home-made *peperoncino* oil.'

Carla drained the pasta into a large warm bowl and ladled some of the rich brown gravy from the casserole over it before tossing it together. Enriched with slivers of boar meat that had shredded from the chunks during the slow cooking, the thick aromatic ragù clung to the wide strips of pasta like a silk robe on wet skin. She divided the steaming *pappardelle* into two generous portions and brought them through to the dining room. Moretti drizzled hot oil over his and shaved parmesan over the top of both plates.

They both twisted forks into some of the unctuously coated ribbons of pasta and tasted them.

Moretti closed his eyes.

'Oh, Carla,' he said, rapturously. 'This is wonderful.'

She laughed. 'You were hungry.'

'Yes, but the sauce is fantastic.' He picked up his glass. 'Salute.'

They clinked glasses again.

'Mmm, Morellino, a perfect match,' she said.

They ate in silence. Moretti finished first and used a *scarpetta* of bread to wipe up the last of the boar sauce.

Carla finished, dabbed the corners of her mouth, and took a deep sip of the wine.

Moretti looked at her, spellbound. 'Why have you never remarried, Carla?'

She tossed back her head and laughed.

'Well, Detective,' she leant on the word. 'If you must know, I'm choosy.' She placed her napkin on the table and folded it while she spoke. 'I've had plenty of offers, from locals and tourists alike – you've seen how men in the bar chat me up. And I would like to get married again.' She lowered her eyes to the table and smoothed the creases on the napkin. 'But after Gigi's father left, I don't know, I lost trust in men, and I've never really regained it.'

Moretti covered her hand with his.

'I'm really sorry to hear that.'

She raised her eyes to his.

'And what about you?' she asked quietly. 'The rumour is that your wife has left you.'

Moretti saw the pulse in her neck beating rapidly.

'She has an important case in the south,' he said, in a tone that convinced neither of them. 'She has to be away for a while – I'm not sure how long.' At least the last part was true.

The hand on the table under his turned and held his. Her thumb rubbed the back of his hand. He noticed her swallow.

'Is that your guilty secret?'

The spell was broken. She saw it in his face and felt it through his hand.

'I'm sorry,' she said. 'It's the wine. It's stronger than I'm used to. Excuse me.'

She slid her hand out, collected the plates and cutlery, and took them to the kitchen.

Moretti sat looking at the wall in front of him as both it and the kitchen noises faded from his consciousness and the sound of Maria's keening filled his mind, alongside the image of her kneeling, doubled over, clutching herself and rocking back and forth.

Dino.

He placed his hand on Maria's shoulder to comfort her but her rocking continued.

Dino.

The unfillable emptiness entered him.

'Dino.'

Carla's voice brought him back. She was standing holding two plates of the boar stew.

'Oh, I'm sorry,' he said, taking one of the plates. 'I was miles away.'

She'd served the stew with polenta.

He filled up their glasses and they both began to eat. The large chunks of boar fell apart with a fork, and they again ate in silence until Carla broke it.

'It's me that's sorry. I obviously opened a door that should remain closed.'

Moretti wiped his mouth, took a deep glug of wine, and shook his head.

'No, Carla, you've given me the first chance I've had to talk about this.'

She laid her cutlery on the side of her plate, placed her hands on her lap and listened.

'You asked what my guilty secret was.' The familiar tightness in his chest returned. He rested his joined hands on the table. 'Well, you know we lost a daughter.'

Carla stiffened a little but made no sound.

Moretti looked at the void somewhere between them.

'She was fifteen. Beautiful – like her mother. Headstrong – like me. She'd asked for a lift to visit one of her friends. Maria had a case in Florence, I was investigating a case in town. We told her that neither of us could take her.' The image played in his memory in front of him. 'She decided to walk there. It wasn't far. About eight kilometres.' He paused and swallowed. 'Then, as everyone knows, her body was found in Lake Maghicchio. It was my fault; I chose my job over my daughter's safety.'

Carla now reached out and placed her hands on his.

'It wasn't your fault, Dino. How could you know?'

Tears ran down both of their faces. He looked up at her.

'I've never admitted that to anyone before, Carla.'

She said nothing but only squeezed his hands a little.

'Maria and I have never spoken about it,' he continued. 'That's why our marriage is where it is.'

They sat in silence looking at each other until Moretti felt liquid running from his nose. He pulled his hands free and laughed, wiping the back of his hand against his moustache.

'Look at us,' he snorted. 'A right pair. Where is your toilet, please?'

Carla had cleared the table by the time he returned.

He joined her in the kitchen where she was rinsing the plates in the sink.

'How to trash a dinner date,' he exclaimed.

She turned round, threw her wet hands around his neck, and kissed him, and kept kissing him until she had to stop for breath.

'I'll remember this night for ever, Dino,' she replied.

CHAPTER FIFTY-EIGHT

Moretti lit a small cigar and enjoyed the cool, moonlit stillness around him – oddly relieved to be free of the tangled investigations at work. He strolled back to his car feeling at once free of a great burden and troubled by his conscience. He'd left before the journey that he and Carla had embarked upon reached the destination it was heading for. He was confused about his feelings for Maria, and for that matter about Carla. The evening with Carla had opened a side of him that he'd locked shut, yet he felt guilty that it hadn't happened with his wife.

When he turned into the quiet little side street and saw his car where he'd hidden it, he laughed. They'd found it, whoever they were, and left a fish – on closer inspection, a red mullet – under his wiper. He was still chuckling to himself as he approached his house and noticed that he'd left a light on. He turned into the driveway and saw Maria's car. His good humour left, replaced by a wrenching in his stomach.

He entered the kitchen and met Maria's suspicious smile and the aroma of the meal she had cooked for him. She was standing at the counter pouring a glass of wine.

'I saw your car arriving.' She held the glass out to him. 'Here.'

He took it and she picked up her half full glass.

'I made us dinner, but I couldn't wait so I've already eaten.' She came round and kissed him on the cheek. 'Have you had a good evening?' She sidled past him with her glass and the remains of the bottle and sat at the dining table which was still laid with one place.

Moretti struggled for words.

'Maria, I didn't know,' he stammered.

'Your phone was off, how could you?' she said archly. She sipped her wine. 'I waited and called you, off and on, until nine. I know that you can't keep regular hours.' She tucked her legs up under her. 'Then I called Gennaro. He told me that you were going out for dinner, but he didn't know where.' She swept a stray hair off her forehead. 'I thought, that's Gennaro, he's probably forgotten, so I called Cristina – nice woman – she didn't know either but tried to reassure me that you were probably in one of the local trattorie.' She topped up her wine and took another sip. 'I called the first one at ten, thinking that you could maybe have a small portion with me, or maybe share dessert.'

Moretti was rooted to the spot.

'I began to worry, and I hated myself for it, because I know that you have to follow leads at insane times of the day and night. So, I tossed a coin to decide whether I should call the hospital or Bar Italia, in case anyone there had seen you.'

Moretti's mouth dried and he clenched his teeth.

'Bar Italia won, and guess what, the barista told me that you were having dinner with Carla.' She put her glass on the table and folded her arms. 'So, did you have a good evening?'

A tiny ember of the memory of the evening glowed in the unfillable void inside him and ignited.

'Maria,' he whispered. 'We talked about Giulia.'

Maria threw her head back, revealing the thick ridge of her windpipe, and let out the same keening wail as when she first saw Giulia's body. Then she crumpled in on herself and fell to the floor.

Moretti dived to her side, and she beat him off with impotent flails of her arm as her body shuddered and tried to find assuagement in the position in which Giulia had been inside her for nine months. Wrapped in his arms, her sobs were silent now, perceptible only through the wrenching contractions of her muscles. He stroked the wet hair off her face, but Maria twisted her head from left to right, refusing his comfort.

They stayed like that, two folded forms – one shuddering, one still – until the coaction of pins and needles and joint pain in Moretti's knees made him shift position. Maria wriggled free of him and used the table to pull herself up to sit on her chair again.

'Sit here, Dino. We've a lot to talk about.'

Moretti hobbled to his feet and sat opposite her.

'What else did you talk about?' she demanded. 'How much more of our private life did you share with this barmaid?'

Moretti had heard her cross-examine witnesses before, and he now felt like he was in the dock.

'Nothing else, only that.'

'How was her cooking? As good as mine?'

Moretti sagged.

'Her food was good. Different from yours. She's Tuscan, you're from the south.' He knew where this line of questions was going. It didn't take long to get there.

'Did you sleep with her?'

'No.'

No reaction from Maria.

'Did you kiss her?'

Moretti thought about making the distinction that Carla had kissed him, but he knew that the lawyer, judge, and jury in front of him had already decided his guilt.

'Yes.'

Maria flinched but recovered and continued.

'What is it about Bar Italia that makes you suddenly irresistible to women?'

His eyes widened and his head jerked back involuntarily. One of Maria's signature questioning techniques was to change attack to disrupt the thought process of the witness and catch them off guard.

'What?'

'You kissed Carla inside Bar Italia, and a Dutch slut kissed you and propositioned you outside Bar Italia.'

Conflating two separate events was also one of her tactics. He decided to change his approach.

'First of all, I kissed no-one,' he said, stabbing his finger into the table. 'Carla kissed me because I helped her serve customers on the day of Domenico's funeral. The woman who kissed me outside was a Dutch woman who was part of our investigation. She also propositioned Cristina. And for the record, tonight, it was Carla who kissed me.'

'You kissed back.'

'Yes.'

'And you told her about Giulia.'

'Yes.'

She looked away from him, fighting to keep the tears at bay.

He hated and feared the stillness around her.

She turned and placed her hands one on top of the other on the table.

'Dino, I think I would have preferred it if you had slept with Carla,' she revealed. 'I could understand it, even. But talking about the death of our daughter was a bigger betrayal.'

He said nothing, watching as a tear ran down her cheek again, and the question that he wanted to ask her about Ricci began to force its way into his mouth. He inhaled to voice it and ran his tongue over his lips.

'And you're suspended,' she declared, stifling his question. 'What the hell has happened to you, Dino? What the hell has happened to us? We used to talk about everything.'

Moretti refocused quickly on the other question that had been haunting him.

'I've been trying to contact you, Maria.' There was a glint of recognition. 'Ever since the day of the funeral.' He regained control. 'The immigrants escaped from custody.'

She showed no sign of surprise.

'I know,' she replied.

'They were helped.' He clenched and unclenched his hand under the table out of sight, unable to bring himself to ask the question. 'Someone had a key.'

'I'm glad,' she said, wiping the matted hair off her face. She picked up her glass and quaffed her wine. 'It was nothing short of a scandal that they were held in prison in the first place.'

'The cells in the Questura are hardly what I'd call prison,' he protested.

She jabbed a finger at him. 'You weren't in them.'

Moretti floundered to recover.

'Yusuf has been in touch, hasn't he?'

She waved away his question. 'Client attorney privilege. Anyway, you're off the case.'

The finality of her closing remark snuffed out further questions.

He left the table and fetched his glass of wine and gulped deeply.

She looked up at him.

'Dino, this isn't finished,' she forewarned him. 'We still have plenty to talk about – if you want to, that is. So, your suspension is a good thing; it lets you choose. You have two choices – you can either stay here and latch onto Carla, or you can come south with me. I have a little business I must deal with tomorrow morning. Sleep in the spare room.'

She stood, drained her glass, and left.

CHAPTER FIFTY-NINE

Moretti couldn't settle. He sent a couple of text messages. So much was going through his head that he rose, looked in on Maria sleeping soundly in their bed, and wondered how fuzzy her head would be in the morning. He dressed without her waking and packed an overnight bag. He paused in the kitchen long enough only to write her a note that he propped up on the counter.

He drove down to Maghicchio and joined the autostrada south, and as dawn lightened the sky in front of him the pieces of the puzzle began to appear, not yet clear enough to put together but enough that he began to see how many they were and how he might begin to imagine their final shape.

With trucks rumbling along in convoy in the inside lane and the occasional self-important businessman in a fast German car screaming along, lights flashing, in the outside lane, the drive for Moretti was easy in the middle lane. After most of the traffic peeled away to the right for Rome, he continued for a short distance then pulled off at a service station for breakfast. The mediocre offerings reminded him how lucky he was to be able to have Carla's coffee and fresh pastries every morning. He shrugged off the contrasting memories of his evening with Carla and Maria and loaded up with water and pocket coffee for his four-hour journey south. While the attendant filled his car with fuel, Moretti bought an air freshener to mask the car's persistent fishy smell that had bothered him on the way down, and on impulse bought a dash-cam at the till as he paid for the fuel.

Now, with fewer vehicles on the road, he made good time and was approaching the outskirts of Naples before Maria woke up.

*

Maria conceded the battle with her repeater alarm and pushed herself up, swung her legs out, and sat on the edge of the bed. The unforgiving mirror doors of her wardrobe confirmed what her thumping head told her. She looked past the wreckage of her own appearance to the reflection of Dino's side of the bed behind her, smooth and unslept in. She groaned and forced herself to stand, needing to empty her bladder and have a shower before she faced him.

She'd fallen immediately asleep with no time to reflect on Dino's revelation. Now, under the cleansing and energising spray, she put his kissing Carla in perspective and contrasted it with her own transgression following Giulia's death – the one that she had felt him perilously close to asking about last night. She turbaned her wet hair and pulled on Dino's thick towelling robe. She needed coffee now and headed into the kitchen where she saw, leaning against an abandoned glass, his note.

There's a third option, Maria. I've gone south on my own.

She filled the Moka and stood re-reading the note until the coffee pot pluttered and hissed. She drank two little cups – the first, straight from the boil, bitter, and so hot that it burned her mouth; the second, loaded with sugar, she sipped more slowly, trying to divine the meaning in the single line. Behind her, on the table, her phone reminded her of her meeting. She quickly tidied up, dressed, and drove into Cassiatorre.

'I'd like to speak with my clients, please,' she declared tersely.

Alfiero reached for the telephone, but Maria's demeanour changed his mind. He collected the key and started towards the cells.

'Sign me in and search me,' Maria insisted, placing her bag on the desk and holding out her arms.

'Of course, Signora De Luca,' mumbled Alfiero, who passed her the book, patted her down, and locked her bag away. 'Follow me, please.'

She waited until he was gone then spoke with Yusuf.

'Please ask the injured man how he is.'

Once she was satisfied that all the immigrants had been properly cared for, she and Yusuf planned how they would arrange for the men still in hiding to come to the Questura and, more importantly, what was going to happen to the Etruscan treasure they had found.

CHAPTER SIXTY

Moretti parked his car in a cobbled side street, and because he was in the south, took a moment to set up the dash-cam. When he'd checked that it was working, he walked past the church of San Valentino to the village square. It was market day, and the area bustled with tourists and locals. The parish priest, Don Vincenzo, had agreed to meet him in Bar Roma. Moretti weaved through the crowds, and a dark-skinned cleric got to his feet and waved him over.

'Don Vincenzo?'

The priest grinned, revealing the whitest teeth Moretti had ever seen, and held out his hand.

'Commissario Moretti, welcome to Borgo di Monte Groppone. May I offer you something to drink?'

Moretti had had enough coffee on the way down.

'Water, please, and maybe something to eat?'

Don Vincenzo looked in the direction of the counter and a bustling woman came over to take the order.

'What can I bring you?' she smiled.

'Grazia, this is my guest, Commissario Moretti.'

Grazia opened her mouth to speak.

'Yes, like the beer,' smiled Moretti, and smoothed first the left then the right side of his moustache as if wiping away beer froth. Grazia looked a bit sheepish.

'He has driven a long way and has a long journey home,'

continued Don Vincenzo. 'Can you bring him something that will tide him over but not send him to sleep on the drive back?'

She beamed at the young priest.

'Leave it to me, Don Vincenzo.'

'Thank you,' Moretti said. 'It's busy here and full of tourists, too. What's the attraction?'

The priest smiled.

'Oh, I'm sorry. I didn't mean to sound so rude,' Moretti apologised. 'It's only that the village is a bit off the beaten track.'

'I understand, no need to say sorry,' said the priest with a shake of his head. 'It's a long story that I'll summarise over lunch. Now, you said that you had a photograph for me to look at.'

Moretti produced the photograph that Carmela had identified as Mario and slid it across the table.

'It's this boy and his mother, Don Vincenzo. They'll have arrived within the past two weeks.'

The priest looked closely at the photograph and frowned. 'I think so, but I'm not sure.'

Grazia arrived with a tray of cheeses, a selection of salami, and three different types of focaccia.

'The cheeses are made locally by the woman in the square over there,' she said proudly, indicating one of the market stalls. 'The salami is also local, and the focaccia was made fresh this morning in the village bakery.'

'Thank you, Signora,' said Moretti. 'It all looks wonderful.'

Grazia turned to go but Don Vincenzo stopped her.

'Grazia, do you recognise this boy?'

She wiped her hands on her apron, picked up the picture and squinted at it.

She tapped the image with a finger. 'That's the Colangelo boy,' she revealed. 'I'm certain of it. His mother Chiara came here looking for a job about a week ago. I already had a full complement of staff and told her to try in the town. She's used to working in a supermarket, so she might have got a start there.'

She handed the photograph back to Moretti.

'I don't suppose you know where she's living?' he ventured.

'I did note her details,' exclaimed Grazia, 'in case I needed someone at short notice. Give me a moment.'

Moretti tucked the photograph away.

Grazia returned with her address book. 'There,' she said, indicating with her finger. 'That's her address and a phone number.'

Moretti copied the details and relaxed into his lunch as Don Vincenzo related the story of the village's success.

CHAPTER SIXTY-ONE

Maria De Luca sat at Cristina's desk. Neither woman had spoken about the previous evening.

'So, to summarise, Ispettore,' Maria said, counting on her fingers. 'My clients are willing to cooperate given the correct assurances, in writing, from both sindacos elect, Donati and Ricci. The men still in hiding will voluntarily give themselves up, you and I will go with Yusuf to collect them and bring them into protective custody here, the immigration authorities will not be informed, and in exchange they will reveal the location of the Etruscan tomb. Agreed?'

Cristina nodded. 'Agreed.'

'I have been informed that a total of four of the men, all Somalis, wish to be allowed to leave Italy,' continued Maria. 'They must be furnished with international travel documents to facilitate that. The other five – that is Yusuf, the remaining two Somalis, and the two Ethiopians – have stated their preference, though God knows why, to stay and settle here. When we have recovered the remaining men, I will confirm these details, and you will see to it that the suitable documentation is arranged. When all is in order and I am satisfied that the men who wish to travel are safely in the care of a refugee organisation that I know, then Yusuf will reveal the location of the gold artefacts that were found in the tomb.'

Cristina frowned.

'Signora De Luca…' she hesitated. 'That is the part I'm not

comfortable with. I don't have the authority to make those guarantees.'

Maria rested her wrists on the desk and steepled her fingers.

'Ispettore, you are an intelligent woman. I suggest that you contact Signor Donati, who has already proclaimed his intention to make the plight of these poor refugees the central plank of his campaign. Achille has been around politics long enough to know exactly who to call to make this happen.'

'And what about the expense involved in transportation, clothing, and subsistence costs?'

Maria smiled.

'That is something that I have already in hand and need not concern the state.'

Cristina collected the key from Alfiero and led Maria de Luca to the cells, where she released Yusuf. Maria gave her phone to Yusuf who made a call to confirm the arrangements, then the three left the Questura and got into two cars. Cristina followed the two in front, expecting to leave the main road onto the track where Yusuf and the injured man had been found, but instead they continued downhill and turned off to the right. Half a kilometre along the track, the remaining men were waiting. Two joined Maria and Yusuf, and three got into Cristina's car. They drove back to the Questura in silence.

As before, Maria left her bag at the desk and insisted that she and all the men were searched. Alfiero frisked them all and let them through. This time, the men went quietly to the cells with Yusuf and Maria, to update everyone and finalise their plans.

CHAPTER SIXTY-TWO

Moretti watched her step back from the door, wide-eyed, and bring her hand to her mouth.

'So, you recognise me, Signora Rosati?' he said. 'May I come in? We have a lot to talk about.'

She looked past him, scanning the street in case others had found her.

'Come in,' she whispered urgently. 'Before anyone sees.'

She pressed against the wall to let him pass before locking and bolting the door. A voice came from beyond him.

'Who is it, Mamma?'

Moretti stopped to let her go first.

'A visitor,' Chiara called back.

Mario came out to see who it was and first froze then clung to his mother's skirt.

Chiara crouched down and embraced her son, cradling his head at her shoulder.

Mario's gaze was fixed on the detective.

Moretti smiled.

'I can't tell you how glad I am to see you, Mario,' he confessed. 'People have been very worried about you both. Signora Rosati, might we sit somewhere and talk?'

Chiara nodded and stood.

'Mario, go to your room and finish the drawing you started,' she cooed, shooing him gently with both hands.

She led Moretti into a small room and sat down, motioning him to do the same. She sat wringing her hands on her lap.

'How did you find us?' she whispered, least Mario heard.

'Quite by chance. Mario's picture was picked up and broadcast on TV. People all over Italy sent in photographs – some bearing no resemblance at all – and this one was sent from here.' He showed her Mario's photograph.

Chiara studied the background and said, 'This is the square. Who sent it?'

Moretti shrugged, palms up. 'I don't have the details. Someone after the reward, I guess. How are you both? You've been through a hellish experience.'

'Mario doesn't know about his father,' she whispered anxiously. 'I don't know how to tell him.'

'I understand. I'll say nothing. What are your plans?'

Chiara's shaking hand covered one eye as her fingertips stroked her brow.

'I don't have any plans, I had to get away,' she tugged the front of her hair. 'I'm so confused.'

Moretti leaned forward.

'That's natural,' he said kindly. 'And I don't want to make your life any more difficult. So, I'll speak for a bit to tell you what I have to do now, all right?'

She nodded.

'There's quite a big operation in place to find Mario – mostly local to Cassiatorre, but also countrywide. I need to let them know that you're both safe and call that off. We're also investigating the circumstances leading to Domenico's death. I hope that you will be strong enough to help to fill in the details of that for me.' He raised his eyebrows as a question.

Chiara nodded again and fished out crumpled tissue.

'Tell me about the funeral.'

Moretti sighed.

'Domenico's cousin Davide organised everything. The church was full, and there was a huge overspill crowd outside.'

She pressed the tissue into her eyes.

'Then there was a funeral procession to the cemetery and another service.' He paused. 'Maybe you can come back with me, then you can visit with Mario.'

Because Mario was playing in the next room, Chiara's sobs were silent.

'I'll bring us both some water,' Moretti said, as he headed to the small kitchen.

When he returned with two glasses, Chiara had found some tissues and had blown her nose and wiped her face. She took a glass and drank deeply.

Moretti sipped his water until she composed herself.

'Here are some of the things that our investigations have thrown up. I can't see a connection between them, and I'm hoping that you can fill in the gaps. We think that Domenico was under pressure to sell your property. We have an idea who from, but we're not sure. We think that you had help to whisk Mario away, but we can't understand why you didn't call for help after the car accident. Do you recognise any of that?'

Chiara twisted a damp tissue.

'Domenico used to run his own business, and he wanted to set up on his own again in Cassiatorre, but he used all of our savings to buy our property.'

'Go on.'

'Money was tight. Domenico was working for somebody else, so his wages were not enough for our bills. I had to go out to work, too.' She looked at her hands and reddened. 'We sometimes didn't have enough money to pay for a babysitter, so we locked Mario indoors.'

She bent forward to take a drink.

'Domenico worked for Signor Ricci after his day job and at weekends. It paid quite well, and Domenico asked if there was anything else. Ricci said he had plans but not now. He knew that we were short of cash and offered to buy our place.'

She looked up at Moretti.

'He offered less than we had paid for it, so Domenico refused.' She looked down at her hands again. 'He called again several times with the same offer, and when Domenico kept refusing, he eventually told him that there would be no more work in future. We had a huge row about it. I asked Domenico why we needed such a large place, but he had big ideas for his own business and said that we would need all the space.'

She took another drink.

'Anyway, Domenico then had a call a few days later from someone else. He didn't identify himself, but his accent was southern. He said that Domenico should reconsider Ricci's offer. Domenico said that he wasn't interested.' She looked again at Moretti. 'He called back a few days later and said that he had noticed that Mario was left in the house alone sometimes and wondered what would happen if there was a fire.'

'When was that call, Signora Rosati?'

'The day before the accident.'

Moretti folded his arms.

'About that, Signora, why didn't you get help after it?'

Chiara held her head in her hands.

'Lots of reasons. If we reported the accident, we'd have been late for work. Domenico had already been warned, but the main reason was I didn't want the authorities finding out that Mario was locked in a house alone.'

'Hardly major crimes, Signora.'

'When I discovered Domenico's body, I panicked, and I knew that I had to get back to Mario. All I could think about was him trapped alone and the house going on fire. I thought that the people who had threatened Domenico would kill us both, so I decided to run away.'

'But your house keys and phone were in the car.'

Chiara looked down at her hands again.

'We hid it in the Partisan's Cave, and I couldn't find my way back to it.'

'We've been told that you keep yourselves to yourselves and didn't have any friends in the village, so who helped you?'

'You're right, I only have a few friends, mainly other mums I use for babysitting.' Her head stayed down but her eyes looked up at Moretti. 'There's another woman, but I don't want to get her into trouble.'

'Signora Rosati, I've driven a very long way to find you. I want to help you, but you need to be honest. Who is she?'

Chiara looked down again. 'Sara Moscardini.'

'Of course,' exclaimed Moretti. 'The locksmith's daughter.'

'Sara told me that there was someone who could help – a man I recognised from the past.'

CHAPTER SIXTY-THREE

Cristina contacted Ricci about getting his written agreement to cooperate in the plan for the immigrants. At first suspicious, he reluctantly agreed to sign the prepared document when Cristina explained that his opponent Donati had already done so. She drove out to the agriturismo and was shown into Ricci's office by Alicia, who waited, holding open the door.

'Signor Ricci, thank you for agreeing to see me at such short notice,' Cristina said. 'I know that this is a very busy time for you.'

She placed the document that had been drafted by Maria De Luca on his desk. He scanned it briefly and signed it.

'Thank you, Ispettore,' he replied in a very business-like tone. 'Now, if you will excuse me, I must get on.'

Alicia closed the door behind them.

'Can we step outside for a moment, Alicia?'

The receptionist looked puzzled.

'It will really only take a moment,' Cristina smiled reassuringly. 'Let me close this screen and I'll be with you shortly.'

Cristina stood in the shade of an olive tree at the corner of the car park and called Maria De Luca to tell her that Ricci had signed the guarantee.

Alicia joined her in the shade. 'How can I help you, Ispettore?'

'When I was here before, you said something to me that has played on my mind since.'

Alicia looked at the ground. 'Oh?'

Cristina tilted her head and leaned over a little, trying to read the other woman's expression.

'Yes, you told me never to get into a situation where I needed something from Signor Ricci.'

Alicia's hand moved immediately to the hair behind her ear.

'And you did that same action before.'

Alicia tilted her head back to look up at Cristina's face. 'What do you mean?'

Cristina touched the hair at the back of her own ear.

'This is where he took your hair from, isn't it?' She placed her hand on Alicia's shoulder. 'He cut a piece off your hair after he had slept with you.'

Alicia's chin sank to her chest, and she nodded. 'How did you find out?'

Cristina squeezed her shoulder.

'I found out that it happened to someone else,' she said tenderly. 'Do you know where he keeps them?'

Alicia covered her face with both hands.

'I found out by accident,' she said, then added quickly, 'And he doesn't know that I know.'

'Where are they hidden, Alicia?'

Alicia looked behind her to check that they were still alone.

'One of his wines won an international competition. The framed certificate arrived, and I had to move some of the other certificates to make space for it. There's a clipping of hair inside the back of every frame on his wall. They each bear a name and a date. His office is his trophy room.'

CHAPTER SIXTY-FOUR

Moretti listened carefully to Gennaro's information.

'That fits perfectly, Gennaro,' he exclaimed. 'You and Cristina bring them both in, and neither of you make plans for this evening. Achille will make the arrangements.'

Moretti avoided the centre of the village and drove to Chiara's address without drawing attention to himself. He checked ahead and behind then got out, knocked on the door, and helped Chiara with the three pieces of luggage. He sat alone in the front, the other two crouched down in the back, until they were safely out of the village. As he passed San Valentino's church, Don Vincenzo and an older priest waved.

After their first comfort break, Moretti insisted that Chiara join him in the front and keep talking lest he should fall asleep. Mario slept for most of the remaining journey. Back in Cassiatorre, Moretti dropped them off at Moscardini's house, parked his car in Piazza Garibaldi, and headed to the small theatre. Two carabinieri, machine guns slung across their shoulders, were on guard. He nodded and handed over his mobile phone as they opened the doors to let him enter.

On the stage were tables arranged in a large rectangle. Moretti made for the empty chair, sat, and poured himself a plastic cupful of water from the cool bottle in front of him.

'Signor Donati, thank you for arranging the accommodation. I know it's a bit theatrical, but I didn't want this meeting to be held in the Questura.' He paused and sipped his water. 'First of all, I'd like to confirm the safe return of Mario Rosati and his mother, Chiara. Both are well and unharmed, and I know that will be welcome news to you all. They are somewhere safe and will stay there until after this meeting.'

The others round the table nodded.

'I believe you may all know each other, but I'll go round the table anyway. To my left, is Ispettore Cristina Furlan, then Agente Gennaro Santoro, next to him is Signor Mancini, and on my right is Achille Donati, candidate for sindaco.'

The members of the circle settled themselves and topped up their plastic cups.

'I asked you all here to listen to various pieces of evidence so that we can find a way ahead. Not all of the following can be proved, I must add, but it makes a strong circumstantial case.'

Donati cleared his throat.

'Almost two weeks ago,' Moretti began, 'Domenico Rosati died in a tragic accident, and his wife and son disappeared. I investigated the scene with Gennaro, and we were baffled because by all accounts Mario had been locked in the house with no possible way of getting out. Chiara's house keys were in their car, Domenico's were in his pocket at the bottom of a fissure in the rocks, and she had no means of getting in. But, as I said, Mario is now unharmed. Before I tell you how, I want to talk about the circumstances leading up to the tragedy, and I'll call on my colleagues to fill in details as we go along. But I'll start.'

He sipped his water again.

'The Rosati's were a hardworking couple who owned a good-sized podere outside the town. They kept themselves to themselves and didn't mix socially with the townsfolk. Their neighbour, Signor Ricci, had the idea to expand his agriturismo operation and contacted Domenico for several building jobs. Money was tight, so Domenico did the work on top of his full-time job in Maghicchio. Ricci contacted Domenico with a view to buying his property, but Domenico refused because he had his own plans to go into business. Go on, please, Gennaro.'

Gennaro opened his notebook and read from it.

'At some point, Chiara had a liaison with Ricci and told him about their finances. Ricci put pressure on Domenico by saying that he wouldn't give him any more work on the agriturismo – he planned to use Signor Erpicone's immigrant workers instead. When even that didn't work, Ricci called Chiara and threatened to tell her husband about her infidelity unless Domenico sold the land.'

Moretti continued.

'Chiara pleaded with Domenico to sell the land, but his mind was made up, until he had a call from someone – probably one of the two Mafia types we saw at the funeral. They made a substantial cash deposit in Ricci's bank account, and they made none-too-veiled threats against Mario. Cristina, what have you found out about Signor Ricci?'

'Ricci has slept with scores of women,' she began. 'There's nothing against that, and no-one has ever made a complaint against him, but Signor Ricci has a curious habit. He collects samples of hair from all the women he has slept with – complete with names and dates.'

Donati shook his head in disbelief. Cristina continued.

'There is one called Chiara, which proves the connection – although Ricci maintains that she came to him. Gennaro referred to Signor Erpicone's workers. Our investigation has discovered that the eight men – six Somalis and two Ethiopians – have been digging on Erpicone's land but searching for Etruscan tombs and not tending crops. We spoke to another Somali, Yusuf, who tends sheep for Signor Giusti. Yusuf has been of great help, acting as translator. He told us that the immigrants found a tomb, removed Etruscan artefacts, and gave them to Signor Erpicone.'

'Erpicone gave Ricci the artefacts to sell,' said Gennaro. 'We brought Signor Erpicone in for questioning, and he eventually admitted to supplying Ricci with artefacts that Ricci sold to his rich guests or to shady characters that he knows from the past.'

Moretti interrupted.

'Let's leave Signor Ricci for a moment and turn to Signor Mancini here. Gennaro?'

Gennaro flicked to another section in his notebook.

'Signor Mancini is living a lie. His real name is Esposito.'

Heads turned towards him, and Esposito shrugged.

Gennaro continued.

'He is a former highly trained detective who was based for a time in Campania. He was working on a huge case involving several Mafia families from two rival clans. So, one of the Mafia clans hatched a plan to get rid of him and to damage the other rival clan at the same time. They spread a rumour and leaked evidence that suggested Esposito was a paedophile. They leaked photographs of him with children, including one from their rival clan. It was ingenious – they used their contact in the Forensics Department to doctor photographs and video and produce paperwork that suggested there was a covert internal investigation into Esposito.'

'None of it true, of course,' Esposito interrupted.

Gennaro resumed his report.

'The papers suggested that the whole case was about to come out, with court proceedings against Esposito. When the second clan got hold of the evidence, they immediately took out a contract on Esposito. Not only did they want to exterminate him, but they also wanted to kill off the story so that it didn't come into the public domain because of the shame that it would have brought on their clan, on the individual families, and the child implicated in the photographs.'

Gennaro scanned the faces around him.

'Signor Esposito has, how can I put it, enjoyed the company of several local women. I've spoken to most of them. They all told me a similar story and one interesting fact. Signor Esposito has no photographs of any family or friends on display anywhere in his house. Unusual for an Italian, you might think, but as his real name suggests, he is an orphan with no living relatives. Unfortunate, but in his profession an enormous advantage, because unlike so many other cops, he couldn't be bought or threatened.'

Moretti added the next part of the story.

'I found out today from Signora Rosati that when she moved to Cassiatorre, she knew no-one, but by chance one day she saw someone through the crowd at the weekly market that she thought she recognised. She carefully made her way closer and confirmed her initial thoughts. She recognised Signor Esposito from many years before, because she had lived where he was stationed as a police detective. She didn't approach him and in fact didn't see him again. She was curious, however, and asked one of the few people that she did talk to about him. That person was Sara Moscardini, who had come to Chiara's house when her father Gianni fitted the new locks.' He stopped and sipped some more water.

'The same Sara Moscardini who's been avoiding us,' grumped Gennaro.

Moretti inclined his head towards the agente, and Gennaro folded his arms.

'Now we come to the day of the car accident and death,' said Moretti. 'Chiara has seen that her husband is dead. Mafia types have threatened to set her house on fire with Mario in it. She has no keys, so she hurries to the locksmith's shop and asks Sara Moscardini for help. She tells Sara about her affair with Ricci and about his threat to tell Domenico. She tells her about the Mafia threats. She needs to get away, but Mario is trapped inside the house. Sara says she'll help. While Chiara gets cleaned up, Sara calls a man she'd slept with – Signor Mancini, or rather Esposito.' He turned to the former detective. 'Why did you decide to help?'

Esposito shifted in his chair.

'I didn't, at first. It was only after I had gone over and met Chiara and realised that she knew who I really was that I decided to get involved. I quickly grasped the possibility that the Mafia guys who were bankrolling Ricci could be part of the same clan who had taken out the contract on me. I certainly didn't want Mafia involvement here, so I decided to help scupper Ricci's plans so that they'd clear off and leave me alone.'

'So, what were your plans?' asked Moretti.

'We'd get Mario out of the house, he and his mother would stay with the Moscardini's, then Sara would borrow Gianni's car and drive them south.'

'Where south?'

'A little village in the middle of nowhere where I had a contact from my police days.'

'A cop?'

'A Monsignor – but as a young man he had Mafia connections.'

'All right, they had transport. What about money?'

'Gianni Moscardini gave Chiara some money to get started. She was supposed to find a job there and make a new life.'

'And did she?'

'No. She had no ID, and no-one would take her on.'

'What did you do?'

'Sara and Gianni told me they faked a ransom demand. But

when I saw it, I knew it wouldn't work, so I sent a second ransom demand. The money was to tide her over and pay for a new identity.'

'So, what changed?'

'With time and distance, Chiara assessed the risk and realised that she couldn't walk away from her land and property. She decided that she didn't need all the land so she could sell some to Ricci, clear her debts, and have enough to live on.'

'So how did Chiara get Mario out of the house?'

Esposito smiled.

'Gianni Moscardini only ever made two sets of keys for customers. But he made another set for himself, in case someone should ever lose both sets. It would save damaging the door.'

'Where did he keep them?'

'At the back of his shop is a cellar dug out of the tufa. There's a steel door hidden behind a stack of boxes. In there he keeps the spare keys. He and Chiara freed Mario while Sara visited Signor Di Vittorio, whose podere directly overlooks the Rosati's, to keep him from noticing.'

'But when Gennaro and I visited, the place was still locked up.' Moretti frowned. 'We saw a video with cobwebs across the locks.'

Esposito smiled.

'Our fight against the Mafia is difficult. They bribe and threaten anyone who could be a potential witness. Their reach even extends into our Forensics labs, where evidence can suddenly disappear.'

He paused to sip some water.

'So, I became expert in making new evidence. It was delicate, but there's a technique that I learned by which I could transfer a few spiders' webs, laying them carefully one on top of another to give the appearance of a cobweb. Mario came out of the front door with his mother, and I made it look like it hadn't been opened for several days.'

Moretti scratched his head.

'That's it. That's the thing that's been niggling away, because there were no cobwebs on the windows inside. I'm speechless.'

'Me, too,' added Donati. 'And to be honest, apart from organising the use of the theatre, I don't know why I'm here.'

Moretti turned to face him.

'Achille, you're important in another investigation and central to what happens next.' Moretti patted his friend's back. 'Your election campaign is very laudably about defending the rights of the immigrants – a campaign that would not have been possible had the immigrants been transported away by the authorities. No, you needed them here.'

Donati shifted uncomfortably in his seat.

'On the day of the funeral, you waited in Piazza Garibaldi until you saw Alfiero leave for a coffee and a smoke, and you released the men from custody when they had maximum chance to escape in the crowds and confusion.'

'You can't prove that,' Donati protested.

Moretti grinned.

'In fact, Achille, I think I probably can. My guess is that you knew how Vice Questore Innocenti had taped his key to the desk. You took the key, released the prisoners through the emergency exit, and used fresh tape to return the key. Your fingerprints will be on the tape.'

Moretti faced Esposito again.

'There's a couple of loose ends that I think you can tie up.'

Esposito shrugged. 'I'm happy to help.'

'There was an older man, neatly dressed, who frequented Bar Italia shortly after Mario's disappearance. He sat there all day reading his newspaper. Now he seems to have disappeared, too.'

Esposito smiled.

'He's the man who arranged my new identity. Until today, only he knew who I really was, and I needed to know that I was safe. He was keeping an eye on things and letting me know what the local rumours were. All he had to do was listen to the three busybodies.'

'I see. And the voice on the burner phone?'

'An actor I found through classified ads in a trade magazine.'

'Aha. All right, here is a list of the main charges that can be brought in this case. Cristina, Gennaro, please feel free to add in any I forget.'

Moretti counted on his fingers.

'Erpicone, digging up and selling Etruscan artefacts. Ricci, reset and fencing of those artefacts. Tourists – as yet unidentified – staying at the Ricci agriturismo, buying Etruscan artefacts. Ricci, threatening behaviour and bribing public officials.'

Donati jerked his head round.

'What public officials?' he asked indignantly. 'To do with the election?'

'Not directly. I'll fill in the details after I've finished the charge list.' He resumed counting. 'Ricci, for laundering money.' He changed hands. 'Ricci, for breaching election spending limits. Ricci, for hindering a police investigation by aiding two suspects to escape questioning. Chiara Rosati, for failing to report an accident, failing to report killing a boar, failing to report the death of her husband.' He returned to the first hand. 'Obstructing a police investigation, accepting money illegally obtained. Sara Moscardini, obstructing the course of justice. Gianni Moscardini, the same plus harbouring a fugitive.'

He looked at Esposito.

'I don't have enough fingers for your charges. Most of those previously mentioned plus faking evidence, destroying evidence, obtaining money under false pretences, ransom. Anything else?'

Esposito smiled and clapped his hands slowly.

'Very good, Commissario Moretti,' he said languidly. 'But we all know that they won't stick. That's why you staged this little performance – to let us know that you know.'

Moretti sighed and smoothed his moustache.

'I have a question for you, Commissario… and an offer,' said Esposito. 'What happened to the ransom money?'

All eyes turned to Moretti.

'I dropped off the Rosati's at Gianni's place then, before I came here, I went to the bank. I called Dante from our last comfort stop and told him that I'd meet him there to return the money. It's safe in the vault by now. What's your offer, Esposito?'

'Call me Pino, but stick with the Mancini surname. I may be able to help with the identification of the two Mafia guys.'

'Thanks, Pino,' said Moretti. 'Now, this is what we're going to do.'

After the meeting Moretti said goodnight to everyone and stood outside the theatre smoking a small cigar. His way forward was clear, and he even managed to smile at the sight of the small octopus wedged under the wiper.

CHAPTER SIXTY-FIVE

Moretti entered Vice Questore Innocenti's office. Achille Donati was already there.

Innocenti pointed to the empty seat.

'Sit down, Moretti,' he snapped.

'I'll stand, if you don't mind, I have a busy morning.'

'Signor Donati told me that you organised a pantomime in the theatre last night. Is this true?'

Moretti shot a glance to Donati.

'Did he tell you what it was about?'

'No, he said to bring you in – you'd tell me everything. So, go on, tell me everything.'

Moretti looked down, hands clasped penitently in front of him. 'I have a confession to make,' he began remorsefully.

Innocenti sat forward to hear better.

'I accessed your bank details without permission.'

Innocenti thumped the table.

'You're finished, Moretti,' he roared, looking at Donati then back to Moretti. 'This means prison. I have a witness.'

Moretti nodded his head contritely, still looking down.

'Yes, Vice Questore. Sindaco Donati is a witness,' he said, as he looked up at Innocenti. 'But he's *my* witness.'

'What do you mean?' blustered Innocenti, wide-eyed.

'You've been receiving money from Signor Ricci for years,' Moretti disclosed. 'I can only guess what for, but clearly you stood to gain if he became sindaco and if his proposed housing development went ahead. At least some of that money has come from sources that are being investigated as we speak by the Guardia di Finanza. In addition, he has accepted Mafia money, which may have been used to pay you. That's why you wanted me off the case, and that's why you banned me from investigating Ricci.'

Before Innocenti could reply, Donati spoke.

'Vice Questore Innocenti, you will write a letter of resignation while I sit here,' he intoned quietly. 'I will accept it and announce publicly that the town is grateful for your years of loyal service. You will retain all pension rights and move away from the area.'

'Who are you to demand anything from me?' Innocenti retorted defiantly. 'That so-called evidence is inadmissible.'

'Before coming here, Commissario Moretti and his officers visited Signor Ricci, who admitted paying you off,' Donati replied. 'You were to be a minor partner in the housing development, I believe.'

'You don't know who you're dealing with,' hissed Innocenti menacingly.

'Oh, indeed we do,' interjected Moretti. 'The two mafiosi have been identified. They're now being investigated by the Guardia di Finanza and, coincidentally, the money they deposited in Ricci's account has been withdrawn.'

'Ricci has withdrawn his candidacy,' said Donati. 'I am the unopposed new sindaco, and I hereby revoke Commissario Moretti's suspension.'

Moretti held out his hand.

'Let me be the first to congratulate you, Sindaco Donati. But if you excuse me, I have some other matters to deal with.'

He hurried to his office where Cristina and Gennaro were waiting for him.

'I'm reinstated,' he announced. 'Let's get on. Cristina, where are we with Ricci?'

'He's denying everything except that Innocenti was on the take. The prosecutor has prepared the charges, but she doesn't think they'll stick. The threats against Rosati are a case of "he said, she said". The trading in artefacts – well, without the artefacts or a witness coming forward, that's impossible to prove. The money side of things will be almost impossible, because the Mafia use shell companies to hide their cash.'

Moretti rubbed his stubble.

'So we've nothing,' he groaned. 'What about the hair trophies? Any news there? Any names we could chase up?'

'It's only a list of names at the moment,' said Cristina. 'Do you want to commit time to identifying all these women? At best we'll find that they are either foreigners who had a holiday fling, or locals who will be too embarrassed to cooperate.'

'Run down the names anyway,' he said, hoping that there were no Marias.

Cristina half shrugged and read out the list. There were two Marias. Moretti said nothing but tried to remember if his wife had ever had a lock of hair missing.

Gennaro snorted at the last two names – Fausta and Rosalia.

'It can't be,' he hooted. 'Not the busybodies.'

'Still waters,' remarked Moretti. 'Thanks, Cristina. Gennaro?'

'I visited Erpicone and told him the plan as we discussed last night.'

'How did he take it?' Moretti asked.

'Much better than I'd anticipated. I might go as far as to say he sounded relieved,' said Gennaro. 'I stuck to the plan and threatened him with arrest and prison for selling tomb goods, harbouring illegal immigrants, and basically treating them like slaves. Then I said that the only alternative to jail time was to accept a deal where Yusuf, the two Somalis, and the two Ethiopians who decided to stay here will run his farm. They'll be shareholders, and he'll pay them fair wages and have proper accommodation built, and he must have cataract operations.'

'How are Chiara and Mario?' Cristina asked.

'That was hard. Chiara told Mario about his father. They have a couple of days together before school begins again, and Maestra Perri says that she'll prepare his class.'

'She's a very caring person who likes Mario very much. I'm confident she'll keep an eye on him.'

'Chiara has agreed to sell the part of her property that contains the tomb to the Comune, so that it can be protected and professionally excavated, and the objects will be carefully removed and added to the museum collection.'

'That will give her financial security at least,' said Cristina.

'How much was in there?' asked Gennaro.

'We'll never know for certain,' Moretti replied. 'Yusuf led us to a spot where some of the smaller gold and silver objects were cached. The immigrants had planned to sell them for travel money.'

'You think that some are missing?'

'Undoubtedly. And we'll never know. These things don't ever leave private collections.'

'What about Esposito and Moscardini?'

'You mean Signor Mancini,' corrected Moretti. 'No charges will be brought, but we'll unofficially use Pino's expertise in the future.'

Moretti's phone rang. He looked at the screen.

'Sorry, I need to take this. Good work. I'll buy us beers later.'

He waited until he was alone in his office with the door closed.

'Maria? How are you?'

'I'm tired and confused.'

'Where are you?'

'I've stopped for fuel and something to eat. I'm heading back south to the case.'

'When will you be back?'

'I don't know.'

He thought about his next question carefully.

'You sold some artefacts for the immigrants, didn't you?' he said. 'Where did you hide them? We searched both cars after you and Cristina came back from collecting the men from the tomb.'

'Ask Alfiero. He searched me and all the men.'

'Where was your bag? Did he search that, too?'

'I put it on the counter. You'll need to ask him if he searched it.'

Moretti smiled. 'I will. Good luck in your case. I love you.'

The signal broke up, and the call ended. Moretti suddenly needed coffee. He crossed Piazza Garibaldi to Bar Italia. All of Ricci's campaign posters had been removed.

Carla smiled and held out his coffee and a pastry.

'Thanks, Carla.'

One of the gossips tutted behind him. He remembered that their names had been on Ricci's list, thought of something to say, then changed his mind.

'What a beautiful day, ladies,' he said charmingly. 'And how lovely you all look today.'

The three fussed and tutted as Moretti passed them carrying his coffee and pastry to an outside table beside a flower tub. It was seldom that all the other tables were empty, but it gave Gigi a good chance to clean and arrange the tables and chairs. He called the boy over.

'Good morning, Gigi,' he said, smiling.

'Good morning, Commissario,' Gigi replied with his lopsided grin. 'May I get you something else?'

'This is fine, thank you. Gigi, I have a question.'

'A question?'

'Yes.' Moretti fixed him with his gaze. 'Why, Gigi?'

The boy blushed and looked towards the open door of the bar. His mother was busy behind the counter.

'My mother is always talking about you,' he admitted. 'I got jealous.'

Moretti nodded and left a large tip under his saucer.

'That's for your honesty, Gigi, but it has to stop.'

'How did you find out?'

'You were caught on camera.'

Gigi picked up the note and left him.

A hummingbird hawkmoth darted beside him, sinking its proboscis deep into the geranium flowers. Moretti smiled, raised his cup to it, and sipped his coffee. The moth rose, curled up its mouthparts and hovered for a moment, its body still, its wings a blur, so close to the detective that he could make out its projecting antennae, its legs held flat under its body, and its fan-like tail before it thrummed over his head.

Moretti used his forefinger to smooth first the left, then the right side of his moustache.

ABOUT THE AUTHOR

John MacDonald writes atmospheric, socially-charged crime fiction set deep in the Tuscan hills. A lifelong lover of Italian culture, language and literature, he spends part of each year immersed in small-town life, learning how modern Italy balances tradition and change.

Inspired by authors like Andrea Camilleri and Donna Leon, John tells stories where small-town secrets, social tensions and personal grief collide – wrapped in gripping mysteries with emotionally complex characters.

The Cassiatorre Quartet, set over four seasons in a fictional Tuscan town, is his debut series.

When not writing, John is drawn to the quiet rhythms of Tuscan life – long walks, slow meals, and the occasional espresso-fuelled plot twist.

John MacDonald

https://www.instagram.com/johnmacdonaldwriter/

@johmacdonaldwriter.bsky.social

Printed in Great Britain
by Amazon